C000001261

First published in the UK by Amazon 2017

For more information about the author, please visit:
www.markchilderley.com

Path To Life

Written By Mark Childerley

Dedicated to one of the greatest scientific minds of our time;

Dr Stephen Hawking.

Well done Leah

Mr Grieg

PATH TO LIFE

MARK CHILDERLEY

Chapter 1 – The Beginning

Jnr was tapping away at the Martian rock face, oblivious to the solar winds raging towards him at thousands of miles per hour!

His team and base were out of sight, tucked in behind the huge, strange, smooth rocks he was chipping away at.

Suddenly, Jnr was slammed into the rock, knocking him out upon impact.

He was caught up in the wind's turmoil. It crashed upon the rock face, then deflected upwards, out into space itself, taking Jnr with it!

Selev spotted it first.

He hailed everyone on the comms: "Look at that dust storm."

He pointed to the area behind them and they all looked up.

"Oh my God! Archer is up there," said Julia.

"We can't do anything now, get inside the base, quickly," said Shaun.

"Chai, get back here asap!"

Jnr was speeding up and away from Mars, still unconscious.

The solar wind had broken his back, both legs and one arm. That wasn't the worse part, though.

Jnr had internal bleeding.

The G-force of such an impact was too much for Jnr's frail human body.

Steadily he came out of his unconscious state; it took a while for him to compose himself.

He was spinning really fast, and it put pressure upon his head: it hurt bad.

Realising he couldn't move without serious pain, he used the booster pack controls with his fingers in short bursts to stop himself from spinning out of control.

He positioned himself to look back at Mars.

It looked so small!

How long had he been out?

How fast was he travelling through space?

How was he going to get back?

There were no comms, not much air left, and no chance the ship had enough fuel to pick him up and get back to Earth – that's if they could even find him.

Jnr had a realisation!

"I'm going to die! Out here, on my own."

Jnr repositioned himself, pointing away from Mars and towards Jnr-X1.

He fired up the boosters on his jet pack for the last time, heading straight towards the black hole!

Jnr knows where it's supposed to be: after all, it was his discovery.

He could see the event horizon, but only just: the faint rays of light that were trapped on the edge for all eternity, light that stood still!

That meant one thing: Jnr was headed into the gravitational pull of Jnr-X1.

Blood started to gather in his mouth and breathing suddenly became difficult.

Panic kicked in.

Tears welled up in Jnr's eyes. The last thing he wanted was this. There was so much more he wanted to do, so much more he wanted to see, to be with his family again.

Jnr knew it was the end but if so, he intended to go where no man had gone before, dead or alive: he had to make it to Jnr-X1.

He started to gasp for air, frantically trying to force air into his lungs.

None left: that's it, the tank's empty!

Jnr's eyes started to bulge, and his body started to thrash around with violent jerks, his veins sticking out of his skin like they were going to burst.

He stared at the huge black hole he was approaching, his black hole; just before his brain gave up and died through lack of oxygen, Jnr managed to say to himself, "I went in."

The Beginning

Anne was sweating, in pain and frustrated. The labour was in its twenty-second hour.

"Breathe hard as you push, love," said Dave, feeling like a spare prick at a wedding.

He was a good husband and had worked hard to get himself and Anne their new home, even putting overtime in to pay for the needs of the coming infant. But right now he was out of his depth. "What do I do to help?" *I bet these people think I'm bleeding useless!* he thought to himself.

—

Every new father knew how it felt being at the bedside with the love of your life who was in pain, screaming down the hospital and at the same time bringing new life into the world.

"Come on, Anne, you're doing fantastic, you're so close, babe," said Dave as he held one hand tight and massaged her back with his spare hand.

"One more push, Anne, and we're there."

Anne took a deep breath and tensed every part of her little body, staring harshly at the midwife as if she could just jump up and pull her head off with frustration, and that was not like her at all. She then let it all out, pushing as hard as humanly possible!

"There you go, Anne, good girl," said Rosy.

Relief came instantly.

"Let me see," said Anne.

Rosy the midwife held up a tiny baby boy, and with a huge smile she passed him to Anne.

"Well done, my love," said Rosy. "He is a bonny one, him."

Dave kissed his wife on her sweaty forehead and told her he loved her so much. They glanced into each other's teary eyes then down at the little boy in her arms. Dave looked at his wife, and for a moment realised she had just gone through hell for the pair of them but Christ, she did look rough.

Now you may be thinking that's a bit harsh, but his Anne had always looked fantastic, no matter what. She had shoulder-length, brown hair shaped into a bob that always seemed to shine like flowing silk; her eyes were a deep brown, too. Her cheekbones sat high up in her face and her jawbone was narrow. She had a small button of a nose and to top it off her lips were blood red-coloured and plump. Her body was slight but perfectly symmetrical. Anne was a stunner: there was no doubt, but she never used much make-up like most other girls her age. That was down to her mother Sophia.

She explained to Anne from a young age that she was a natural beauty and didn't need 'tarting up', as her mother called it.

"It only attracts unwanted attention, my love, and besides, you have no need for it: you are perfect as you are," Sophia always stated.

"He is a little small, isn't he?"

"Yes he is, my love, but he looks as healthy as any I've brought into the world: you'll need to feed him up," said Rosy with a smile.

3

The newborn and his mother were to stay in hospital overnight, so Dave took off home to get some much-needed sleep.

He was overjoyed: he wondered if he could be too excited to sleep.

First job is to ring our parents to spread the good news, he thought, *as they have been calling what seemed like every twenty minutes or so.*

"Hi, Dad, it's me, David." He always had to tell his dad that it was his own son on the phone.

"You are now a granddad."

"Oh that's good, son, yes, great news," replied Roy. "I'd better tell your mother, then. What did she have?"

"A beautiful little boy," said Dave excitedly.

"Hey, Jean, you have a grandson!" shouted Roy.

Dave could hear her cheering and his mother's feet slapping the wooden floor has she made her way to the phone.

"Oh David, I'm so proud of you both. Is the boy ok? Is Anne ok? Did everything turn out fine?"

"Yes, Mum, don't be panicking: everything is good. He's healthy but a little underweight, 6.2 lbs, they said, but he's fine and so is Anne, so no more worrying, ok?"

"Oh, I can't wait to see them both. Can we come over today?"

"No, Mum, they are keeping them in overnight so you should be able to come tomorrow."

"Ok, son, I'm so happy for you both."

"Thanks, Mum. I wish Dad would have sounded as happy as you."

"You know him as much as me, David. He will be excited, but you know he won't show it."

"Yeah, Mum, you're right. I'm going now, Mum. I need some kip, I'm knackered, so love you and I'll see you tomorrow."

"Ok, David, I'll call before we set off, ok?"

"Ok, Mum. Bye."

"Bye, love," replied Jean.

Roy was a quiet bloke even with his own family, never mind strangers. Dave wondered why he was like he was: quiet, grumpy, stone-faced even, but it had never stopped him looking up to his father. Roy had always worked hard from fourteen years of age in the mines. Never really had any lengthy periods off work and he always provided everything his family needed.

Dave loved him for that.

He retired at 52 due to an injury at the pit which nearly ended his life and now spent his time fishing close to their home; if he wasn't fishing, then he'd be sitting in his shed. A radio, kettle and plenty of fishing tackle which keep him happy, plus the odd cigar. Roy stopped smoking fags years ago, but he sneaked a cigar every now and then when he thought the coast was clear, but Jean was no mug – she knew.

Roy made up his own hook lengths. He preferred four-inch for his feeders but used fifteen- to eighteen-inch for his waggler or slow sinker work. Roy competed in the local competitions once a week on a Thursday. So Monday through to Wednesday he prepared his tackle.

He must have had at least a dozen rods from old bamboo three-piece to ultra-tech, two-piece carbon rods, nine foot to thirteen foot, to suit all types of fishing scenarios. Roy only employed baitrunner reels. He liked to relax in his huge, comfortable carp seat and drift away with his thoughts and of course a cigar. If he used a traditional reel and he got a huge take, his rod could be ripped off the rest and into the pond. Roy didn't want to watch the rod tip all day. When he got a bite the baitrunner would let him know: only then would he snap out of his daydreaming.

He didn't actually care if he won or not: it was the relaxation he enjoyed with his fishing buddies, plus they usually grabbed a pint together afterwards.

Oh my God, thought Dave after drifting away with thoughts of his dad. *I nearly forgot to tell Anne's parents. I can never tell her that: she would be furious with me.*

Tapping out the number on his mobile, he felt a little embarrassed with himself.

"Hello, Mr Asher, it's David."

"Hello, David, do you have news for us?" asked Anne's father.

"Yes, I have great news: you are both grandparents to a gorgeous baby boy," explained Dave.

"Fantastic, I'm really chuffed for you both: is my daughter ok?"

"Yes, both of them are doing well but have to be kept in overnight just as a precaution, but you can come and see us tomorrow as soon as they are home."

"Great, can you let us know when that will be?" asked Mr Asher.

"Yes, I will, of course," replied Dave.

"Very well, then, I'll speak to you tomorrow, ok?"

"Yep ok," said Dave, and then hung up.

Tosser, Dave thought to himself.

"Is my daughter ok?" He never even asked about the child. Dave didn't have time for posh Charles Asher.

Ever since he put Dave down as a no good nobody, Dave knew he could only just tolerate the man. If he hadn't been in love with Anne, knowing he wanted to spend forever with her, then he would've broken Charlie boy's nose the first time he had met him.

Ah well, he thought, *I've had the last laugh. Anne is my wife now and lives with me –* which worked great for Dave as Charles would not even visit.

Before he knew it he'd dropped off to sleep on the sofa: he was more tired than he realised.

Anne and her baby had a nice, comfortable night.

It was seven-thirty and in walked Rosy.

"Good morning, Anne, how do you feel, my love?"

Anne had been drifting in and out of sleep all night, worrying if her newborn infant was ok as most new young mums do.

So she opened her eyes and pulled herself into a slightly elevated position so as to see Rosy more clearly.

"I feel fine actually, Rosy, and thank you for all you've done for me: you have made this birth easier for me than I thought anyone could."

"You don't need to thank me, it was my pleasure and besides, I love what I do, it's what I was born for," replied Rosy with a warm, caring smile.

What a lovely woman, thought Anne. *She must have delivered thousands of infants into the world and it seems like she cherishes each and every one.*

"The great news is that everything is going as expected and if you like you can call David to pick you both up at about one o'clock: how's that sound, lass?"

"That sounds good to me, Rosy."

"Would you like me to call him for you?"

"No, not yet, he will still be asleep but you could later if you may," replied Anne.

"About ten, then, shall we say?"

Anne nodded again with her lovely smile.

"Right, I'll go and fetch Jnr for you now, eh?"

Hmm, pondered Anne. *We haven't decided on a name yet as we didn't check the sex of our child before the birth, as we both agreed we wanted a surprise. We have narrowed down a shortlist, but I like that name: David Jnr. Yes, it has a nice ring to it,* she thought, *plus Dave would unbelievably proud of his son having his name.*

Dave woke up suddenly to the phone ringing. As he closed in on it, he worried.

"Hello."

"Hello, David, it's Sister Rosy here from Barnsley Hospital."

"Is everything ok?" he asked.

"Yes, love, I was just calling you to let you know both your wife and child can be picked up around 1.00."

"Oh great, thank you Rosy very much."

"You're welcome, David. I look forward to seeing you later," replied Rosy.

"Ok, thanks again, bye."

Right, thought Dave, *it's ten-fifteen. I'd better get some breakfast and then double-check everything is in place ready for my family's return and I'll call the parents and fill them in before I set off. I'll have my mum and dad here first, then the tossers can come afterwards,* he chuckled to himself.

At the same time he realised he'd taken to Sophia as she had secretly been calling to his home to see her daughter. Sophia had realised too, that, David was after all a really nice, hard-working guy who idolised her Anne, so she now felt comfortable with him in their home.

He knew one thing for sure: he would never feel like that towards Anne's dad, never.

It was approaching 4.00 as Dave's parents turned up.

—

7

As he expected, his mother was infatuated with the birth of her first grandson and well, Roy managed a quick glance, a smile and a 'Well done' handshake before he sat to watch TV.

Jean cradled the baby in her arms and with a loving smile asked, "What are you going to call him? Have you decided yet?"

"No we haven't," replied Dave.

"Yes we have!" interrupted Anne.

Dave turned and looked at his wife with huge surprise.

"We have?"

"Yes we have, his name is David Jnr." Anne smiled.

Dave's jaw dropped so far open that Anne swore she could see down to his stomach. His face beamed the biggest smile he could muster. Walking over to Anne who lay on the sofa, he crouched down beside her and whispered into her ear.

"You I love more than anything and always will: thank you, love." He kissed her, not noticing a tear running down his cheek.

"I love you, too, babe, always." Again with that lovely gentle smile of hers.

The Ashers came over a little after six. Dave let them in.

A kiss on the cheek off Sophia which raised an eyebrow from Charles but alas, no handshake offered.

It didn't go unnoticed.

Just another silent insult from the tosser.

They didn't stay long. Just like before, Anne's mother was all over her grandchild and there was not much notice from Charles.

Dave thought Charles and his father would get on. They were both stone-cold: *must be their generation of men,* he mused to himself.

They left after only visiting for twenty brief minutes.

Sophia made the excuse of wanting to leave their family in peace on this their first day with Jnr.

It didn't bother Anne or Dave because that's exactly what they wanted: to be together, all three of them.

Chapter 2 – Growing Fast

Jnr was growing up quickly. Both his mum and his dad had taken so naturally to parenthood. Jnr was now three years old and had just started junior school.

He was a quiet but pleasant child, always smiling and generous, sharing his toys with anyone who played with him. His teachers were impressed with his attitude and willingness to learn; even at this young age, he was ahead of his peers in all the various activities they engaged in, and by a long way. He seemed to be able to build something from nothing with ease. He liked to draw and paint. Jnr always tidied up after himself, too, with no prompting from anyone.

Anne and Dave Snr were very happy with their lives. Snr had his own business: he had been a mechanic since he could remember. It started with scrambler bikes and go-carts when he was only seven years old, and by the time he was ten he could take apart and rebuild a motorbike engine within a day or two, so his future was mapped out for him whether he liked it or not.

He did enjoy being his own boss within a business he knew so much about, which had been in his blood for what seemed like forever. He could work the hours he wanted, plus, because he was in demand, he could afford the family a good lifestyle, not extravagant but comfortable. Soon he would take on a couple of apprentices to take some of the weight off, and maybe even take a day or two off to spend with the family.

Anne, on the other hand, had never worked a day in her life, not that she wouldn't have, but the fact was her parents were quite well off, as her father was a university lecturer in the field of science at Sheffield University. Anne's mother was a senior school headmistress, again in Sheffield, so between her parents they earned a very good income, which they invested wisely to give their daughter the best start in life, that every parent would want for their child. Of course, when Anne's father found out she was secretly dating a mechanic he was really disappointed: it didn't matter to her father that she was now old enough and could make up her own mind on whom she would like to marry, and spend the rest of her life with.

At first he argued every night with Anne and her mother who was obviously on her daughter's side, even though she didn't let on. He told Anne that if she went to uni and did well, that she could practically take her pick of the crop and ensure her future with a solid family, but Anne would have none of it. She loved Dave and that was that, and nothing her father could say would change her mind.

He was frustrated because he knew they would struggle through life, probably having to borrow money every now and then to get by: he was sure of it.

It was the 22nd of July 2010, the day of Anne's 19th birthday. She popped her head into her father's study.

"Dad, can I please ask David to join us tonight for my birthday dinner?"

"Certainly not," replied her father. "I have invited quite a few of my colleagues from the university and your mother's work colleagues are coming, too. How would David fit in? No, Anne. I'm sorry: he may not be invited!"

"But Dad, it's my party, not yours!" she screamed, slamming the study door behind her. Charles was startled by Anne's exit. He knew it would sooner or later fizzle out, this young romance, and he knew he was right. *She will realise later in life*, he thought. He just wanted the best for her, his only child.

Anne watched from her bedroom window as her parents went shopping to stock up on wine and food for the party.

Right, thought Anne. *I'm leaving, so I'll pack and leave before they get back.* So Anne packed and set off for Dave's parents' house, hoping they would take her in.

They did reluctantly, especially Roy. He was against it from the start, but Jean wore the trousers, so Anne was allowed to stay but on two conditions: 1) Anne slept in the spare room; and 2) Anne had to call her mother every day to reassure her she was ok – more so for Sophia's sake, really.

That is history now as Anne and Dave are married with a child and are doing well for themselves.

Anne stood outside her son's classroom waiting to collect him when she felt a slight tap on her shoulder. She turned to face a lady of similar age facing her. "Hello, love, my name's Susan. I live three doors down from you."

"Ah," Anne replied, "I thought I recognised you, how are you? My name is Anne." Polite as usual.

"I'm well, thank you, how about you?"

"Yes, I'm ok thank you. I've seen you in your garden out front: that's where I recognised you from," said Anne.

"I've seen you, too, passing by – small world, eh?"

"Yes it is." They both chuckled together like little schoolgirls.

"I'm so glad," said Susan, "that our boys are in the same class together. Maybe when school's off they can play together at mine if that would be ok?"

"Oh yes, that would be great, I'd very much like that and I'm sure Jnr would, too. There are not too many children of his age on our street, are there?"

"No there ain't," replied Susan. "Let's hope they get on in class, then. I'll ask Mark about your son: what's his name?"

"It's David Jnr."

"That's nice, after his dad obviously," replied Susan. "Do you spend time with anyone on our street at all, Anne?"

"No, not really, we've been there for four years now, but no, I speak to people but I don't really visit anyone."

"Ok," said Susan, "that's decided then. We shall have to get our boys together which will give me an excuse to get out of mine for a cuppa every now and then."

"Fantastic. Oh, here come the children. Hi, Jnr." Anne smiled and Jnr ran to her side and cuddled her legs.

"Here's our Mark."

Each kid stood by his mother's side, smiling at each other. The women look at each other and smile, too.

"That answers our question, then, Susan."

"Yep, it would seem so. Right, Anne, I'm off. Got to stop by my mum's: my sister's over visiting so I better show my face"

"Ok," replied Anne. "We shall speak again soon, I hope."

"We will, don't you worry, lass."

With that, they departed.

On the walk home Anne asked her little Jnr if he played with Mark in class and to her surprise he replied, "Yes, Mummy, we're friends." She smiled and wondered if it was fate – you know, meant to be. *Of all those kids in class they happen to be friends, but then again Jnr gets on with everyone he meets, it's his nature,* she thought to herself.

As soon as they got home Jnr shot off upstairs to his books. He loved his books that his Granddad Charles had given him. His favorite was entitled *Our Solar System.* Of course he couldn't read the book: all that scientific language a child of his age could not possibly fathom. It was the pictures that stuck in his mind. He was mesmerised with their beauty, even though he didn't quite understand what it all meant: the colours, the blackness of space, these beautiful images he could never get enough of. Jnr would sit for hours drawing the planets.

He would draw rockets on the moon, and only when he was completely satisfied he'd done a good job would he stick the picture on his wall. As night came Jnr would sneak quietly out of bed and stare up at the night sky through his bedroom window. He'd sit on the window ledge hoping he could see the planets. Obviously he could only see the moon and stars, but that was good enough for Jnr for now.

As Anne was cooking she noticed Mark on his little bicycle riding along the pavement across the road. She shuddered at the thought of a three-year-old out on the streets at five o'clock. *What's Susan thinking?* she thought. *Or does she even know? Well, whether she knows or not, Jnr wouldn't be joining him out like that, not her little gentle Jnr.*

Dave came home and was starving, he proclaimed. "Good, love, because I've cooked us a lovely steak dinner with chunky chips and home-made onion rings with a crunchy coleslaw."

"Wow," said Dave, "what have I done to deserve that?"

"Silly, you do plenty enough to earn a good meal, my love," said Anne with that never-ending great smile of hers.

"Come here, you," he said, standing with his arms open wide. "I need a kiss, my princess." Anne blushed and jumped into his arms: they kissed as passionately as though they were together for the very first time.

After dinner they sat on the sofa watching their favourite soaps and Dave asked, "What's Jnr doing? He hasn't come down to see me."

"The usual, love," said Anne. "Hey, I met one of the parents today from a few doors down. Her name's Susan. She has a son in the same class as Jnr and guess what?"

"What?" he asks.

"Well, her son Mark and our Jnr have hit it off, so Susan and I agreed to let the kids play together after school or in the holidays. Isn't that great?"

"Yeah chick, that's great, he'll like that. What's he like?"

"He seems nice but, funnily enough, I saw him riding a bicycle at about 5.00 over the street. He was on the pavement, but still I wouldn't let our Jnr do that at his age."

"No way, love, I bet he's a street kid, then, eh?" chuckled Dave.

Anne smiled back but her face said it all: she was a little apprehensive about it already.

"Don't worry, love. If they do end up being friends, then they play within the house or the garden, ok?" Dave stated.

"Of course, love, I'm fine with that."

Over the next few years the boys became very close friends: they jelled well and instinctively. Mark was the streetwise one, and Jnr was the brains of the outfit. Many times at junior school other kids would pick on Jnr, but Mark would jump in without blinking to help Jnr. They were that close: no way would Mark allow anything to happen to Jnr. On the flip side, Jnr would help his friend with reading, drawing, maths, tidying his room, etc. It worked for the boys, this system, with neither of them having to put an ounce of thought into it.

Everything was right in Dave Snr and Anne's world. The grandmas popped round every chance they got. Charles never called, which suited Dave just fine. Roy did, but not often and not for long, and yes, he didn't say much as usual. Dave only went to the garage four days a week now: his recruits had learnt well and if they were stuck he was only a call away. Dave liked to do a bit in the garden on nice days, so he'd take care of the grass and hedgerows while Anne sorted to the flowers. They like to do the gardening together: quality time, Dave called it.

———

Sometimes, though, Dave would disappear into the garage on the side of their home working on his latest restoring projects. He could spend a whole day in there but he was the only one allowed in, so Anne didn't mind too much because, as Dave always delighted in telling Anne, these little projects brought in extra cash. "And better than that, tax-free cash," said Dave with a smile and a wink.

He went to an auction once a month and usually came home with a bargain, knowing with his expertise that he would make at least two grand profit. He had always explained to Anne that's twenty-four grand a year, under the carpet, tax-free money. The money they used for bills, food, clothing, furniture, etc. The fact was that the money earned from the business was immediately invested for their futures. Money for their retirement, plus to get Jnr through uni, because they both knew deep down that's where Jnr was headed.

Chapter 3 – An Astronaut?

Snr walked into the kitchen and grabbed his little wife by the waist and kissed her softly upon the nape of her neck.

"Hi, love, you ok?"

"Yes, I'm fine," said Anne with a smile and a kiss.

He smiled back and asked, "Where's Jnr?"

"He's outside playing in the garden, I think."

Dave wandered outside to look for Jnr who was now seven years old and always out exploring. He noticed that his garage door was slightly ajar and quietly made his way over to the entrance. He could see Jnr in front of a 1988 3.0S Capri he was restoring.

"Jnr, what the hell are you doing in my garage?"

Jnr stood up and smiled. He was just about to explain as his father grabbed his arm and smacked him hard on his bottom in anger.

"Get out of here and don't come in here again! Do you hear me?" roared Snr.

The young lad ran but he didn't hear his father because he was crying and screaming as he was running towards the house with the sting still throbbing in his pants, shouting for his mother. He didn't understand as his dad had never hit him like that before.

To Jnr he'd done nothing wrong.

Snr looked down at what his son had been doing in his garage and was stunned. There on the floor was the twin carburettor from the Capri which had been stripped bare by Dave, but now it was completely rebuilt!

How the hell did he do that? wondered Snr.

He'd never shown him and surely he'd not been shown at school. Snr felt ashamed at what he had done. True, the lad shouldn't have been in his garage. *Dangerous things in a man's garage for a child to be messing with*, he thought to himself.

Dave should have checked before spanking Jnr first, but it was too late now.

He better go and explain himself right away.

As Snr walked into the room he saw Jnr sitting on his mum's lap sobbing, holding tight to his mother, looking at his father in a way Snr had never seen before.

"I'm sorry, son, I didn't know what you were up to until you had gone and you damn well know my garage is off-limits!" bellowed Dave. "I saw what you did, Jnr, and I don't understand how you've done what you've done. It wasn't until I was around fifteen that I could rebuild a twin carburettor and that's after spending many years trying and failing," explained Snr. "How did you know how to build it, Jnr?"

"Stop getting at him," snapped Anne. "You've hurt him, Snr, for nothing really: he wasn't doing wrong."

"I know, Anne, I overreacted. I'm sorry, Jnr, but if I knew that you could do that, I would've encouraged you to help me out. How did you know, Jnr?" asked Snr yet again, eager for his son's reply.

"I didn't know, Dad, I just looked at it and worked it out for myself: it wasn't hard really, a bit like a jigsaw," replied Jnr. "It took ages, though, nearly an hour."

Snr started laughing out loud. "You're joking, son: you're seven years old, it's impossible. You must have researched it or had some help from someone."

"No, Dad, I just worked it out. Is it ok, Dad? Did I do it right?"

"Did you, my boy! It's like brand new and in fact it's given me an idea. Looks like it's in your blood, too, Jnr so as soon as you finish school you have a job with your old man waiting for you. How does that sound, eh?"

"Thanks, Dad, but I've decided already as to what I want to do when I grow up: I'm going to be an astronaut."

Snr laughed really hard and said," Did you get that idea from your grandpa? Has he been filling your head with his science bullshit, lad?"

"Dave, stop your swearing."

"Grandpa talks to me about science and what he teaches, but no, I have learned a bit at school and I've used the internet and books to learn things about space and planets. Do you know what the nearest star is to Earth, Dad?"

"I haven't got a clue, son, enlighten me."

"It's the sun, it is 94 million miles away, Dad. I learned that." Jnr smiled.

"Well, my clever little star," said Anne, "it's time for bed. Shall I take you up?"

"Ok, will you please read a story for me, Mum?"

"Yeah, go on, then."Anne smiled.

"Come here, star man. Can I get a hug?" asked Snr.

Little Jnr ran and jumped into his father's arms.

Snr kissed his head and again said he was sorry for the smacked bottom.

"It's ok, Dad. I won't go in there again, I promise."

"I'll be proud of you, son, whether you become an astronaut or not. I'm really proud of you already."

"Thanks, Dad. Goodnight, love you."

"Love you, too, son."

Anne entered the room after putting Jnr to bed, standing in front of Dave and looking cross.

"Dave, you don't be teaching him to swear, please, even if you're angry for whatever reason. I don't want our Jnr learning that from you," she explained.

"I know, love. I panicked because he had his back to me: I couldn't see what he was doing. There are bottles of sulphuric acid in there, Anne, and sharp tools etc. I don't know why I panicked because our Jnr ain't stupid, but I dunno, love, I panicked, I'm sorry."

"Ok, just think before you jump in again."

There it is, thought Dave. *That loving, warm smile of hers, back across her face yet again.*

"I will, my princess, now would you grab me a can please, and then bring that sexy ass of yours over here? There's a good film starting soon."

Anne got her hubby a can of his favourite bitter.

She poured herself a glass of red wine, Cabernet Sauvignon 2015.

"Hutch up, then," said Anne. "Let a little one in."

Dave put his leg down and made room for his princess.

"Aw thanks, love: nice and cold."

"I'm going to have a glass, too, love. I quite fancy one."

Smiling, Dave looked at his gorgeous wife and replied with, "I quite fancy you, ya know."

They both faced each other and giggled as they always did when feeling slightly giddy.

They kissed, sat back and relaxed into the film.

The next morning Dave had a brainwave. He still felt guilty about Jnr, and he lay thinking until the early hours how he could make it up to him.

"I'm going into town, Anne. Do you need 'owt fetching home, love?"

"What you going into town for?"

"Well, I feel bad for Jnr. I didn't sleep well: it played on my mind all night and I'm going to treat him. A sorry present, I suppose."

"Oh ok, what you thinking of?"

"It's a surprise, but he will love it," Dave explained excitedly.

"Can you pop in the corner shop for a whole meal loaf, beans and some semi-skimmed milk please?"

"Yeah no probs. I'll see you later, ok, love?"

As Dave drove he was getting more and more excited because he knew right where to find the item he was looking for, and he realised this could be the best present he'd ever bought for Jnr in Jnr's eyes.

Maplin's was the shop he wanted and there it was. He parked his car and trotted off in.

As usual, he thought to himself: there were two sales assistants at him before he had got ten feet inside the shop.

"Hello, sir," said a young, happy chappie.

"Hi," replied Dave.

"Can I help you with anything?"

"Yes you can, actually. I would like to buy my son a telescope."

"Ah ok, right. This way, then, sir."

Dave followed the young lad over to the corner at the back.

"Here we are, sir. Do you know what you want?"

"I ain't got a clue, it's for my son."

"Ok, how old is he?"

"He's seven."

"Has he used a telescope before?"

"I don't think he has, no."

"Ok," the lad continued. "We have three different ones for sale starting with this one" (he pointed to a smallish telescope). "It is a TS Starscope which has a magnification up to 170 times and will cost £90."

"The next one is a Sky-Watcher Explorer-130 M. It has a maximum magnification of 180 times. That's £187."

Dave jumped in. "That's a big price difference for 10 times more zoom, isn't it?"

"Yes, sir, but this scope has many more features than the previous one."

"Oh ok, I see."

"Next is a Celestron NexStar 5 SE," the young lad continued.

"This one has a massive price increase to the previous two you've seen, but this scope is not really for someone of your son's age, it's for a more advanced user. It incorporates some very intelligent software called SkyAlign. To set it up you point it at a certain star, the on-board computer detects what star it is, and will then automatically adjust the scope to pinpoint accuracy. This one, sir, is £650."

"Bloody hell," splurted Dave.

"Well, sir, the other two are priced well and they would easily be good enough for your son, as he is a beginner."

"Yeah, I see what you're saying."

He didn't want to appear stupid, buying a seven-year-old the best telescope in the shop, but Dave knew that his Jnr would never get bored with it.

He knew that Jnr would learn inside out how to use this scope to its maximum potential as he grew older.

"I'll have the Celestron, please," Dave motioned, pointing to the best one.

"Right, sir, I'll go and fetch you a brand new and boxed one, then."

Dave asked, "What warranty do these things have?"

"This one has a three-year full manufacturer's warranty, sir."

"Ok, that's the one, then, thank you."

"No problem, if you want to go to the counter I'll be over in a couple of minutes, ok?"

"Yeah ok, thanks," replied Dave.

He stood waiting for what seemed like ten minutes as he weighed up what he was doing.

£650 for a slap on the arse, he muttered to himself with a grin. *I wish I'd got just £10 for every slap I ever got, I'd be rich*, he thought.

He paid in (tax-free cash) for his item and the young lad carried it to the car for him, for which Dave thanked him and shook his hand: he couldn't wait to get home.

"Anne, where are you?" shouted Dave as he entered the house.

"I'm in the kitchen, love. What's up?"

"Nothing's up, love. Come here, I want to show you something."

Anne walked through to the hallway intrigued as to what Dave had bought Jnr.

"Oh my God, Dave, is that a telescope?"

"Yes, love, what ya think?"

"Wow, our Jnr is one lucky guy. He will be over the moon when he sees that."

"I know, love, I can't wait to see his face."

"Me, too. How much was it?"

"£650!"

"You what? Are you crazy? We didn't spend that much on him at Christmas."

"I know but we can well afford it and besides, this is one of the best you can buy: Jnr will get years of use from this, you know."

"I know, Dave, but…" Anne shrugged, not really knowing what to say.

"Did you get the food I asked for?"

"Aw shit, no, I forgot. Let me put this in Jnr's room and I'll pop back out, not take me long."

"Ok, love." Anne walked over and planted a kiss on his cheek. "You're a good catch, you. Love ya."

Dave smiled from ear to ear, feeling really proud of himself. "Love you, too, babe."

"I'm going to get Jnr from school, Dave. You'll be in when we get back, won't you?"

"Yeah, it will only take me ten minutes to the shop and back."

"Ok, see you later, then."

Susan and Anne were there ten minutes early to have a little natter.

"Anne, our Mark has asked if Jnr can come over later to play on his Xbox, what ya reckon?"

"He would love that: he has an Xbox, too."

"Ah but I've just remembered he can't tonight: his Dad has a surprise waiting at home for him, but I will ask Jnr if he wants to make it maybe tomorrow night?"

"Ok," said Susan. "I'll tell our lad: he's never off the bloody thing."

Anne laughed. "Well, it's what they do nowadays, isn't it?"

"Yeah true, lass, as least they're out of mischief when you know where they are," stated Susan.

Looking a bit bewildered, Anne replied, "I always know where our Jnr is, Susan. He doesn't go out much really."

"I wish I could say the same. Our Mark will get in, eat his tea and then he's off out, same every night. I don't think he's getting up to no good: no coppers have turned up yet," Susan explained jokingly.

"Oh that's good, then," said Anne as she waved goodbye.

Dave opened the door for Anne and Jnr.

"Hi, kiddo, you ok?"

"Yeah, Dad, I'm starving, though. What we got for tea, Mum?"

"What would you like, son?"

"Erm, can I have fish fingers and chips please?"

"What do you think, Snr?" Anne asked, smiling. "Can he have fish fingers and chips?"

"Yes, but he has to eat six fingers, loads of chips with two slices of bread and butter. Is that a deal, Jnr?"

"Ok, Dad, I bet I can eat it all, I'm properly hungry."

"Ok," said Anne. "I'll get cracking, then."

"I'm going to my room: will you shout me when they're ready please, Mum?"

"Of course I will, dummy. About twenty minutes, son, ok?"

"Ok, Mum!" Jnr shouted as he climbed the stairs.

Both parents stood still, listening hard, not even daring to take a breath.

"WOW!" they heard, loud and clear. Bang, bang, bang, Jnr was down the stairs in less than three seconds.

"Mum, Dad!" Jnr shouted as he ran straight at them, arms open wide ready to grab his folks. Tears flooding down his cheeks, his face red raw with emotion: he couldn't breathe.

"Thank you, thank you! I've been reading about telescopes and I was going to ask for one for Christmas but I don't need to now."

Jnr blabbed it out so fast it was hard for them to make it out.

"I take it you're happy, then?" asked Snr.

"You bet, Dad. Will you help me with it, please, to set it up?"

"Yeah, star man, let's go!"

As his dad was setting up the telescope, Jnr was telling him about certain planets. He could name most of the main ones within our own system, such as Mars, Jupiter, Neptune, Venus, etc. He even knew some of the distances of them from our own planet. Of course it all flew straight over Dave's head.

He could himself remember from school lessons a few of the planets' names but that was it, nothing else; he'd never been interested really. Sure, he watched major events like launches on the news, but as for Jnr, well, he was going to have to learn by himself. His dad could teach him how to fix a car – that was about it.

The telescope was in position. Jnr sat on his bed waiting patiently for the dark to come: it was September so it would be pitch-black by seven.

Jnr was tapping his hands on his knees, willing the darkness to come.

I can't wait to see the planets, Jnr thought to himself.

I wonder how far the telescope will be able to reach.

I wonder if I will see Mars?

That was Jnr's favourite planet.

He'd read that Mars was once thought to have contained water, and scientists thought that maybe it could have also once contained life. Now that really puzzled our Jnr: if it did once contain life, then where did that life go?

To Jnr, Mars seemed a mysterious planet.

He wanted to know more.

He read the manual and learned that with the handheld unit he could tap the name of a star or a planet and the telescope, coupled with its clever on-board computer, would automatically point to where he had commanded.

Come on, Jnr asked the darkness. *Where are you?*

Chapter 4 – Jnr's Love Of The Universe

Jnr had seen loads through his scope but now he needed more. The computer had told him what he was looking at, and there was a lot to take in.

He was tired now and it was almost 10 o'clock. Quietly he climbed into bed, images flooding through his mind: there were so many stars up there.

I wonder if they all have names, thought Jnr. *I'm going to have to speak to Granddad Charles to find out more.*

The next evening Jnr found himself in Mark's bedroom; his mum was downstairs chewing the fat with Susan.

"I've got the new *Call of Duty*: do ya wanna go on that? We can play one-on-one or go online and take turns: what do you think?" asked Mark.

"I've never played *COD* so I dunno, it's up to you," said Jnr.

"We'll go online, then, first so you can practise: it won't be fair if we play against each other, I'll waste ya." Mark laughed.

They took turns, but from the offset Mark had the upper hand.

"You're good at this, Mark."

"I should be: I've spent hours at it."

Jnr wasn't quite concentrating on the game: he had puzzles to solve.

Jnr wanted to get home asap to research as much as possible about what he'd seen the previous night, and besides, the weather was bad, raining hard outside, so Jnr knew there would be no stargazing tonight. Instead he'd use the internet to investigate his findings.

"Quiet up there, them two, Anne."

"Yeah true, Susan."

"You know what – why don't you call me Sue? Everyone else does."

"Ok, then, Sue. Might take some getting used to, though," replied Anne with her usual smile.

"What does your husband do for a living, Sue?"

"He drives lorries long-distance, love. I like it 'cos I don't have to see him very often!"

Both ladies giggled at that one.

"Do you not get on?" asked Anne.

"Oh yes, we do, but he gets on my nerves if he's around me too much. He earns decent money driving and, like he's says, there's not much round here for him. Mark's used to it, too, he don't mind. Stu always takes him out when he gets back."

"What does your hubby do?" asked Sue.

"Dave's a mechanic, he has a garage near town."

"Ah good, that will give the guys something to talk about at barbecues, then."Sue laughed.

"Yes it would, Susan, I mean Sue."

Stu and Sue: she imagined how funny it could get at times in this house, especially after a couple of glasses of wine.

"Jnr?" asked Mark."Here, do you want a chocolate egg?"

"Yes please. You're lucky, Mark: my mum wouldn't let me eat in my room."

"Why?" asked Mark with a surprised look on his face.

"In case I made a mess: I'm not allowed to eat food upstairs at all," said Jnr.

"My mum doesn't mind as long as I bring my dishes down. Besides, she doesn't know I've got these."

"Why?"

"'Cos I nicked two from the shop," explained Mark with a mischievous look on his face.

Jnr gasped. "You stole?"

"Yeah, all the kids do it, it's no biggie."

"What if the man caught you?"

"Dunno, never thought about it."

"Well, I think you shouldn't do it, Mark. If you got caught, your dad would kill you!"

"I won't get caught, silly."

"Hey, Mark, you should come to my house next time, I've got a telescope."

"What for? You can see the moon without one."

"No, a proper one," said Jnr with a glint in his eye."You can see everything with it, not just the moon."

"Like what?"

"Well, on a clear night you can see other planets and thousands of stars."

"What for?" asked Mark.

Jnr was stunned. "What for?" he said. "Because they are so cool: it looks fantastic through a telescope."

"Oh right," replied Mark as he turned his attention back to his Xbox.

Jnr wondered why anyone would not want to gaze towards the stars.

"Jnr, come down, it's time to go ok!" shouted Anne from downstairs.

"Right, Sue, thanks for tonight: next time come to my house with Mark."

"Our Jnr has a Gamebox thing so they can play on his, too."

"Alright, Anne, I'll bring some wine and snacks round. We'll have a proper girlies' night, eh?" remarked Sue.

"Yes, we will, love, but no need for you to bring anything. I'll cook us a little something nice."

"Settled, then," replied Sue.

"I've got to go, Mark. See you tomorrow."

"Right," Mark replied. "Bye."

"Come on, kiddo, get your coat on, it's raining out there."

"Mum, can Mark come to our house one night please?"

"Of course he can, Jnr. Sue and I have already started organising it," replied Anne, with both ladies smiling.

"Great, let's go, then, I've got some homework, Mum."

"Steady, tiger," laughed Sue.

"Wish my Mark would be so excited to get his homework done."

Anne just smiled.

"Right, thanks, and I'll see you at school tomorrow."

"Yep ok, lass. Bye, Jnr."

"Bye, Mrs Childs."

"Isn't he polite?" Sue ruffled his hair.

Even though they lived only fifty yards away from the Childses' house, they were both soaked as they burst through the door.

"Mum?"

"Yes, love, what is it?"

"When is the next time we see Granddad Charles?"

"I don't know, Jnr. Why?"

"Well, I want to ask him some questions, that's all. I like it when Granddad talks to me about space, and besides, I have some queries he could help me with," replied Jnr.

"Oh ok, Jnr. I'll arrange something at the weekend if he's not too busy. Is that alright with you, my little star?"

"Yep, that's fine by me," he replied as he was halfway up the stairs.

Jnr jumped straight onto his laptop.

Right, time to do some research.

Over the next few years Jnr had soaked up so much information that he thought he could enter university now and pass, even at only fourteen. He knew everything about our solar system: he could name every planet in order from the sun, working away to the last planet. He knew the radius of each planet, distance to Earth from each planet, atmospheric details of each planet. Jnr even knew by name each of the moons that surrounded the planets.

But Jnr's biggest interest – apart from *Is there life anywhere in the universe?*, which every human being that ever lived on this blue planet of ours would ponder at some point in time – was the black hole.

He admired Dr Stephen Hawking and would read every word that he had ever written.

Albert Einstein first predicted black holes back in 1916, with his general theory of relativity, but it was Kip Thorne, a great physicist, who discovered the first black hole in 1971 – Cygnus X-1, it was named.

In fact, both Hawking and Thorne had a little friendly bet between themselves.

Hawking bet against the finding of Cygnus X-1 as a black hole. Hawking lost: he conceded his bet in 1990.

But to Jnr the fact that Mr Hawking hadn't been the first to find one didn't matter: it was the professor's undeniable interest and theories of the black hole that set him apart from all other physicists for Jnr.

"Hi Granddad, hi Grandma!" shouted Jnr as he entered through their front door with his mum.

It was Saturday so the grandparents were home.

"Hello, Jnr," replied his grandma. "Are you ok?"

"Yeah I'm fine, thank you. How about you?"

"I'm also fine, my love."

"Where's Granddad?"

"He's in the garden, Jnr, right down the back end. There's a mountain of dead leaves down there and they are smothering the grass: your granddad is sorting them out."

"Ok, I'll go and help him, then."

"Don't get dirty, Jnr! "his mum shouted. "Ask your granddad for some wellies."

With that, Jnr set off down the garden.

"You ok, Mum?" asked Anne with a kiss and a cuddle.

Anne loved her mum deeply. Her dad had always been a stubborn old so-and-so and a man's man, so he never really got into too much conversation with Anne: if she needed to talk seriously to anyone, then it was her mum.

"Yes, dear, I'm fine. Why wouldn't I be?" replied Sophia.

"Ok, Mum, I'm only asking. How's school?"

"It's alright actually. I don't think it could run any better."

"This coming year we've been given a government grant for some new buildings which should reduce child numbers per class: our sports centre is going to have improvements, and a new science department is being commissioned," said Sophia.

"Oh good, I bet Dad shows some interest now!"

"I'll not hold my breath." Sophia smiled.

"Hi, Granddad."

"Hello there, Jnr. Watch your step, it's very slippery on these leaves," replied Charles.

"Do you have any spare wellies?"

"Yes, in the shed on the left."

"Ok, shall I bring a rake, too?"

"Yes, why not? The two of us will finish this job quicker, Jnr."

Granddad's shed was huge and he spotted the boots straight away but couldn't see a rake. He spotted a model of the planets (you know the ones: the planets are balls attached to wires that move around each other). He smiled to himself. *Granddad had got the sequence wrong,* he mused. Jnr put things in order: no way would he tell his grandpa that he'd had to be corrected by Jnr.

Ah, there's the rake. He was talking out loud to himself.

"Got it, Granddad, where do you want me to start?"

"You go to the left as I've already started here, ok?"

"Yep, ok."

27

"Take a sack and fill it up, Jnr?"

"Yes, Granddad."

After just under an hour they were back inside and cleaned up.

"Wow," said Sophia. "You two have done a wonderful job between you."

She could see all of her lovely garden again.

"We filled twelve black sacks with leaves, Grandma," said Jnr.

"Fantastic, what are you going to do with them?"

"Both Jnr and I will take them into the woods next to Barny's farm, that is after you've made us a nice sandwich for our hard labour," said Charles with a wink at Jnr.

"Are you hungry, Jnr?"

"I could eat a sandwich: have you got any ham?"

"Yes, love, do you want it plain or with some salad on?"

Charles spoke first.

"I'll have salad with mine and some mustard on, please!" he barked.

"Yeah, Grandma, I'll have the same as Granddad, please."

"Ok, do you want a pot of tea, too?"

"Yes please," the guys replied at the same time.

"Wait, Mum," said Anne. "I'll help."

Off they trotted into the kitchen.

"Granddad, do you know much of the phenomenon called the event horizon? And what goes on inside black holes?" asked Jnr.

Instantly his granddad's eyes lit up.

"Why yes, Jnr, I know a little. The event horizon is the outer edge of a black hole – the rim of it, if you like. Once anything passes this point it simply disappears within."

"Even light cannot escape once it's crossed this point. As to what exactly happens when things enter black holes, well, I should imagine they just disappear. Why do you ask, Jnr? What are you working on?" asked Charles, excitedly waiting for Jnr's answer.

"Oh, it's something from school, Granddad. I've been working on a theory myself for a long time now and I've read so much information and learned a vast amount on black holes, but still I cannot get a burning question from my mind," explained Jnr.

"What is the question, Jnr?"

"Stephen Hawking theorises that a person could pass through a black hole."

"Ridiculous, Jnr, he would be torn to a million pieces in an instant," replied Charles with that look of certainty across his face.

"Ok, Granddad. There are many physicists who believe it to be true. Obviously it's all theory until proven," continued Jnr.

"Now Hawking believes that if one did indeed manage to make it through this event, then it would propel you to another universe."

"Ok, Jnr, but this theory has been a theory of many for years now: it's nothing new," said Charles.

"Yes true, Granddad, but Hawking says if a person or indeed a ship, for example, did make it through, then he believes it would be impossible for them to make it back to our own universe. I don't believe that, Granddad," said Jnr, getting excited at the prospect of telling his granddad about his own theory.

"We know there are two types of black holes. I believe that both work internally slightly different from each other, I think there lies the secret: maybe interstellar travel is possible using the two different black holes. We also know there are millions of them scattered throughout the universe, so I am absolutely positive that it would be possible to return into our own solar system!"

"In fact, if I could go through one to prove it, then I wouldn't hesitate, I'd do it right now," belted out Jnr.

"Wow, ok, Jnr. Good theory, but again it's a theory that's probably been used a thousand times over," explained Charles.

"Tell you what, use your young years wisely, do well at school and onto university, then I believe you will become a great physicist. So I would like to ask a favor," said Charles.

"Yes of course, Granddad, anything."

"Prove your theory to the world, Jnr!"

Chapter 5 – University

"Hurry, Amandeep!" shouted Jnr. "We're going to be late."

"Gosh, David, calm down, it will only take two minutes to reach the lecture."

"Yes, but we have Professor Machin in today and he does not suffer fools easily: as we are late, in his eyes, we are fools," barked Jnr.

Amandeep is of Indian heritage: his parents hailed from the Punjab region of India, and moved to England around 30 years ago to build a better life for themselves.

Amandeep had taken Biological Science.

For years his interest in biology had built from being very young, very similar to Jnr. As a young child he was obsessed with the creatures great and small: he would spend hours in his garden catching insects, observing and cataloguing his finds. The diversity of creation on our planet is Amandeep's passion. Many evenings they would sit and chat for hours about their interests.

Our Jnr, on the other hand, as you've probably guessed, had chosen Physics and Astronomy.

Both boys started uni at eighteen and they didn't take a gap year – eager boys to get to work with their chosen subjects. The need for knowledge was undeniable for both; plus, the quicker they got stuck in, the quicker they could pass and progress onto employment. It was then that their lives would excel, they hoped.

They met in the first week at uni. There had been an after-class club for newbies for the purpose of making new acquaintances. Jnr took a liking to Amandeep straightaway. Of course, they spoke to just about everyone in attendance but well, the boys just clicked!

Amandeep hailed from Derby, so he had to share student accommodation in Sheffield quite close to town and only a quick bus ride to uni.

Jnr meanwhile travelled in from Barnsley.

His dad obviously provided Jnr with his first set of wheels, a 2014 BMW 1 series in black with only 32,000 on the clock. Jnr passed his test first time, which he put down to his father's many driving lessons taken around local B roads just outside of Barnsley. Of course, all the lessons in the world can't help you pass first time, it's down to the day and whether or not you can compose yourself, not letting nerves enter the equation, not cracking under pressure. Needless to say, Jnr passed with flying colours: even the test instructor commented on Jnr's composure during the test.

"Well," exclaimed Amandeep, "that was pointless!"

"Why?" asked Jnr.

"Well, did you get anything from that lecture?"

"Erm yes, I suppose so."

"Oh good, because I didn't."

Jnr laughed. "Well, you wanted to go: I wasn't that bothered really. I'd rather stick to what I know: that way I feel I can contribute to some extent."

"Let's go and eat, Jnr, I'm starving. I might as well fill myself with food, because I'm not full of knowledge after that shambles."

"What do you fancy, Jnr?"

"Well, normally I eat at home. My mother always prepares me a meal, so I'd better call and ask first."

"Ok, hurry up, then, because if you ain't coming then I'll have to go by myself!"

"Wait then, I'll find out," added Jnr.

"Hi, Mum, it's me."

"Hi love, are you ok?"

"Yeah, Mum, I'm fine. My friend Amandeep wants to go for food. Would you mind if I eat out tonight?"

"Oh Jnr, of course I wouldn't mind and besides, I've been to my parents' house for my tea. I needed to see your grandmother so I haven't even started preparing anything yet."

"Dad won't mind, will he, Mum?"

"No, I'll pick him some KFC up on my way home: he likes one every now and then," replied Anne.

"Wicked. Ok, Mum. I'll see you later."

"Sorted, Amandeep. What we having, then?"

"I fancy a curry myself, what about you?"

"Erm curry: I don't usually eat curries, are they really hot?"

31

Amandeep laughed. "You white boys make me laugh. You all think us Asians eat hot chillies like sweets and shit flames."Both lads were crying with laughter.

"Now, Jnr, come, let me educate you, my friend, on culinary art."

"Near my place we have an Indian restaurant with an impeccable reputation and they deserve it! I've been a couple of times with my flat mates: no complaints what so ever," said Amandeep.

"Ok, then, stop talking and start walking!"

Jnr eyed the menu intently. *Hmm, I don't know.* He was thinking out loud.

Amandeep grinned. "You haven't been to a curry house before, have you?"

"No, like I said, I always eat at home: we have takeaways sometimes but not very often. Pizza or fish and chips mainly. My mum loves cooking, so my dad and I have our meals planned out."

"What you having, Amandeep?"

"My usual, I like butter chicken: it's a dish from my area of India."

"Oh right, I'll have the same, then. It's not hot, is it?"

"No, it's quite mild: it's the flavour I like."

"Believe it or not, Jnr, not all Asians eat hot curries all the time, you know. Sometimes I fancy a hot dish, but mostly I prefer milder dishes. I enjoy the milder curries when I want to indulge in flavour."

"Is tandoori hot?"

"Not really, no. Again it's a flavoursome dish: the meat's cooked in a clay oven, it's really nice. That dish comes from Punjab, too," added Amandeep.

"What shall I order with it, then, just rice?"

"Don't worry, Jnr, leave it to me, I'm gonna educate you."Amandeep smiled.

After their meal Jnr dropped his friend off and headed onto the M1.

As he drove home he felt uncomfortable: he had eaten loads. Amandeep ordered a pickle tray with poppadoms to start. Jnr enjoyed that, which surprised him with the look of some of the contents on the tray. One was too hot, though: lime pickle. He wouldn't be having that one again. Next came the curry and rice complete with pear drop-shaped naan bread, garlic and coriander, all washed down with a pint of Cobra.

Jnr only had a half. He was not used to alcohol and no way would he risk drink-driving: his dad would kill him, full stop.

It took Jnr forty minutes to reach home.

"That you, Jnr?"

"Yeah, Mum, it's me."

"You ok, love?" asked Anne.

"Yeah, Mum, I'm good. I've been for a meal with my mate. It was nice, we had a curry at a restaurant that he goes to."

"A curry? Didn't know you liked curries."

"I didn't, I had the same as my friend: butter chicken. I enjoyed it,"explained Jnr. "Not hot at all!"

"Hi, Dad, you ok?"

Jnr's dad was half-asleep on his man chair.

"Hi son, I'm alright, bit tired," he replied. "So you've been out, eh, lad?"

"Well, not out, Dad. I went for some food, that's all. Not out, like out!"

"Well, if it's a nice place and the food's good maybe we should go one night, love. What ya think?" asked Snr.

"Yeah, why not? I don't think I've ever tried a proper curry," remarked Anne.

"Well, let me know and we can go together," added Jnr.

"I'm going up, Mum, I've got some research to do."

"Ok, love. Do you want a drink fetching up?"

"Yeah, could I have a hot chocolate please?"

"'Course you can. I'll fetch it up."

"Thanks, Mum. Night, Dad."

"Goodnight, lad."

The next morning Jnr set off earlier than usual: his mate Amandeep needed a lift into uni because the buses were down for some reason or another.

"Hi Jnr. Do you mind if my flatmate gets a lift, too?" asked Amandeep.

"No, course not, jump in!"

Amandeep introduced his flat mate as Raph, short for Raphael.

"Hi, my name's Jnr."

"Nice to meet you."

"Yeah, you, too, pal," added Raph.

"Seatbelts on, guys?" asked Jnr as he set off.

"What do you study, then, Raph?"

"I've taken Biological Science, same as Jib here."

"Jib?"

Amandeep laughed. "It's my nickname!"

"You never told me to call you that."

"Well, I normally introduce myself with my full name, but Raph started to use 'Jib' and it's stuck, it's growing on me." Amandeep smiled.

"Ok, Jib," laughed Jnr. "I may get it wrong every now and then, but Jib it is!"

All three chuckled as they weaved in and out through the bustling traffic towards uni.

It turned out that Raphael was a Greek Cypriot. He was a cheeky, happy-go-lucky chappie, a ladies' man, too. Always there was a lady or two in Raph's life.

His grandparents come from the Aradippou region of Cyprus (not too far from Larnaka, for you holiday makers out there). They moved here over 60 years ago to Birmingham. All the family before him, his grandparents and now his parents, ran fish and chips shops. Raph was not going down the same route: he had seen enough to tell him that fish and chips shops were not for him. Ever since he could remember he never really saw that much of his dad: it was Raph's mother who basically brought him up.

His dad would set off to his shop around eight in the morning and wouldn't be home till nearly one the following morning. It's a demanding business to be in and fourteen- to sixteen-hour shifts weren't uncommon for the fish shop owner.

Hence the reason Raph hardly saw his dad.

"Ok, guys, shall we meet at lunch?" asked Jnr.

"Yes ok," replied Jib and Raph.

Jnr's morning was taken up with geophysics.

Geophysics seeks to understand Earth in terms of simple physical principles. To do this, you will learn principles of magnetism, heat, waves and radioactivity in order to develop an overview of Earth's structure, the processes it is affected by and the techniques used to observe them. Jnr's brain was like a sponge soaking up every ounce of information fed to it.

Jnr had taken on four modules for his degree, Geophysics as we now know, Quantum Physics, Space and Time, and, last but not least, Relativity.

He discussed with his parents the options available to him. At first he decided on for a three-year-long course leading to an honours degree, but after the discussion with his mum and dad, our Jnr knew in his heart that wouldn't have been enough. So Jnr went the whole hog: a four-year-long MEng or MSci course leading eventually to an integrated Masters degree. To pass with full honors, our Jnr would need a score of 480.

Jib and Raph were already seated when Jnr entered the cafeteria. Jib waved him over.

"Hiya, guys." Jnr sat down.

While unpacking his cutlery he asked how their day had been so far.

Raph replied first. "It's been ok, same old. Can't wait till our course intensifies: bit dull at the moment!"

Jib laughed. "That's why you seemed not to be paying much attention, then, eh?"

"Well, I don't need to. I'll just ask you later to fill me in!"

"Don't think for the next three years I'm going to bail you out, my friend." Jib smiled.

"What you been up to, Jnr?"

"I've had Geophysics this morning, it was good."

"So three years, Raph. Honours you're after?"

"Yes, it will be enough for me, I think. If not, I could always extend or take another year later," replied Raph. "Anyway, it means I get into the world of employment before you two! I'll probably land a position in London and, well, just party like it's my birthday, it's my birthday, I hope!"

All three lads sat munching and laughing like a bunch of ten-year-olds.

Over the next three years the boys became inseparable.

Although both Jnr and Jib were a bit nerdy, Raph was outgoing.

He went out often with other students, you know, the usual stuff: student nights at certain bars, bowling, etc – as usual, a girl hanging off his arm.

Both Jnr and Jib mostly stayed in.

If they were to go out it would be for a meal (Jnr's parents often joined them) or they would attend an evening club of some sort, or be battling against each other online through their Xbox consoles.

That's the way it stayed until it was graduation time for Raph.

Jnr and Jib were there, right at the front with Raph's family, whom looked on at their son with teary eyes: proud they were.

"Who would have thought it?" remarked Raph's dad. "My son, a biologist."

Even though he wanted to pass his business on to him and felt a little sad that Raph had turned his back on their way of life, he couldn't have been more proud at what he'd achieved. He knew his son had a bright future ahead of him.

As they watched Raph up on stage, Jib turned to Jnr and said, "I've got some good news, Jnr!"

"What's that?"

"I don't know if you remember but myself and Raph put our names down for a NASA-planned colony position at the start of uni. There were thousands of names, as you can imagine, on the list, but my name has come up! It doesn't mean I'm accepted yet, it just means I've been shortlisted," explained Jib.

"Wow, that's fantastic! When you say 'colony', where do you mean?" asked Jnr.

"Mars!"

"You're joking. I've read about that," explained Jnr. "That's a one-way ticket!"

"Yes it is."

"Gosh, you'd better start really thinking about what that implies, my friend."

"Oh Jnr, I have, believe me. As a biologist it's a dream of mine. Imagine: I will be part of a team that will in essence create life on Mars! Ok, it will be plant life, but still, I will be part of something huge, if I were to get offered the chance to go, I'll be off, Jnr."

On the way home Jnr couldn't help thinking of what his friend had just announced: Jib would leave Earth forever. Of course, that's even if he was selected.

Firstly he had to graduate and he must achieve a top score to even qualify. It wouldn't be for a few years yet, plus it would mean Jib would have to undertake astronaut training, which was brutal. He would have to be 100% fit in body and mind.

Jnr didn't doubt his friend in graduating, even with such a high target to achieve. It just was, well, Jib, an astronaut: it just didn't fit with Jnr.

With a shake of his head, Jnr thought he was getting ahead of himself.

"Thanks for dropping me off, Jnr."

"You're welcome, mate. Listen, Jib, have you really thought this through?"

"I knew you would panic. Well, don't, I haven't gone yet."

"See you tomorrow."

Raph had already left to begin his career with the Royal Society of Biology.

He jumped on the first employer to take him on, but he was happy with his position.

His idea was to stay on for a year or two then take a look to see what was on offer.

With six months left to go, Jib applied for a position at Goddard Institute for Space Studies, which lies in Manhattan.

The reply came, with which he was overjoyed.

Provided he graduated with distinction (he expected nothing less), then the position was his. Jnr was, of course, over the moon for his friend, even though he would be moving to the US.

Nowadays we have mobiles, internet, FaceTime even, so they could still speak everyday.

They would always remain close friends, even if Jib did get to Mars!

Our Jnr applied to Kennedy Space Center which is in Cape Canaveral, Florida.

As we can expect, Jnr would graduate, Jnr would exceed his expectations, and Jnr would leave for the US. This would not be easy for his parents, especially his mother and grand parents, but they knew this day would come.

They also knew Jnr's destiny and it wasn't in Barnsley!

Chapter 6 – Becoming A Reality

"David!" shouted Markus, one of Jnr's colleagues."Wait for me!"

Markus quickened his step to catch up.

"I hate that walk from the car park."

"Keeps you fit," replied Jnr," and besides, until we can be beamed up, we haven't much choice in the matter."

"I'm gonna buy a Segway!" Markus smiled.

"What's on the menu today, then, David?"

Our Jnr is a team leader already, so other than Dr Professor Shultz who plans out the group's studies, Jnr dictates what would be studied on the day.

"Same as usual, my friend: Titan."

Titan is a moon surrounding Saturn. NASA had theorised about Titan even more so after the Cassini-Huygens mission arrived in 2004.

It was discovered in 1655 by a Dutch astronomer called Christiaan Huygens: what makes Titan so interesting is the fact that it contains liquid, maybe even seas like our own.

Jnr is a part of a small team of three scientists; Markus and Andrea make up the rest of his team. Jnr's theories would have to wait for now. Dr Shultz believes in Jnr, even with his theory, but at that moment NASA were concentrating all their efforts on two things. One was Titan: hopefully a future mission to land on this interesting rock.

The next was the Mars landing which is being meticulously planned as we speak. Jnr would love to work on that project, but alas, it was nothing to do with Dr Shultz and his team.

Jnr found an apartment only four miles away from base so it didn't take long for the drive to work. Just before he left his home in the UK, his mum and dad presented him with a parting gift which he was not allowed to open until he had set up in the US.

Jnr took the apartment as soon as he saw it: FountainVillas it was called, in Rockledge, FL. It had two bedrooms, one with an ensuite, kitchen/diner, spacious living room, laundry room, study and, best of all, a balcony, for stargazing, of course. It was a little expensive ($275 per week), but his salary could cover it no problem, as long as he was careful not to waste money.

Jnr sat on the only stool in his new place, as it was unfurnished. He started to think of what he'd left behind when suddenly he remembered the envelope his father had given him.

Ok, thought Jnr, *I'm allowed to open it now, I suppose.*

While carefully opening the envelope, the cheque that was enclosed in a short letter dropped to the floor. Jnr just stared at it as it lay on the floor face-up. He couldn't believe what he was seeing! £25,000. *What the hell? Why have they done that? Why so much?* wondered Jnr.

Jnr knew his father was always careful with the money he had worked so hard for, but he didn't realise Snr had done that well.

Must be all those cars he bought at auction and restored, thought Jnr.

His dad always explained that the restorations were a tax-free profit income to be used as rainy-day money.

"I'm going to call them now!" said Jnr, out loud to himself.

It was 10.15 pm in Florida so Jnr calculated in his mind: *we are nine hours behind the UK so it's 7.15 back home. Great: they will be up.*

After speaking with his parents, Jnr carefully placed the cheque into his wallet. He arranged the opening of a bank account before leaving for the US. First job in the morning was the bank. He would use taxis until the money had cleared into his account.

On the phone his dad told him what kind of car he should buy. He knew what he was talking about: after all, he was the expert in that particular field.

His mum told him to buy furniture for the apartment and clothing for his new job. Even though she wasn't there, Jnr's mum wanted him to dress impeccably: shirts, trousers and comfortable shoes.

Bless her, thought Jnr with a warm smile.

He decided to rent a room at a nearby motel on a pay-per-day basis until he could properly move into his apartment. For the next few days he would familiarise himself with his surroundings.

The cheque had cleared, time for Jnr to embark on a serious shopping spree.

Firstly, furniture, a bed, TV, kettle, toaster, sofa, etc.

He went to Costco and brought everything he needed from under one roof and paid extra to have it delivered and installed the next morning.

He was there for the delivery and advised the delivery guys where to put his new furniture.

When finished, Jnr sat on his new sofa feeling quite proud of himself.

The apartment now resembled something like home.

Right, time to sort a car out, thought Jnr.

The first car sale he came toand there on the forecourt was a nerdy kinda car he could see himself in. It was a Volkswagen Beetle in silver, 2016 model, 1.8 diesel with 48,000 km on the clock.

The salesman took him out for a little spin.

"Well, what do you think, buddy?"

"Yes, I like it," replied Jnr.

His dad had told him everything he needed to know about buying a car.

Check the bodywork for repairs, check the seat upholstery, make sure the foot pedals and gear shift don't look more worn than they should be for the mileage.

Ask to see any documentation that comes with the vehicle. Does it have a service history? Make sure it has two keys, and always ask for discount.

If none offered, then ask for the warranty to be extended: just make sure you get something out of the deal.

With the job done, Jnr pulled out of the garage an hour later.

I must remember to drive on the right!

On his test-drive it looked so easy, but in all honesty Jnr wasn't taking notice of the salesman's driving: he was too busy listening to the engine, checking for any nasty noises.

He headed back to the area of his apartment. Jnr knew most of the area there now, so driving would be easier to learn around his own estate.

After about an hour he decided to head home: shopping for clothes could wait for now.

Meanwhile, back at work, a message is sent to Jnr from Dr Shultz with a junior physician who works in the astrobiology lab.

"Dr David Archer?"

"Yes, that's me."

"Ah good. Dr Shultz would like to speak with you in his office."

"Ok, guys, I'll leave you to it. Got to see the boss!" explained Jnr.

Knock knock.

"Come in!" shouted Dr Shultz.

"Ah David, come in, take a seat."

"Thank you," replied David as he sat waiting for Shultz to engage in conversation.

While waiting he looked around the doctor's office. Trophies on the bookcase, diplomas hanging on the walls, and beautiful pictures of planets on every wall.

"Ok, David, sorry about that, always something to sign, emails to read, phone calls to make, busy, busy," remarked Dr Shultz.

"David, I need to ask you a question to which I need a direct answer, ok?"

"Yes, Dr Shultz, fire away!"

"How would you like to go to Mars, David?"

Jnr smiled and said, "Ok, Dr Shultz, when's the next bus?"

Dr Shultz laughed. "Oh David, I do enjoy your wit. I am being very serious here. We have been asked by NASA to put forward a scientist of your qualification. You're very bright David, and I believe you are the right person to fulfill this position! The reason that I have asked you in particular is because I don't want to leave anything to chance. I need someone with calm determination and the upmost professionalism. David, I know in my heart that person is you!"

Jnr was visibly shocked at what he had just been told.

"Well, Dr Shultz, I would like time to think before I choose to take the opportunity. What would be expected of me?"

"Don't worry about that now, just take time to digest what has been asked, but please, you must keep this matter to yourself for now, David, ok?"

"Yes, Dr Shultz, no problem at all."

Jnr lay awake for most of the night pondering the situation.

Why me? How long would I be gone? What about Mum and Dad? When would I get back?

Poor Jnr just couldn't sleep.

He got up for a drink of juice.

Quietly he sat in the dark, still pondering.

This decision would be his and his alone. Even though in time he would discuss it with his parents and close friends, it would be our Jnr who ultimately must decide.

41

Jnr opened his laptop and emailed Jib.

Back to bed now, gotta get some sleep, he reminded himself.

As requested in his email, Jib called him the following evening.

"Hi Jnr, you alright?"

"Yeah, I'm good."

"I'm glad you called me, I need to ask you some questions."

"Ok, David, this sounds serious."

"Nothing serious really."

"What's happening with the Mars landing? Are you going?" asked Jnr.

"I find out within the month."

"Oh right. How long does it take to reach Mars?"

"Well, it depends on a few factors really, like the speed of the launch, alignment between Earth and Mars, and how much fuel we have to burn. It takes anywhere between 150 and 300 days, Jnr. Why do you ask?"

"Oh nothing really, just out of interest."

"Come on, you don't just email me out of the blue to ask me that, especially when you can just Google it!" exclaimed Jib.

Jnr was dying to splurt it out but no, he couldn't!

"Well, I just wanted a chat really. We haven't spoken in weeks: have you spoken to Raph?"

"No, but we text often: we should get together and Face Time him, Jnr."

"Yes, good idea. Ok, I'll speak to you later in the week then, .I'll ask for a few days off and I'll come to yours. It'll be fun!"

"Ok, Jnr, that sounds good to me."

For the next few weeks Jnr tried to forget his dilemma.

This question was in his thoughts constantly, no matter how hard he tried to push it back in his mind.

The team continued their work set out by Dr Shultz.

It was at that time that Jnr noticed something strange beyond Mars!

He examined the photos provided courtesy of the Spitzer Telescope.

The Hubble Telescope, which is probably the most famous one that people recognise, only sees images in visible light, whereas the Spitzer Telescope sees in infrared, and something had appeared!

Jnr noticed a tiny distortion to the side of Mars.

Obviously it could be millions of miles away, but on the pictures it looks close.

Hmm, he wondered. *That's strange.*

It could be anything. As the planets and moons continue on their orbits, they often produce distortions within the images taken.

Jnr put the images away.

"Right, guys, I'm off. See you both in the morning."

Jnr had just walked in when his mobile sounded. He had had to get a new one because the network was different in the US.

It was a text from Jib. It read: *call me as soon as you get this, it's important.*

Jnr didn't reply with a text: he rang the number.

"Hi Jib."

"Oh Jnr, I'm so glad you rang, I wasn't sure if you'd finished work yet," replied Jib, sounding excited. You know a few weeks back you were asking me questions, Jnr, about the Mars thing!"

"Yes, I remember."

"Was there something you weren't telling me?"

"No, mate, like what?"

"So you knew nothing of it from anyone at all?"

"About what?" asked Jnr, getting curious.

"I've only gone and been accepted, Jnr! I'm going on the Mars mission!" Jib announced.

Jnr gasped. "You're joking! That's awesome news, mate!"

"So you thought I maybe had been tipped off, then. I promise, Jib, I knew nothing of it. To be honest, though, I'm excited for you and I feel sad already that you'll be leaving."

"Listen, Jnr, it takes up to two years to be fully trained as an astronaut, plus there are no guarantees to whether I'm going to qualify or not, so don't worry," explained Jib.

After the conversation with his friend, Jnr all of a sudden felt alone. One of his best friends could be leaving the planet.

Wow, imagine that, thought Jnr. *My friend going to Mars.*

Even though technology meant contact could still be made, it would be hard to think that he was alone in the US once Jib had left –if he did leave.

Jnr decided a chat with his mum might help but it was too late now. *I'll give her a call tomorrow.*

He then decided to call Raph: he was always up till late.

Jnr needed to hear his friend's voice.

Would you believe it? thought Jnr. *No answer!*

After leaving a message he opened his laptop. *Let's look at those images again,* he muttered to himself.

Back in the laboratory, Jnr decided he needed to have Dr Shultz look at his findings.

Even though Jnr wasn't quite sure of what he was looking at, he had his suspicions.

Jnr lifted the receiver and dialled 08, which took him straight through to the doctor's office.

"Hello."

"Hi, Dr Shultz, it's David here. May I come and see you, please? I have something I would like your opinion on," asked Jnr.

"Ok, can you enlighten me? Is it Titan?"

"No, I'm afraid not. It's not Titan but it is important," replied Jnr.

"Ok, give me twenty minutes, please, David, then pop in, ok?"

"Yes, Dr Shultz, twenty minutes, then, thank you."

Knock knock.

"Enter!" he shouted loudly.

"Ah David, you have me intrigued. Come and tell me what's on your mind."

Now, Dr Shultz thought Jnr was there to answer the question put to him a few weeks prior: how wrong he was.

David placed on the table multiple images of Mars in front of his boss.

"Take a look, Dr Shultz, to the left of Mars, just there!"

The doctor drew close.

"What am I looking for, David?"

"Ok, let me show you. If you look at this point" –Jnr pointed with his pen –"keep watching it as I pass the pictures along," explained Jnr.

"Ah yes, David, I see it!"

"It seems to appear in some of the images and then disappears in the later ones."

"So what is it, then, David, any ideas?"

"I'm not sure, sir.I could theorise as to what I think it is, but I will need to view many more images and do some serious calculations before I could determine an answer," replied Jnr.

"How did you spot this?"

"Well, as you know, Jupiter has blocked our vision of Titan at the moment, so I was just flicking through some images that we have when it caught my eye."

"Well done, Jnr."

"I think it could be nothing but research this, please, it may be of significance," stated Dr Shultz. "Can I ask a question, David?"

"Yes, sir, of course you may."

"What do you really think it could be, David?" The doctor knew exactly what Jnr was about to say.

"Well, Dr Shultz, it's hard to say without further evidence, but if I had to answer your question with the knowledge I have on the subject, then I would have to say in my opinion that it could be a black hole!"

Jnr took a deep breath: he felt a little anxious.

"Ok, David, and if it is?"

"Well, sir, if it is, then it's a new one to science, but like I said, it needs investigating fully before we could come to that conclusion."

"Very well. Now, David, may I ask you the same question that I've already asked? This time, think of your answer with this new knowledge in mind."

Jnr looked at his boss and smiled. "My answer is yes, Dr Shultz!"

Chapter 7 – Jnr's Findings

Over the next week it was madness in Jnr's otherwise quiet existence.

Dr Shultz contacted one of his very good friends at NASA, who was one of the senior professors at the Ames Research Center, heading the department of lunar science. They were told to speak to no one and to attend a meeting to discuss the finding.

Jnr was so excited.

He wanted to tell everyone on the planet but, until it was explained, Jnr's discovery, no matter what it was, had to be kept quiet – top secret, even.

Jnr picked up Dr Shultz at 9.00 am on the dot: the airport was only a ten-minute drive away.

"Morning, David."

"Good morning, Dr Shultz."

They had over a two-hour flight so that gave rise to plenty of chat on the way.

"Ok, David, we're going to see Professor Martin Seabank. He's the foremost scientist in the detection of any new phenomena at NASA: if anyone can help us decipher your blip David, then he's the one."

Dr Shultz asked Jnr if he could use his ecigarette in the car.

"Yes, sure, I didn't know you used one of those."

"Yes, well, I smoked tobacco for many years: it helped calm my nerves but I never really smoked around work. Not that I was ashamed, David, you understand," explained Shultz. "Besides, vaping is healthier and I don't smell of tobacco anymore."

"Well, Dr Shultz, I never knew and neither did Markus nor Andrea."

"Are they safe?"

"Oh yes, quite safe, provided it's used properly and bought from a reputable supplier. I order online: there are plenty of flavors and nicotine strengths to choose from and it's kept me off traditional cigarettes up to now. Been eighteen months since my last real smoke," explained Dr Shultz.

"Ah, very good," replied Jnr.

"Now, David, tell me, in your professional opinion, why do you think it's a black hole? Surely NASA would have spotted it by now. It cannot have just materialised?"

"Well, it's certainly hard to tell from the photos we have."

"The way you described that, the image seems to appear then disappear. That relates to the distortion of the images caused by gases left over by the orbit from Jupiter, hence the need for more detailed pictures. What we need is more specifically targeted images using infrared: that way, we may spot X-ray signatures around the object or indeed moving away from the object," explained Jnr.

"Ok, David, I see what you're saying. So if it were a black hole, anything falling into it would burn up, emitting x-rays from its core."

"Yes, Dr Shultz, you're correct. A lot of study is needed. Many hours of footage need collecting before we can even determine whether it's a black hole or not!"

They got through security pretty quickly and were on the plane within 30 minutes.

The flight was ok, not much turbulence to mention. Jnr didn't mind flying but the professor liked his feet firmly planted. They collected their hire car from the airport car park and were soon on their way.

On arriving at NASA, the security guard asked to see their permits.

"Ok, car park A please." The guard pointed.

Jnr parked up and gathered his files.

Reception ordered a golf cart to drive the pair to the far end of the complex, which was huge.

"This is nice, David, eh?"

"Yes, Dr Shultz, express delivery."

Standing outside the entrance was Dr Seabank, waving towards the cart. Dr Shultz waved back and turned to Jnr with a smile and said, "He's a character, this one."

"Hi Peter, how the devil are you?" asked Dr Seabank.

"I'm fine, Martin. You look well!" Seabank laughed. "You mean I've put on weight, don't you?!"

"Always polite to you, Peter. Ah, this must be Professor David Archer." He offered his hand out to Jnr.

"It's a pleasure and an honor to meet you, Dr Seabank. I've read so much of your work," explained Jnr.

47

"I like you already, young man, but your opinion may very well change in due course working with myself!"

"Work with you?" asked Jnr.

"If this turns out to be of interest, then both you and I will have to dedicate ourselves to many hours of grueling research," replied Dr Seabank.

"Oh yes, sir, of course," said Jnr – he wasn't expecting that!

Jnr was impressed with the man's greeting. He expected a limp handshake like most men of his intelligence, but no – strong and tight. They can solve unbelievable mysteries, but human interaction seems to be hard for most of the more eccentric types. Jnr's dad taught him that within a handshake you can instantly tell whether you will take to a person and a strong handshake is vital in projecting confidence.

"Well, don't dawdle, let's go in," remarked Seabank.

Wow, Jnr thought to himself as they entered the building.

There was a small reception desk where they needed to collect their identification badges and sign in.

He saw beautiful images adorning every wall in the waiting area.

To his left, the Mystic Mountain from the Carina Nebula.

On his right, the Hourglass Nebula.

Stunning, clear images which he'd seen on the internet and from books given to him by Granddad Charles.

The best by far was on the facing wall: it must have been twenty feet by ten feet, and seemed to project as if in 3D. It was covered in some type of glass which enhanced the image even further.

The background was from our own solar system, and the planets were there in all their magnificent glory, in order and scaled to perfection. Jnr gazed at the picture: he couldn't take his eyes off it.

Dr Seabank moved to Jnr's side.

With hands on hips, he too stood, quietly taking in the natural beauty in front of him. *Funny, really*, he thought as he looked at Jnr's response to the art above. Seabank had seen these pictures a thousand times, but now he never really took the time to enjoy them anymore.

"Glorious, David, don't you think?" asked Seabank.

"Sir, for me, it makes me realise just how small we are in the greater scheme of things," replied Jnr. "These are some of the clearest images I've ever seen."

"Brought to you by our good friend the Hubble Telescope," replied Seabank.

"Simply beautiful," said Jnr.

"Come, you two must be parched with the drive over. We have some of the best coffee on the planet here, too!"

"Oh yes please," said Dr Shultz. "I do enjoy a quality roast every now and then."

All three guys walked over to the coffee prep area: the coffee machine itself was bright gold, and Jnr had never seen anything like it.

"I'm going to have an espresso. What would you guys like?" asked Seabank.

"I'll have the same please, Martin," replied Shultz. "One sugar, though, in mine!"

"Same as Dr Shultz please," added Jnr. "What kind of coffee-maker is that?" he asked Dr Seabank.

Seabank laughed and added, "No expense spared here, David. It's one of the finest coffee-makers in the universe."Both the Professors chuckled as they sipped the beautiful Italian roast arabica coffee.

"It's an Elegant Elektra Belle Epoque, worth around $18,000!"

Jnr coughed as he took a sip: the froth shot out from his cup. "Oh, I'm sorry about that, I nearly choked then."

"Come, let's take a seat," added Seabank.

In the lounge area sat two large leather sofas and a couple of coffee tables with odd copies of *Astronomy* neatly stacked on them. As Jnr sat he noticed that the coffee tables were supported by two huge balls. One of the coffee tables had the Earth and Moon, and the other had Mars and Neptune.

Jnr pointed to the underneath of the tables and asked, "Were they your idea, Dr Seabank?"

"No, David, I'm afraid not but a wise choice made, don't you think?" replied Seabank.

"Yes, sir, I do agree, I would love one for myself." Jnr smiled.

"I'll tell you what, David, if you can carry one, then you may have it," said Dr Seabank.

Both professors laughed out loud and Jnr could see what Dr Shultz meant about his friend: he was a bit nuts.

"Ok, David, Peter has sent me copies of what you have discovered. I have looked over images taken previously of that particular region and I must admit that what you have spotted has not been seen so far."

"What is it?" asked Dr Seabank.

"Ok, sir, I'll try to explain what I see in the images."

"David, my name is Dr Seabank, not 'sir'. Everyone simply calls me 'Doc' around here, ok!?"

Jnr nodded."Ok, Doc." Jnr was bought up well and taught respect for his peers, so 'Doc'didn't sit well with him.

So our Jnr explained his theory of the object or lack of it to the professors. He had spotted heat signatures, plus gamma rays behaving oddly around the image, but it was hard to tell through the haze. It is widely known that we have a massive black hole in the centre of our own MilkyWay, but that's it, no more. Science knows that there are literally millions of black holes throughout the universe. Our understanding of black holes is vast now thanks to the efforts of some great minds in science both past and present.

Such people as Isaac Newton, Galileo Galilei, Albert Einstein, Charles Darwin, Nikola Tesla, Niels Bohr, and probably the greatest mind of this generation, the great Dr Stephen Hawking.

All these fantastic minds have helped mankind understand what goes on in our world and even out there, in space. At times they were thought crazy with their new, revolutionary concepts, but their belief was strong and their determination even stronger.

What they struggled with many years ago is now common knowledge, thanks to them.

After about 30 minutes of chatter the team went off into the building. Jnr tagged along behind the two men in front, taking in the splendour around him. *The cost of such a place must be huge,* thought Jnr.

There were small labs here and there: offices dotted around, too. Scientists in their distinctive white coats scurrying from place to place. They finally reached Dr Seabank's office.

"Come, take a seat, I have something to show you," said Seabank.

On the big desk in front of them were some large photos.

"Ok, after the conversation with Peter, in which I'd received the coordinates of this object, I asked my friends over at NASA to have a few images taken from the Spitzer scope and sent directly to me." Seabank spread the images out towards the two men.

"These have not been seen by anyone but ourselves," explained Seabank.

"Now, as we know, it takes Jupiter just over 11 years to orbit the sun, so Jupiter has just moved past our finding here, giving us a distorted image."

"At the moment, as you can see from the photos, there is something going on there, but it's hard to determine because of the gases left behind from Jupiter: the image is blurred somewhat."

"Also, the object or image of what you have found, David, could be millions of miles past our own system: that we cannot explain until the space clears of gases. Only then we will be able to obtain clearer images from Spitzer, and that, my friends, could be a year or so."

"So the fact that David spotted this is really down to luck?" asked Shultz.

"It seems that David has a keen eye. These images have been viewed many times over by myself included, but yes, David spotted something that everyone else missed! But don't get me wrong, it doesn't mean everyone else was blind, no," explained Seabank.

"If you look closely, you will notice that the object appears in only two of the photos, that's why I believe it was missed! No one was looking at that region in detail because it was believed to be void of anything of interest."

"Ah yes, I see. So, Dr Seabank, what do you think you were looking at?" asked Shultz.

"I'm not going to speculate, my old friend, until we have more to go on. It could be a number of things. So for now I want a tight lid kept on this: we must keep this to ourselves. I'm assembling a team as we speak for this project which will be headed by" – he turned to Jnr –"Dr David Archer."

Chapter 8 – The Conclusion

As requested by Professor Seabank, Jnr was to head a team of three to work on his finding: Jnr, of course, Dr Sarah Blank and Dr Steven Marriott.

Dr Seabank never intervened unless he was asked. He trusted that Jnr would be up to the job. He knew David had the credentials and the determination to see this through, and to come to a satisfactory conclusion as to what it was Jnr had found.

Jnr had to move to Ames to complete his work. He had a single-room studio within the complex, so no travelling needed.

He brought some clothing, his laptop and his favorite picture of himself with his entire family. Here Jnr could work twenty hours per day if needed, and when the day had finished, just a short walk to his suite was all that was required.

Three months had passed since arriving.

"Ok, Sarah, I would like you to come to my office at 3 o'clock and bring your files with you. Stevie will be there, too. It's time we collaborated on the results of our findings."

3 o'clock came and the two young assistants arrived spot on time.

Stevie knocked on the office door. "Come in!" shouted Jnr.

"Hi guys, come over to the table, will you? I've already arranged a few of the most obvious photos," said Jnr.

All three scientists placed on the table the evidence gathered over the last three months. All the pictures had to be compared and analysed to the most minute of details.

"We cannot go to Dr Seabank until we are 100% sure of what we have here. I know you have probably come to the same conclusion as myself well before now, but it's time we cleared this up."

"Ok, guys, straight answers please!" asked Jnr.

"Dr Archer," replied Sarah, "the answer I've come up with is the same one as yours!"

"And you, Stevie, what's your conclusion?"

"Well, David, I've ruled out the obvious and I'm going to have to admit that I too, think the same as Dr Blank," replied Stevie.

Jnr laughed and added, "So both of you have collaborated with your findings, you then present them to me, and neither of you dare say it, do you? I do, on the other hand, understand why you struggle to say it," continued Jnr, becoming more and more excited as he built himself up.

"'Black' and 'hole' are the words you're looking for, guys!" He held his breath as he awaited a reply.

"Yes, Dr Archer, you are correct," replied Sarah.

Dr Marriott nodded his head and with a smile said, "Ok, I dare say it now. Yes, David, I agree, a black hole and very big one at that, but there are some huge questions we are going to have to face, if and when we announce our results to Dr Seabank."

Jnr let out the air in his lungs: it was like a great weight had lifted from his shoulders. He stared at the image. All the years Jnr had dreamed about this very moment, what would it mean? What would happen next?

Once the information leaked out, a formal announcement would need to be made in front of the press, plus every relevant scientist in the world!

"I'd better give Dr Seabank a call," said Jnr, looking slightly apprehensive.

"Dr Archer, why do you look so worried? There is no other conclusion to come to: you are correct," said Sarah.

"Ok, then, here goes."

Jnr called Seabank and asked him to join his team in his office.

"Hi, Dr Seabank, I hope I haven't interrupted you."

"No, David, you haven't at all, now how can I help you?"

"Would you please come to my office, I have an announcement to make!"

"Yes, of course, David: is this the one we've been waiting for?"

"Yes, it is," replied Jnr.

"I'm on my way!"

Click: the phone went dead.

Dr Seabank entered without knocking and moved straight towards the images displayed neatly upon the table.

"Ok, let me have it, Dr Archer!"

Jnr stepped forward, feeling a little apprehensive as he did so. For years now he had dreamt of this moment, but with the little bit of evidence lying on the desk he started to feel nervous, anxious even: *What if I'm wrong,* thought Jnr.

Well, if Jnr was to misdiagnose the object in question, it could spell disaster for his future in science and discovery, especially from NASA'spoint of view, so he took a deep breath!

"Dr Seabank, what we have discovered is indeed conclusive to my prediction from the very first observation. My team and I"– Jnr smiled at both of his colleagues –"have discovered a black hole!"

"Ok, David, what process has brought you and your team to this decision?" asked Seabank.

"No matter how many times we look using Hubble and Spitzer, we only have two images with any signs as to what we have concluded," explained Jnr.

"Now I believe this is because the area in question is vacant of any planets, stars, etc, so surrounding our object is basically empty space: that is the reason why this black hole has never been detected."

"Ok, David, so with the flimsy evidence you have, how can you come to the conclusion you have? We will at some point, and sooner rather than later, have to announce this to the scientific world, Dr Archer. This has to be a definitive answer, so are you sure?" asked the doc.

Jnr blushed: he was so nervous. Could he be wrong?

The whole team had worked so hard to get to this point. Yes, sure, it had only been a matter of months since the first sighting, but there could be no other known answer.

"Yes, Dr Seabank, I'm willing to bet my life on it!"

"Right, David, please explain to me why you are so adamant and sure this is a black hole!"

Jnr explained to the doc.

Black holes cannot be seen, even with the most powerful telescopes known to science because they are exactly as it says on the tin: black holes.

The only way possible to detect a black hole is when x-rays are emitted from them which we can detect. Now this usually occurs when something is drawn into the black holes' gravitational pull. Nothing escapes from a black hole once past the event horizon (the leading edge of the black hole): this is what has happened to our Jnr.

As you may remember, Jnr was looking at images of Titan: it was then that he thought he'd seen something to the left of Mars.

He had indeed just seen the x-rays emitted from the black hole, because as Jupiter passed by, some of its atmospheric gases had been caught in the black hole's gravitational pull.

The second image collected was again from x-rays, but this time a portion of interstellar debris had drifted into the black hole's path. Without these two events the black hole may have continued to be unknown.

"There are two questions I have to work out now," said Jnr. "How long has it been there? And how big is it?"

"Well, David, Sarah and Stephen, you better get on it! I'm going to make some calls," said Seabank.

With that, Dr Seabank left the room and Jnr felt himself relax. There were more questions now than before! So many more months of research to do, if not years!

That evening his team were joined by Dr Seabank and went for a celebratory meal. They would discuss their finding and the meaning of it to science. Black holes appear when a star dies; normally the size of the star needed to create a huge black hole would need to be thousands of times bigger than our own sun. The star would implode on itself, becoming only the tiniest of a fraction of the size it once was, creating a super-dense black hole with an unbelievably strong gravitational pull. Everything within distance would be pulled in, and even light doesn't escape.

"How do you feel about it all, David?" asked Seabank.

"Well, even though I'm obviously excited, I'm still confused, to be honest. I mean not confused, but I have more questions than before its discovery now!"

"All in good time. Now what are you calling it, David?"

"Good question: I haven't thought about that yet."

"Stevie and myself have, Dr Archer: we have used the name without your knowledge for awhile now," said Sarah.

Stevie smiled and said, "We have named it Jnr-X1."

Dr Seabank turned to Jnr and added, "That's settled, then. I like that, it has a nice ring to it."

Jnr sat contemplating his team's decision. *Fancy that, a finding named after me. I will be remembered in history – well, until the NASA boffins decide otherwise and change it,* thought Jnr.

"Very well, if you guys think it's ok, then yeah, Jnr-X1 it is."

Jnr added, "A toast, then."

All four raised their glasses.

"For all four of us who believed in our research, spent many long hours with equations and diagrams, photos and drawings, day and night, to reach a pivotal moment in humanities history, I say 'Salute'!"

The team raise their glasses: with the clink of glasses they drank and laughed the night away.

Jnr walked into his office with the biggest headache known to mankind. It was the first time in his life he had been properly drunk: he had a bruise on his elbow and a scuff to his knee, but for the life of him he couldn't remember how he'd got it.

With his morning coffee to hand he downed a couple of painkillers and sat back to ponder the previous day's events.

Jnr will now have to write a paper to present to the scientific word at large. Obviously this was his first, so Dr Seabank had offered him his help on the paper. First an announcement would be made here at Ames, in front of a very distinguished audience of fellow scientists, which Jnr didn't relish at all.

I'm going to call my family: they will be the first to know!

Chapter 9 – The Aftermath

The date was set for the big unveiling of Jnr-X1. It would be announced at the forthcoming American Astronomical Society event at Ames.

Anyone and everyone would be there in the world of science and, of course, plenty of press. Jnr was having his family flown over from the UK: his granddad Charles so desperately wanted in on the action. He would rub shoulders with some of the greatest minds our era had to offer.

Of course, Raph and Jib would be there: Jnr hadn't spoken to his friends of late, which he felt guilty about, but his time had been well and truly deserved elsewhere.

Jnr had spent many hours with Dr Seabank preparing his speech: they had covered all aspects of questioning they knew would be coming. Preparing was the key in keeping calm: Jnr was taught that from his granddad Roy. He might have been a quiet, stubborn type of man but he never lost his cool. Roy never crumbled under pressure.

On the day before the unveiling his family arrived at the San Jose International Airport, Jnr rented a minibus to collect them in person: it was only around ten miles from Ames.

He patiently waited outside the arrivals: it seemed so long ago that he had seen their faces.

Jnr rammed his hand into the air, frantically waving it around.

"Mum, Dad!" shouted Jnr.

"Hello, son, you ok?" asked his father as he dragged the luggage trolley behind him, with what looked like everyone's suitcases piled up high.

"Yeah, Dad, I'm great, thanks. Come here, Mum." He wrapped his arms around his mother, squeezing her hard, and, at the same time, kissing her cheek.

"So nice to see you, Mum."

"You, too, David, I've really missed you," replied Anne.

Jnr went round to each of his grandparents with the same greeting. Even though he'd FaceTimed each one of his family members almost every week, seeing them in the flesh was a blessing.

"Raph, how are you, mate?"

"Not as good as you, Jnr. Where's ya suntan?"

Jnr laughed. "No sunshine for me, my friend, too busy."

"Follow me, everyone: your chariot awaits in the car park."

"You what, Jnr? You haven't discovered teleporting yet?" Raph laughed.

"Working on it: one discovery at a time," replied Jnr.

All the luggage packed, family seated, Jnr headed off towards his home. On the way Jnr pointed out the attractions to his grandparents while his mother sat quietly taking in the warmth of the sun on her face.

Raph sat with Jnr's dad chatting about their stint at university.

"Most of us knew, Mr Archer, that your Jnr would make a name for himself in science. It was only a matter of time," explained Raph.

"Well, lad, I suppose our Jnr was at the right place at the right time. He told me that he was extremely lucky to spot this thing in the first place," added Snr.

"Sometimes it just needs a fresh set of eyes, I suppose, a new perspective if you like."

At the gate to Ames the security guard asked to see the visitor permits and allowed them to pass.

Jnr pulled into his parking spot and told everyone to leave the luggage and follow him to his quarters. Jnr thought he would show them where he worked and then obviously the pictures, to which he made his astonishing discovery, before heading out for a get-together meal, after which he would drop them all off at the hotel Jnr had booked them into.

"Nice facility," remarked Raph and that was before they entered the building. "Do they have a museum here, Jnr?"

"No, but we will visit the Kennedy Space Center: they have the best one in the world there!" said Jnr.

"Here's my office. In you come: there aren't enough chairs obviously, so we won't stay here too long."

Everyone muddled around the photos which Jnr had proudly fixed in frames onto the wall. His family stood looking at what seemed to them as nothing but empty space, so Jnr explained what was happening within the pictures.

"Ok," said Jnr, "let's go into the seating area and grab a coffee. We can all take a seat there and I can explain further to you about these pictures in comfort."

Both sets of his grandparents were glad to hear that. It had been a long journey for them, and they were starting to tire.

Jnr led the way to the lounge, and as the family walked in, they saw the beautiful scenery all around them.

"Wow," said Raph and Charles at the same time.

"What fantastic pictures, David."

David Snr said to his son, "I bet the globes were your idea, eh, Jnr?"

"No, Dad, they were here long before me."

"Come and sit down, everyone, I'll make you a nice cuppa."

"I'll help, David." Anne joined him at the bottom end of the lounge.

"What's that, David, a mini-rocket?" Anne smiled.

Jnr smiled and told his mum all about the expensive and beautifully made coffee machine in bright gold before them.

With drinks made they all sat with eyes on Jnr as he explained his theory behind the finding of the Jnr-X1 black hole. He told them of his team, who they would meet, and the great Dr Seabank to whom Jnr owed a great deal.

"Right," said Jnr, "I will drop you off at the hotel so you can relax and get ready for about 6.30. I've booked a table for us at Slice n Dice steakhouse which is only a short drive away."

"What about a grand tour around this place, Jnr?" asked his father.

"Dad, don't worry, you're here for a week. Tomorrow is the big announcement day for which you'll need to be up early, so as soon as that's out of the way, we can visit as many places of interest as you like," stated Jnr.

"Ok, son, keep ya wig on!"

Jnr dropped everyone off and asked them to be ready on time, for now he had to attend a meeting with Dr Seabank to go over the finer details of the next day's proceedings.

All sorted, now I'll have a quick shower, get dressed and pick everyone up, thought Jnr.

Jnr packed his family into the rental bus again and set off for the restaurant: it only took fifteen minutes to arrive.

"Here we are."

"Looks nice, David," said Sophia.

His grandmother had dressed herself up to the nines as usual: there was no need, as this was a casual gathering: tomorrow would be the day for formalities.

"Yes it is, Grandma. I've eaten here many times: they do a mean rib eye here, Granddad Roy!"

Roy said, "That's me sorted, then, Jnr."

They all had a laugh at Roy's comment and headed on into the diner.

The menus were being carefully examined: we knew what Roy was having!

Raph and Jnr were passing comments as to what they were going to eat when Raph got a tap on the shoulder. He turned and looked up at the guy behind him.

"Jib!" Raph cried out and tried to get up.

Jib reached down and embraced his friend before he had time to rise from his seat.

Jnr walked over and all three lads stood with outstretched arms: they hugged and giggled like little school girls.

Jnr's family looked on with great pride: at university, these three were such good friends.

As they all ate their meal, banter was passed back and forth over the table.

Jnr sat next to Raph and across from Jib: they talked amongst themselves mostly about university, and which road their chosen paths had taken them so far in their young lives.

"Jnr, both Jib and I have spoken about this before: we knew you would do something incredible with your science. It was, pardon the pun, written in the stars!" Raph smiled.

"Don't be silly, you two: this could have come from any scientist or astronomer, or whoever saw what I saw at that very moment in time!" replied Jnr.

Jib added, "No one else did, though, Jnr. You discovered it!"

"Look, let's not get ahead of ourselves here. It wasn't just me, remember: I have two teammates to thank, too. We all worked hard on this project, so tomorrow I'm going to share the admiration between us," explained Jnr.

"Jnr, they named the hole after you, my friend –that's history right there!" said Raph. "You will be remembered in history forever!"

"Yeah, yeah," replied Jnr. "Eat your food and stop your rambling, my friend. Let's talk about us for tonight: there will be enough science jargon to last a lifetime tomorrow."

"I know, Jnr, but I love it when science gets a jolt from a new discovery, it's exciting. Remember last year when Caltech researchers found PlanetNine? There was a right buzz around the world!" added Raph.

"Of course I remember. As technology moves forward, new discoveries are bound to become more common place, not like years ago. It happens so often in science now that it seems rather short-lived when something is discovered. Centuries have passed and only two planets have been discovered in that time. We marvelled at the discoveries. Now look, a third planet is discovered and it's old news already!" said Jnr.

"So what are you saying, Jnr?" asked Jib.

"I suppose what I'm saying is, it's just not that big a deal anymore. It's like we need a discovery to be made on a super-high level to get people's interest now," added Jnr.

"Like what?"

"I dunno, erm, like proof of dark matter, life on alien planets… I don't know, guys, but you know what I'm getting at, don't you?" asked Jnr.

"I suppose I do, Jnr, but ya know what? That's human nature for you!"

Everyone enjoyed themselves that evening: the food was good and a bottle or two of wine afterwards was even better. None for Jnr, as he had to drive them all back to the hotel.

After bidding his friends and family goodnight, Jnr drove back to the campus. He ran through the next day's events in his mind: *Up at six, lots to do!* he thought.

As well as sorting out his guests, fetching them and getting them seated, he would have to meet beforehand with his team to go over the final details.

Jnr got back to his suite just after ten.

His next job was to make sure he was ready for the morning: jeans and t-shirt to start the day, then into his brand new tweed suit for the main event. Jnr was quite calm, he thought. *No sign of nerves yet!*

Next morning, Jnr was up before his alarm: he headed for the canteen for a breakfast with Dr Seabank and his team. Today he was going to have to work like clockwork, precise!

Breakfast first, then fetch the family, then get changed again, then onto the main hall, more checking: have I got my notes. When's my cue to enter the stage? etc.

9 o'clock came and everyone was seated.

First to take the podium was Eugene Tu, the director at Ames Research Center.

Eugene spoke to the audience with such clarity and confidence, thanking the American Astronomical Society for holding its annual meeting at this great location.

He, of course, thanked everyone else for coming and gave a special thanks to the many staff and volunteers for their contribution to such a memorable event.

A few other people from Ames spoke, and finally it was Dr Seabank's turn.

Dr Seabank told the audience about the young scientist who made the discovery and his team. He told them of the brilliance and commitment the team had made to science in general.

Jnr stood to the side of the stage, double-checking his notes: he noticed that there were still no shakes or nerves to think of.

Surely our Jnr should be shaking in his boots by now!

"Ok, Dr Archer, you're on," said one of the technicians.

Jnr steadily walked to the podium, and for a second or two he looked out at the audience. *Wow!* thought Jnr. *They're all here because of me. Crazy.*

"Hello and a very good welcome to you all," belted out Jnr.

He took out his notes and read. Throughout the lecture he pointed to the huge screen, explaining what was represented in each photograph. The cameras kept clicking right through his speech. As Jnr spoke he could see smiles on some faces and bemusement on others: he knew there would be doubters out there, but nevertheless Jnr continued.

Jnr put most of the praise on his team because that was Jnr for you.

As he was coming towards the end of his speech he noticed that nerves had kicked in. The reason was that he had just spotted through the haze of flashes from the cameras, sitting together, Dr Stephen Hawking and Dr Kip Thorne!

They were Jnr's ultimate heroes of theoretical physics. Sure, there were so many that Jnr looked up to, but these two professors were for Jnr the pinnacle of excellence on theories about black holes.

He concluded his speech to rapturous applause from the audience. He had dealt with the flurry of questions thrown at him, and cameras were flashing like crazy! Jnr smiled and waved, then moved off to the side of the stage.

Backstage, Jnr was joined by Stevie, Sarah and the doc.

"Well done, David, well done indeed," said Seabank.

Both Stevie and Sarah reinforced the congratulations.

While they celebrated, the scientific world sat in the audience mulling over and questioning what they had just been told.

You could hear the hum from space, thought Jnr.

Seabank told his team to go and relax as later the hall would be cleared, and tables would be set for an evening feast in Jnr's honour, plus the AAS have their own agenda to get through – it was going to be a long day!

David Snr led his family into the hall and they found their table very easily. On Jnr's table were his family, Raph and Jib, Dr Seabank, Stevie and Sarah.

The food rolled out to the table, waiters were buzzing around like charged protons, dashing in this and that direction with ease. Jnr had a funny thought: *If he could look down from the ceiling, the image below would look very similar to space: the tables would be the planets and the people milling around them would be like particles, whirling around in their orbits!*

After the meal was finished, the AAS took to the stage.

The meeting held recognition for new advances within science and space exploration. Names were mentioned, Jnr was mentioned, his theory was debated: all in all, a good meeting, said the director of the AAS.

As Jnr sat facing the stage he noticed that Dr Kip Thorne was walking towards him, looking straight at Jnr with a smile upon his face.

"Hello, Dr Archer, it's a pleasure to make your acquaintance," said Dr Thorne.

"Dr Thorne"–Jnr couldn't believe he was shaking the hand of one of his most admired heroes –"believe me when I say that the pleasure is mine alone," replied Jnr.

"Would you walk with me?"

"Yes, sir, but of course," said Jnr.

"Dr Archer, please call me Kip, would you?"

"Alright, Kip, but if you could return the favour and call me Jnr, then we have a deal."

Both scientists walked out of the main hall and into a corridor leading away from the noise behind.

"Jnr, I have a few questions for you – well, to be honest, *we* have some questions for you."

Just before Jnr could ask any questions himself, Kip opened a door and asked Jnr to enter the room.

Jnr looked a bit baffled and thought, *We?*

As Jnr entered the room he realised who exactly was the second person in the equation.

There was Dr Stephen Hawking waiting to question him.

Jnr now started to tremble!

Chapter 10 – Mars

Over the next week Jnr spent every minute with his family and friends: they went to the coast which pleased everyone immensely. Relaxation on a beautiful beach with the warmth of the sun's photons pounding their flesh – just what they all needed. Ok, the UK is a nice place to live but the weather – well, you know the score.

As promised from Jnr, a visit to the Kennedy Space Center was full filled. Jnr, being a bit of a celebrity now, had arranged a guided tour for his friends and family, and to top it off the tour was given by none other than Neil Armstrong, one of America's most famous astronauts.

Although no one relished the intercontinental flight, more queuing, more checks, more waiting and two flights in one day, everyone enjoyed the visit.

For Charles it would be a massive tick off his bucket list.

"What a fantastic day, Jnr," said Charles. "Thank you. Neil is such a lovely person, too: nice touch, kiddo!"

"You're welcome, Granddad." Jnr smiled: he knew how much that visit meant to him, and he would never forget it.

Charles would now be the talk of the university for quite a while to come, and that pleased him.

It had been a busy week for everyone but a very enjoyable one, especially for Jnr. At the same time he wanted to spend quality time with his family, but there was something nagging at him, about which he needed to come to some sort of resolution, and soon.

They all decided another day on the beach was in order. It was the last day before departure so a few more rays wouldn't hurt.

Anne asked her son if everything was ok.

Jnr simply told her he was fine, but that set off everyone else with the same question. They had all noticed a difference in him over the week.

"Stop with the questions please, I'm ok," said Jnr.

"No, Jnr," said Jib. "Ever since the day of your announcement you've been acting weird." Jib was laughing and he continued with: "Not the normal nerdy weird like we're used to, but you seem to be away with the fairies!"

Jnr sighed and rose from his towel. He stood looking at the sky with hands on hips, taking in the gorgeous scenery before him.

He turned around and faced his family.

"At the Ames meeting you may remember Dr Thorne and I disappeared for a while," said Jnr.

Everyone nodded in agreement.

"Of course everyone noticed, Jnr. It's not every day that Kip Thorne comes to your table, is it?!" replied Raph.

"Yes, yes, but we took a walk. Obviously Thorne wanted to ask questions about my find: after all, he's one of the foremost thinkers on the subject!"

"We entered a room adjacent to the main hall and to my surprise, Dr Hawking was waiting with questions of his own," continued Jnr.

"Bloody hell, Jnr, why didn't you tell us? That's amazing. What did he ask?" asked Charles.

"Dr Hawking had preprogrammed into his speech synthesiser a list of direct questions for me regarding black holes and mostly questions surrounding his theories regarding them," said Jnr.

Everyone was stunned into silent thought.

"Both professors asked me a life-changing question to which I still haven't found an answer."

"Come on, then, Jnr, stop with the suspense and spill the beans, would you?" blurted out Snr.

"There is a mission happening in three years' time – a mission to Mars!" explained Jnr. " It's a six-person mission which will consist of two PLCs (PayloadCommanders), one shuttle commander, one mission specialist, one astro biologist and, finally, me," added Jnr.

Everyone except Jnr's mother jumped up excitedly from the sand to congratulate him. They all cheered as each of the men made a cradle of arms, chucking Jnr high into the air with loud shouts of *Hip hip hooray!*

When the commotion had settled down, Anne, who had remained on the sand, looked at Jnr and asked, "What does it all mean exactly, Jnr?"

"It means, Mum, that if I want to accept then I would be going to Mars!"

"Oh Jnr, I see," replied Anne. "Well done, son, if that's what you want, then great, I'm happy for you."

Jnr hugged his mum: he could tell with the expression upon her face and with the absence of that never-ending smile of hers that it was not ok! This latest announcement was a bit too much: she was not at all happy with the prospect of her only son leaving Earth for Mars.

"But Jnr, you're not an astronaut. Why have they asked you?"

"Mum, if I accept, then I will have to undertake astronaut training, and if I pass, then yes Mum, I will be an astronaut." Jnr smiled.

Anne just nodded and forced a smile!

For the rest of the day they all sat listening to Jnr explaining why he was asked to go and what he would be asked to do during the mission.

Both Raph and Jib were terribly excited at the prospect, Jib even more so because, after all, this mission to Mars, apart from an exploration aspect, was the first stage in building a base on the planet for a future colony, which he was going to be a part of: that was the reason why two Payload Commanders were required.

The next morning Jnr said his goodbyes to his friends and family and headed back to base. On the way home he pondered about the upcoming decision he would have to make.

Jnr knew a lot already on the subject, having spoken to Jib, and while at the visit he managed to speak at length with Armstrong.

Jib was in the middle of his own training which was much more complex than Jnr's. Jnr's training would be as follows:

At NASA, following the selection phase, the so-called "AsCans" (astronaut candidates) have to undergo up to two years of training/indoctrination to become fully qualified astronauts. Initially, all AsCans must go through basic training to learn both technical and soft skills. There are 16 different technical courses in:

Life-support systems
Orbital mechanics
Payload deployment
Earth observations
Space physiology and medicine
Astronauts train in the Neutral Buoyancy Facility at the Johnson Space Center in Houston, Texas.

AsCans initially go through basic training, where they are trained on Soyuzand ISS systems, flight safety and operations, as well as land and water survival. Pilot AsCans will receive training on NASA's T-38 trainer jet. Furthermore, because modern space exploration is done by a consortium of different countries and is a very publicly visible area, astronauts receive professional and cultural training, as well as language courses (specifically in Russian).

Following completion of basic training, candidates proceed to NASA's Advanced Training. AsCans are trained on life-sized models to get a feel of what they will be doing in space. This was done both through the use of the Shuttle Training Aircraft while it was still operational, and through simulation mock-ups. The Shuttle Training Aircraft was exclusively used by the commander and pilot astronauts for landing practices until the retirement of the Shuttle, while advanced simulation system facilities are used by all the candidates to learn how to work and successfully fulfill their tasks in the space environment. Simulators and EVA training facilities help candidates to best prepare their different mission operations. In particular, vacuum chambers, parabolic flights, and Neutral Buoyancy Facilities (NBFs) allow candidates to get acclimatised to the microgravity environment, particularly for EVA. Virtual reality is also becoming increasingly used as a tool to immerse AsCans in the space environment.

The final phase is the intensive training. It starts at about three months prior to launch and serves to prepare the candidates specifically for the mission they have been assigned to. Flight-specific integrated simulations are designed to provide a dynamic testing ground for mission rules and flight procedures. The final intensive training joint crew/flight controller training is carried out in parallel with mission planning. This phase is where candidates undergo mission-specific operational training, as well as experience with their assigned experiments. Crew medical officer training is also included to effectively intervene with proactive and reactive actions in case of medical issues.

Mars One's teams of prospective Mars inhabitants will be prepared for the mission by participating full-time in an extensive training programme. This will be their full-time, paid job. The training is split up into three programmes: technicaltraining, personaltraining, and group training.

Technical training

The astronauts will be required to learn many new skills and gain proficiency in a wide variety of disciplines. At least two astronauts must be proficient in the use and repair of all equipment in order to be able to identify and solve technical problems.

At least two astronauts will receive extensive medical training in order to be able to treat minor and critical health problems, including first aid and the use of the medical equipment that will accompany them to Mars. At least one person will train in studies on Mars geology, while another will gain expertise in 'exobiology', the biology of alien life. Other specialties like physiotherapy, psychology and electronics will be shared among the four astronauts in each of the initial groups.

Mars One will ensure that, in each group, at least two crew members will be trained in each essential skill set in case a member becomes ill. Their training and preparations will take place between their admittance to the programme, and the start of their journey to Mars.

As the population on Mars increases, each new arrival will be able to bring with him or her an area of expertise. In time, this will reduce astronaut training time and requirements.

Personal training

The ability of astronauts to cope with the difficult living environment on Mars will be an important selection criterion. For example, an astronauts mobility will be restricted for a long period of time, and they will no longer be able to speak to friends and family on Earth face to face of course. They will be able to receive psychological assistance from Earth if they wish, via long-range communications. The astronauts will initially be chosen for their inherent ability to cope with these situations, and will receive training on how to deal with them most effectively.

Group training

Group training will take place in the form of simulation missions. A simulation mission is an extensive, fully immersive exercise that prepares the astronauts for the real mission to Mars. The simulated environment will invoke as many of the Mars conditions as possible. Immediately after selection, the groups will participate in these simulations for a few months per year. During simulations, astronauts will only be able to leave the base when wearing their Mars suits. They will have to take care of their water supply and keep the life-support systems up and running. They must also cultivate their own food, and all communications with the outside world will be artificially delayed by twenty minutes.

There will be several simulation bases, some easy to access for early stages, while others will be located in harsh environments on Earth, providing realistic desert terrain and drastically cold conditions. These trials will demonstrate whether they are suitable for all elements of the task ahead. Can the astronauts keep the group functioning? Will they keep a cool head when confronted with a challenge? Can they effectively and efficiently solve given andemerging problems?

I wonder if Jib has what it takes to qualify as one of the Mars One candidates. Do I have what it takes to be able to pass my training? wondered Jnr.

Jnr entered his suite and lay upon the sofa with hands behind his head, his mind working overtime: questions, questions and more questions!

Jnr decided to call George Alambritis who is head of mission control for the Mars landing. Dr Kip Thorne had given him the mobile number direct to George, knowing the outcome of Jnr's answer.

He dialled the number.

"Hello, Mr Alambritis."

"Hello, how may I help you?" asked George.

"My name is David Archer. I was given your number by Dr Thorne. I hope I'm not intruding at all," replied Jnr.

"Ah, Dr David Archer. I was told to expect your call."

"Ok, first things first, to you my name from now on is George, and no, you're not intruding. It's an honor to make your acquaintance, even if it is over the phone for now," explained George.

"Likewise, George, you may now call me Jnr then, if we are on first-name terms already."

"George, I have many questions to ask of you, but if you're busy right now I could call at another time to suit."

"As it happens I am quite busy at the moment, but you could call me this evening, say, sevenish? And would you mind if I call you Archer: I struggle with forenames!" replied George.

"Yes, you may call me Archer, and yes, I'll call around seven. And thank you."

"Ok, I look forward to speaking with you later, then, Archer. Bye."

Jnr opened his laptop: research time. He wanted to know more before a final decision was reached.

How long would the mission be likely to take? How long to reach Mars? What would the effects on his body be, living without gravity? What could go wrong out in space?

YouTube videos were readily available to anyone wanting to witness astronauts in action up on the ISS. It was so cool how people just seemed to float effortlessly from one point to another within the space station, even though he knew this was just an illusion, an effect of gravity.

If Jnr accepts this mission then he, too, would be one of the lucky few that would feel weightlessness for himself.

As well as making videos that the public could watch, answering everyday questions like: How does one brush their teeth? How does one take a leak? How do astronauts eat and what do they eat? Simple questions but not really anyless interesting procedures for what we take for granted here on Earth.

On the ISS, more important research is conducted by astronauts: they aren't there simply to mess around making videos of mundane events.

Many experiments are conducted while in space, such as finding out what effects space has on the human body, what effects occur in the growth of plants, the study of how worms age, etc.

All these experiments help those who question the effects of space, and the answers are important, as research helps the human race with problems we face here on Earth.

Jnr's phone rang: he picked it up and saw that Dr Seabank was on the other end.

"Hello, Doc."

"Hi, Dr Archer. I thought I'd give you a call to ask about the Mars trip. Have you decided yet, David?" asked Seabank.

"Yes, Doc, I have and the answer is yes, I'm going!" replied Jnr.

"Fantastic, David. I'm so pleased for you: this is truly amazing news."

"Yes, Dr Seabank, it is but what is the purpose of my involvement? I haven't been told. I'm to speak with Alambritis this evening, so hopefully I will know more."

"Alright, David. Anytime you need to talk or indeed if you need help at any stage, then please call me, ok?"

"Thank you, Dr Seabank. I will pop into your office first thing Monday morning and fill you in on the details from my talk with Alambritis," said Jnr.

"No problem, David, see you Monday. Bye."

There were so many questions running through Jnr's mind. After a few hours on the net Jnr made himself a meal: he needed a break. He would get answers soon enough.

Six forty-five came and Jnr could not wait any longer: he dialled George's number.

"Hi George, it's David Archer. I was to call you if you remember our conversation earlier today."

"Oh hi, Archer. Yes, I was expecting your call. I should imagine you have a lot to ask, Archer, but first let me ask you a question."

"Have you come to a decision yet?" asked George.

"My answer, George, is yes – it was always going to be yes!" stated Jnr. "But I do have questions!"

George laughed and said, "I'm sure you do, Archer, but this is where our telephone conversation ends. Pack your belongings: I'll arrange your accommodation at this end. I would prefer that we speak in person!"

"I see, George. Ok, but I must speak with Dr Seabank first: my research needs to be continued here with my team and..."

George interrupted. "Archer, I will speak with Seabank: your research can be conducted without you actually being at hand. Leave all the technicalities with me," said George. "I'll book the earliest flight available on Monday, get your stuff together, Archer: you're going to Mars!"

Chapter 11 – Trip Of A Lifetime

Jnr packed his belongings and headed off yet again. This time he was headed for the Johnson Space Center in Houston, Texas, to begin his astronaut training.

He was told by George to let him know as soon as he had arrived: it only took around four hours for the flight. By the time the plane had reached altitude it seemed to be on its way back down again in no time.

Jnr had eaten lunch before take-off, so just a coffee sufficed on the trip over.

"Hi George, it's Archer. I'm outside the main building," said Jnr on his mobile.

"Hello, Archer, that's good. Did you enjoy your flight?"

"Yes thank you: nice and smooth, no problem at all."

"Ok, wait there, I'll be down in a jiffy. I will have to sign you in, too."

The Johnson Space Center is a massive place: in fact, it occupies 1,620 acres. It started its life in 1961 as the Manned Spacecraft Center and headquarters for mission control to the US. Its name changed in 1973 to what it is known as today after President Lyndon B. Johnson.

George came out of the main entrance and recognised Jnr straight away from this month's article in *Astronomy* magazine, in which our Jnr had a four-page spread.

"Hello, Archer, very pleased to meet you at last," George said, holding out his hand.

"Likewise, George."

"Ok, I'll get you sorted at the reception and then a guided tour, I suppose. Unless you prefer to rest a little first?"

"No, I would sooner take a look around," requested Jnr, "but I don't relish the thought of dragging my luggage around this enormous site."

"I should think not." George smiled.

"I could ask reception to hold it for us until we're finished: I'm sure they won't mind," he added.

"Before we go in, please be aware, Archer, that you are somewhat a hot topic at the moment with your recent discovery, so I hope you will not mind the attention you're about to receive."

"No, I don't mind at all, and besides, until people get to know I'm here, I'm sure I'll pass unnoticed," remarked Jnr.

George laughed. "Sorry Archer, I spilt the beans before your arrival."

After signing in and receiving his name tag, Jnr left his belongings with the receptionist and began his tour.

He was really excited to be there: that was where the magic happened for all space flights out of the US.

George was also excited as he was chatting to Jnr and introducing him to everyone in the mission control room, of which George was the commander.

Now Jnr had seen this room on various films such as *Apollo 13* and *Interstellar* (interestingly enough, Dr Kip Thorne's work was used for *Interstellar*).

Being in the room was so different, though: there were rows of computer screens – God knows how many. Upfront were huge screens which mission controllers could watch in great detail as to what was happening during a space flight.

Jnr could only imagine what it must be like in there when a tense moment occurred: he could sense how the atmosphere would be electrifying.

Fortunately for Jnr, not too many handshakes were needed as it was pretty quiet in there. Only a handful of people were there keeping in touch and monitoring the astronauts up in space in the ISS.

Next came the astronaut spacewalk simulation area: a large-sized pool with a replica of the ISS outer shell that sat on the bottom. Trainees were put into their space suits and submerged under water to get a feel for weightlessness and to practise the obvious tasks an astronaut would have to carry out, such as repairs on the ISS.

"Wonderful, Archer, isn't it?"

"Yes, sir, it is, I can't wait to get started."

"I was going to take you to my office as we really need to talk but I'm hungry. Have you eaten, Archer?"

"Earlier today, yes, but I'm a little peckish now, I must admit."

"Ok let's eat first. We can talk there anyway, then I'll show you to your new home for the next couple of years."

The canteen was huge and very impressive, as you can imagine. There was a full range of options available from the menu from vegetarian, gluten-free, curries, spaghetti and pasta dishes, pizza, burgers, steaks, etc. The coffee choices were good, too.

George opted for a lasagna with garlic bread, while Jnr decided on a good old steak 'n' chips!

While they were eating, George explained as to what the procedures were for astronaut training, but Jnr wasn't really taking much notice. He wanted to ask George what the real reason was he'd been asked to go.

There were so many more candidates available and probably better suited for this mission than Jnr.

Jnr had always been fascinated with space but never in his wildest dreams, even for a second, imagined himself on a shuttle bound for space.

As George was waffling on, Jnr jumped in.

"George, can I ask a serious question please?"

"Yes, Jnr, what?"

"Why me?"

"Good question, Archer."

"It seems that after your initial find our good friends Hawking and Thorne have persuaded NASA to put you on-board for the upcoming mission, to orchestrate the positioning of a new telescope called Brightstar St-1."

"What's it for, this new telescope?"

"To further our knowledge into black holes, Archer."

"With your discovery of Jnr X-1 it has got the world of science all beefed up, none more so than the esteemed professors who assigned you to this project."

"This scope, Archer, will enlighten us as to the mystery surrounding black holes."

"It sees in various spectrums of light with the potential to view everything, from the event horizon itself to the magnificence of Hawking's radiation," explained George.

"Imagine, Archer, because of you we can now actually see a black hole which, in turn, will hopefully answer many fundamental questions of our time!"

"Wow," said Jnr, "I now understand."

"You are to place the telescope in a specific latitude just outside of the Mars orbit. As you can now understand, Archer, NASA plans on killing two birds with one stone."

"Yes, George, I do: two missions consolidated into one with huge savings to boot, I imagine," replied Jnr.

"Exactly, Archer."

"But still why me? Surely someone who helped with the construction of the telescope would've been more suitable?"

"The find was yours, Archer, and you're the latest kid on the block, so I imagine that's why they want you in on the act, and besides, there are many experiments you'll be involved in, so I suppose they think you must be the one to bring in the results!"

"Right, we're finished here for now, let me take you to your quarters, Archer, so you may unpack and rest."

"Very well, George, lead the way."

Jnr follows George back to reception to collect his belongings, then over to an adjacent block where he will be living with the rest of his new team.

"Archer, tonight I request yourself together with your colleagues at my home for dinner, will that be ok?"

"Yes certainly, it will be my pleasure, George. Plus I want to meet my fellow astronauts."

"Good, that's settled, then: about six be outside to be picked up, ok?"

"Ok, George, see you later."

"Bye for now, Archer."

Jnr unpacked his suitcase, carefully hanging his shirts so as not to crease them. All the while Jnr's mind was doing overtime.

Once he finished unpacking and familiarising himself with his new surroundings he called his parents to fill them in.

His mother sounded worried as per usual, but his dad, Snr, sounded excited for his son. Men don't seem to have the same capacity for worry like women do when it comes to their children.

After the call, Jnr headed out to the foyer to await his lift to George's. As he exited the building he saw five others standing waiting. Nervously he wandered over.

"Hi guys, you going to Georges, too?" asked Jnr.

"Yes indeed, Dr Archer, we are. Nice to meet you," said one of the team.

"Pleasure to meet you, too."

"Here comes the cab."

They all jumped in and headed off. On the way they made small talk and all of them questioned Jnr about his success surrounding his discovery. For Jnr it was getting a little tedious now; not that he didn't appreciate the applause he was awarded, but it seemed like all anyone spoke to him about was that: Jnr X-1!

On arriving, the cab driver spoke into the intercom on the gate to ask permission to enter the premises.

"Check out the mansion," said Shaun (one of the new assembled team members).

"Come on up," a voice billowed out from the intercom.

George stood outside his home with his wife Irene, waiting to welcome the team into their home.

Everyone jumped out of the cab and George squared up with the driver.

"Welcome, guys and gals, to our home, please come on in," said George with a warm, welcoming smile.

Once seated in the living room Irene offered drinks. Everyone opted for juice or water. Jnr noticed the Greek theme to the room with pictures from Greek mythology to statues of various Greek gods. Aristotle proudly held the main wall. There were old pictures, family pictures, probably from the early days in Cyprus.

Irene came into the room with the drinks: she was a lovely-looking woman with a very kind and elegant smile.

Everyone stood and thanked Irene.

"Ok everyone, you've met Archer, I take it, if not properly, then please take turns in introducing yourselves," asked George.

First to stand was Shaun.

"Dr Archer, my name is Shaun Witter. I'm one of the PLCs on our mission."

Jnr nodded and replied with "Hello."

Next up was Julia. "Hi, Dr Archer, my name is Julia Simpson. I'm the astro biologist."

Next stood a Russian fellow. "Hello, my name is Selev Breshkinov, I'm also a PLC." Selev sat.

"Hello, Selev," replied Jnr.

"Hi Dr Archer. May I say it's a pleasure to have you join us on our mission? My name is Xai Sin Mo, I'm the mission specialist for our journey, and you may call me Chai."

"Very well, Chai, thank you."

Finally the last rose.

"Dr Archer, my name is Simon Wilson, I'm the shuttle commander."

Jnr stood.

"Hello, everyone, thank you for your introductions. I'm sure with the press surrounding me just lately you know who I am. I'm sure you've been briefed. If any of you would like to ask questions of me, then please feel free. Thank you."

With that done they all sat and relaxed; they all seemed a nice bunch and obviously hand-picked, so Jnr had no worries at all about the mission at hand regarding his crewmates – from first impressions anyway.

"Irene, may I ask a question?" asked Jnr.

"Yes, David, of course."

"The pictures from your family background: are they your parents?"

"Yes they are, David. These are my parents and in the next picture are George's parents. Back in Cyprus they actually lived quite close to each other," replied Irene.

"Beautiful pictures, Irene."

"Thank you, David."

"Now if you would excuse me, I will go to see how the food is doing."

With that Irene headed off into the kitchen.

"Ok, guys, get acquainted with Archer. I'm off to help my wife with the food," explained George.

The crew were summoned to the dining room which again was decorated to the highest quality.

After taking their seats, George said, "Dig in, guys."

The first course was Florina peppers and squid accompanied by a Greek salad and fresh, home-made bread.

The main consisted of three traditional Cypriot dishes, moussaka, souvlaki and finally kleftiko served with rice, potatoes and vegetables.

Last but not least was moustalevria, a dessert made from flour and grapes, typically found in Cyprus.

The drinks to accompany the meal were a fruity red wine or the most famous of Cypriot lager, Keo.

Juice and water were available for those who didn't drink.

"Irene, may I say that was one of the most enjoyable meals I've ever eaten: thank you very much," stated Jnr.

"You're welcome, David. If this was your first introduction to Greek home-cooked food, then it was indeed a pleasure to cook for you all."

The rest of the team joined in with the thank-yous, and everyone helped Irene clear the dining table. Irene told them there was no need to help, but our bunch had been brought up with respect and manners, which cost nothing.

Everyone moved into the lounge area to get comfortable and begin the task of bonding as a team and with their mission commander George.

George told the team what was expected from the mission, and how it was going to play out.

Eighteen months flew by and now came the last few months which in astronaut training terms are the most important part to the mission.

Now they would concentrate their training efforts around the details which each person was assigned, to perfect their skills prior to launch.

Jnr took to the training like a duck to water – in fact, so did the rest of the team. All were young, fit and strong, especially of mind, which is very important out there in space. You need a full bag of marbles up there! If one team member could crack, then it could possibly spell disaster for the rest.

Jnr's main job was to put the St-1 into space on a precise latitude within the Mars orbit. Selev was trained to use the Canadarm3, which would take the St-1 from the ship and let it go into space. Jnr would then use boosters to correctly position the telescope onto its correct orbital path.

Launched on STS-100 in April 2001, the next generation robot arm, called Canadarm3, is a bigger, better, smarter version of the robotic arm that was on previous Space Shuttles. It is 52.5 feet long when fully extended, and has seven motorised joints. This arm is capable of handling large payloads and helped build the entire orbiting complex. It has latches on either end, allowing it to be moved by both ground controllers and the expedition crews to various portions of the payload bay. It has even been used to move astronauts around during spacewalks, which you can see on YouTube videos and on the main NASA website.

The Mobile Base System is a work platform that moves along rails covering the length of the shuttle. It provides lateral mobility for the Canadarm3 as it traverses the main trusses.

Selev needed to be very proficient with the use of the robot arm: any mistakes and billions of dollars could be wiped away in a split second – not to mention the let-down to future astronomical research the St-1 would bring.

The date was set for the launch, 9 August 2021, only a few weeks away now.

Two weeks before the launch astronauts are placed in quarantine and are monitored by doctors constantly to make sure they don't fall ill. This was when it really hit home to the team: soon they would be on their way.

On the previous day to quarantine, Jnr spent as much time as he could speaking to his family and friends, who were obviously there to witness this once-in-a-life time event for their Jnr.

Again the women worried and, although they wouldn't admit it, the guys had butterflies in their stomachs, too.

It was an emotional time for Jnr and his family. Of course no one could predict the outcome of this mission: even the launch could go horribly wrong, but nevertheless it was going to happen, no matter what!

The team spirits were high, as were the whole of mission control, George especially.

It was George's job to make sure nothing went wrong!

Over the coming two weeks in quarantine, the team started to feel like a small family, not just team members. They had jelled well. All spoke of what they were consigned to do once on Mars: in more ways than one, history was going to be made on this trip.

Jnr with the St-1 and Chai with the first-ever biological plantation on Mars! Exciting times indeed.

And last but not least, the first chapter in the colony-building process of Mars in which everyone would take part.

Six-thirty and the team were up: it was launch day! Today was going to be frantic for our team.

First job: food. They would need every particle of energy they could get! This would be their last real meal until arriving back on Earth, which is a long time away.

Once finished, the astronauts suited up: this took hours, as it's not like putting on your t-shirt and jeans.These suits take ages to put on and are quite heavy – on Earth, that is. Once in space and away from the Earth's gravity, the suit weighed nothing at all, but just remained hard to manoeuvre in.

Did you know that astronauts wear space nappies? They are not called nappies by NASA, there called Maximum Absorbency Garments, or MAGs for short. Think about it for a moment. Imagine you're strapped to your seat waiting for take-off: there's a problem at mission control, so you may be sitting there for hours until the problem is cleared. What if you need to take a leak? What if you need a dump? One cannot simply go to the loo!

All strapped in and ready for launch, the technical team who helped strap in the astronauts leave the area in their bus.

"Hi guys" (it was George's voice coming from the shuttle intercom). "We are at t-minus one minute. Proceed with final checks please."

"Good luck, everyone, let's get the job done and get back home safely, ok?"

"T-minus 30 seconds."

The shuttle now switches to internal power and the shuttle's computer takes over the launch from mission control.

"T-minus ten seconds."

Now all the crew felt unbelievably excited. In around eight minutes they will be ejected out of the Earth's atmosphere and onwards, out into space.

They had waited their whole lives for this moment.

"Go for main engine start," stated the launch announcer.

"T-minus six seconds."

Next the three main thrusters from the shuttle kick in, one followed by another, 0.25 of a second apart.

The crew heard a rumble as the engines burst into action.

Spectators, friends and family, mission control and the rest of the world look on in anticipation at the amazing event unfolding before their eyes.

The shuttle now shakes and jerks forward only around a metre, still being held down by the clamps that hold the shuttle upright.

"T-minus 0!"

Boom!

The massive rocket boosters kick in: from the outside it can be heard for miles, but from the inside it was just a loud rumble.

Underneath the shuttle, huge clouds of smoke billowed out in all directions. The team could not see this, but could certainly feel it!

Finally the clamps let go.

"We have lift-off," said the launch announcer.

The shuttle shook, rattled and rolled as it climbed upwards towards the stars.

Jnr could feel G-forces working against him as the shuttle sped upwards: for our Jnr this was the scariest moment so far.

Next stage was a controlled roll of the vehicle to align the shuttle onto the correct flight path out of our atmosphere.

As soon as 35,000 feet were acquired, *Go* for throttle was announced and the shuttle was then propelled to full power until our atmosphere had been breached: only then would the throttle be let off slightly, as they made the transition into space.

Mission control team members could now relax: their part was mostly over, especially the most critical part, the launch.

George came in over the comms.

"Congratulations, guys, everything is going to plan, no problems to report, all system checks complete. Enjoy, my friends, your historic journey to Mars!"

Chapter 12 – Touchdown On Mars

A month had elapsed since our intrepid astronauts launched from Houston.

For the most part they spent getting used to zero gravity while conducting the many hundreds of experiments required by NASA and the scientific community in general.

Everyday the team had to undergo a two-hour exercise regime to keep their bones and muscles strong. This was very important as 1-2% bone mass is lost on average per month out in space. So regular exercise plus added calcium and vitamin D were supplemented into the astronauts' diet.

Bone mass increases where stress is put on a particular part of the bone, such as exercise. In space, however, because of zero gravity, there aren't enough pressures applied to bone structure for regrowth.

The team adjusted nicely to the new struggles of zero gravity. Everything was so different to that on Earth; it was great fun, too.

Brushing teeth, for example. What do you do with the mouthful of spittle when you've brushed?

1. Either spit out the contents of your mouth into a tissue and discard it.

2. Simply swallow!

How do you go to the toilet?

1. For a number one there is a flexitube with a cup on the end: simply hold in place and fire away. Easier for guys than girls, I'm afraid. The flexitube does have suction, so this helps with the procedure. Don't miss, though: there would be blobs of piss floating around the ship!

2. Number twos are easier because it's very much the same as down here on Earth.

Jnr loved the feeling of weightlessness. Sleeping was weird, though: it doesn't matter in space which way you are while sleeping, because there is no up or down without gravity.

Eating was fun, too. All the mealtimes were taken together so the team could have quality time discussing their experiments and experiences so far on the trip.

There was a wide array of food to eat which was stored in airtight packs: just add water, so to speak, and bingo, dinner is served.

The first time the team had dinner they all nearly choked with laughter. Imagine letting go of your utensils to fetch some ketchup, and they are still floating in the same place when you got back!

You cannot spill your drink, for example: you would simply suck it up while it floated. It takes a little while to adjust to this kind of experience.

The team worked well, everyone knew their role, and it was carried out with precision.

As it was expecting to take another three months to reach Mars, everyone tried to interact with each other as much as possible. Firstly, it helped with the boredom and also strengthened their bonds as a team.

The shuttle was hurtling through space at a constant 25,000 mph.

On-board you would think it was more like 20 mph because space was so massive that you couldn't get a visual on anything close enough to judge the speed by.

Many times the team would find themselves looking back at Earth through the view finder. You just cannot imagine how beautiful our little blue planet looks from space unless you were there yourselves: it was a breath-taking sight.

Houston came on the comms every now and then, giving new instructions and asking for certain procedures and checks to be carried out.

George would often ask to speak to each member of the team in turn, to check the well-being of each individual on-board, to make sure they were ok and everything was going according to plan.

George was a professional in every aspect: as the mission commander, he cared for his team.

Three months later.

"Seeker, this is Houston, please respond."

"Yes, Houston, this is Seeker, received loud and clear," replied Shaun.

A pause of around 20 minutes before the next message arrived because of the distance from Earth.

"Two days approx. for the scope deployment: please commence with payload extraction checks."

"Ok, Houston, received. Checks will begin shortly. Results will be relayed thereafter."

"Ok, Seeker, thank you, out," said the announcer after another lengthy delay.

"Right, guys, time to get some proper work done," said Chai.

The first job was to open the payload doors and power up the Canadarm3 to check its functions were all working correctly for the extraction of the scope.

This was Selev's task: he had trained meticulously for this moment alone. He was so proficient with the arm that he could pick up a glass of water and pass it around the shuttle, without applying so much pressure that the glass would shatter or spill its contents.

The scope had an abstraction point midway along its body which the arm would gently take hold of without causing damage, and more importantly, without upsetting the complex magnification section within.

If Selev got it wrong, billions of dollars would be wasted in a split second!

"Houston, this is Selev of the Seeker. Checks complete, no faults to report. Brightstar extraction shall begin on schedule, respond?" asked Selev.

"Seeker, this is Houston. Continue to the set co-ordinates of Mars orbit, await further instructions, thank you, out."

The Mars orbit is an elliptical one and the heliocentric coordinates are programmed into the Seeker's computer, so the alignment will be perfect and precise.

Jnr floated through the inner section of the shuttle to join the rest of the team who were having a meeting in the 'office area', as they called it.

"Come on, Jnr, we've been waiting for you."

"Sorry, guys, made a mess with my last test, had to clean up."

"Ok, so we have a little over twenty-six hours before we embark on the orbital positioning outside of Mars. Checks are complete on the cargo: does anyone have any questions or thoughts about the upcoming events?" asked Shaun.

No one spoke.

"Right, ok, so after the completion of phase one, we will have a two-hour window before proceeding to phase two.

We will check the suits now and we'll use the time between phases to go through procedure details of the landing, ok?"

Everyone nodded in agreement.

"Exciting times ahead, my friends. May I suggest that we all get some rest after we've eaten: we are going to need it."

Jnr wondered to himself about what impact this new scope would bring to science. It would firstly bring ultra-high definition images: clear because they are out in space, with nothing to obstruct the scope's viewing capabilities.

Maybe they could even get an image of the event horizon surrounding the Jnr-X1: now that would be cool.

"Ok, guys," announced Chai, "let's do this."

"Houston, this is Wilson of Seeker. Phase one is a go, out."

"Opening cargo bay doors now," said Chai.

Selev stood by the controls for Canadarm3.

"Selev, proceed with stage one, attachment of Canadarm to the Brightstar please," asked Chai.

Selev manoeuvres the arm perfectly into position: the number of times he'd practised this, he could do it in his sleep.

"Canadarm3 in position."

"Unlocking holding clamps now," explained Chai.

"Unlocking clamps complete, over to you, Selev."

Selev uses the joystick to lift the telescope from the cargo bay while watching on a TV monitor screen.

The rest of the team who aren't involved watch through the shuttle window at proceedings unfolding outside.

"Extending arm to full reach at a seventy-five-degree angle."

"Ok, in position, releasing the grip now," continued Selev. "Brightstar St-1 is now on its own."

All the crew cheered.

"Well done, Selev, nerves of steel, you buddy," said Simon.

Everyone else joined in with congratulating Selev on a job well done –after all, one knock could have spelled disaster.

Next, Jnr took control of Brightstar using the boosters: within a few maneuvers the telescope was quickly moved into position: it was now in orbit around Mars.

The results were relayed to Houston: the St-1 was now in their control. Now onto phase two.

The next job for Selev was to lift the lander and connect six habitat modules, which was a simple task. They automatically clamped onto the craft's outer shell which would hold them in place during the descent to the lunar surface.

These modules contained all the tech gear, life-supports, food, tools, etc for the mission, and would also double up as home once connected on Mars.

Once assembled, Selev would tilt the lander 90 degrees and bring it to the shuttle to dock.

The team would then suit up and board the lander. This was no easy task: they would help each other suit up, and when only one remained, Selev would secure the suit for them and check they were strapped in correctly.

Next procedure was to pressurise: they must breathe pure oxygen for two hours straight, removing nitrogen from their bodies. If they didn't do this, the nitrogen in their bodies would cause bubbles within their blood, around the joints: it was extremely painful, known as 'the bends'.

Selev speaks to the crew over the comms to keep their minds occupied while pressurising.

"Guys, I'm so jealous of you while at the same time excited for you: being the first human beings on Mars is mind-blowing, and knowing I'm so close but so far away, well, I envy you," stated Selev.

"Selev, this mission cannot take place without you, remember that. We are all in this together," said Jnr.

"I know, David, thank you."

"I wish you all a safe journey. I'll be monitoring you closely," said Selev.

"Ok, it's time. Please let Houston know we're beginning phase two," said Shaun.

Selev took to the controls as the team were strapped in and awaiting departure.

First task, undocking, went without a hitch.

Next Selev used a gentle thrust of the lander's booster to take them away from the shuttle; next, he rotated the craft 90 degrees, straightening their position in space.

The lander was now pointing towards the martian surface.

"T-minus one minute," announced Selev.

The crew sat patiently waiting.

"Anyone want to change their mind?" joked Selev.

"Too late for that, Selev," replied Julia.

"T-minus 30 seconds."

Silence.

Nervous silence.

"T-minus ten seconds."The booster ignition commenced.

"T-minus six seconds."

"T-minus zero seconds."

"Mars lander successfully underway, boosters working at full capacity."

"Have a nice flight, guys," added Selev.

The whole team heard the rumble of the boosters and felt the lander shaking as it made its way through the Mars atmosphere, which is much thinner than our own.

As soon as it broke through the atmosphere and rolled over, Selev activated the huge parachutes that would slow down the descent of the lander: only when it was close enough to the surface would the boosters be used to slow it down before landing.

Selev worked his magic and brought the lander down smoothly through the Martian sky.

"30 seconds to impact," Selev announced over the comms.

"Ten, nine, eight."

They could hear the boosters roar into action yet again.

"Seven, six, five, four, three, two, one."

"We have touchdown," announced Selev.

The team looked at each other with relief and then the excitement hit home: they all cheered and patted each other.

"Lander to Seeker, thank you, Selev, you were amazing," said Shaun.

"You're welcome Shaun, continue with extraction."

The message was sent back to Houston: landing on Mars had been completed.

Everyone in the control centre cheered really emphatically: George was a happy man.

"Well done to all of you up there on Mars. What an achievement: we're all proud of you." George asked Marino, the comms technician, to relay the message.

Marino did as he was asked, while crying with joy at the same time.

For science and human exploration this is a huge event. Dreamed of over many years, it had now finally happened. The only thing now which will be bigger than this is when Shaun, to whom it was decided, would be the first human to step foot on the red planet.

Shaun exited the lander first, but as he climbed down the ladder he stopped and gestured to the rest of the team.

"Come down, guys. I've decided we're doing this together, all four of us," said Shaun.

Simon, Julia, Jnr and Chai made their way down and all four astronauts linked arms.

"Houston, all four of us from the Mars lander team have linked arms. This is four small steps for mankind we're taking together, but it's a massive step for humanity's future," exclaimed Shaun.

"Ok, guys, after three: one, two, three!"

All four touched down together: they all cheered and patted each other so excitedly that they got the giggles. They'd done it: what was a dream for years was now a reality, man on Mars!

"Houston, we have successfully touched down on the surface of Mars."

Selev was screaming and cheering to himself as he was looking on a monitor at the historic event that had just taken place below him.

After twenty minutes they received the message from Mars: the astronauts had touched down together on the surface. What a significant moment for all involved. The whole of the control centre jumped, clapped and cheered. George was an immensely proud man at this moment in time.

The next couple of days were used to set up home.

The modules were connected to one another and formed into a straight line.

There was a decompression chamber connected to the first module: this was the main entrance.

There were six modules in total.

The first one was the entrance.

The second one housed the equipment that maintained life-support systems, which included oxygen production.

Third was the main laboratory where all experiments were worked upon.

The bedroom-cum-changing room was number four, and next door in number five was the bathroom.

The sixth module was the garden.

Here food was to be grown, if it was at all possible: it worked in space, so why not here?

Also it made sense to reuse the water from next door.

Day three came and now it was time to start work. Hundreds of experiments needed to get completed in the two weeks they were to stay on the surface.

Regular contact was kept with the Seeker to update Houston on their progress.

Jnr was conducting experiments with the rocks. He wanted to know how much radiation they contained, plus their exact chemical composition.

He noted that about a thousand yards away stood a huge mound, hundreds of feet high: there seemed to be a lot of loose rock built up at its base.

He reported to the team over the comms that he was going to check it out.

"Archer, be careful and do not go out of range. Chai, please go with him," said Shaun.

"Okey-dokey," said Chai. "Lead the way, Jnr."

Both astronauts bounced their way over, which only took a few minutes.

"Chai, I'm going to have a look up top. Will you collect some sample rocks from here please? Make sure they are of interest, ok?" asked Jnr.

"What do you mean 'interest'?"

"Rounded if possible, like they've been weathered," replied Jnr.

"Ok."

Jnr climbed up the huge face of the mound which obviously was easy. The gravity on Mars is around a quarter of our own, so Jnr could literally bounce his way up if he needed.

The top was a little jagged but easy to get across, but looking down at the other side, Jnr was amazed at what he saw.

The rock face on this side was smooth.

He explained over the comms to Chai that he was going to lower himself down to around fifteen feet upon the face.

"Why, Jnr?" asked Chai.

"Well, it looks two-tone in colour at that point. I need samples. Don't worry, I'll put in a peg at the summit: it will only take five minutes," replied Jnr.

"Ok, Jnr, be careful."

Jnr laughed. "What's the worst that can happen? I'll float down if I fall."

So Jnr hammered in a safety peg at the top, then proceeded down the slope on a tether.

He cannot get a piece out no matter how hard he hit the smooth surface: it was like iron.

Further down he noticed the colour of the rock changed.

I'll have to go down further: he was talking to himself.

He stopped his descent and started to chip away at the surface.

To his amazement it worked.

Jnr was tapping away at the Martian rock face, oblivious to the solar winds raging toward him at thousands of miles per hour!

His team and base were out of sight, tucked in behind the huge, strange, smooth rocks he was chipping away at.

Suddenly Jnr was slammed into the rock, knocking him out upon impact.

He was caught up in the wind's turmoil: it crashed upon the rock face, then deflected upwards, out into space itself, taking Jnr with it!

Selev spotted it first.

He hailed everyone on the comms. "Look at that dust storm."

He pointed to the area behind them and they all looked up.

"Oh my God! Archer is up there," said Julia.

"We can't do anything now, get inside the base, quickly," said Shaun.

"Chai, get back here asap."

Jnr was speeding up and away from Mars, still unconscious.

The solar wind had broken his back, both legs and one arm: that wasn't the worse part, though.

Jnr had internal bleeding.

The G-force of such an impact was too much for Jnr's frail human body.

Steadily he came out of his unconscious state: it took awhile for him to compose himself.

He was spinning really fast: it put pressure upon his head.

Realising he couldn't move without serious pain, he used the booster pack controls withhis fingers in short bursts to stop himself from spinning out of control.

He positioned himself to look back at Mars.

It looked so small.

How long had he been out?

How fast was he travelling through space?

How was he going to get back?

There were no comms, not much air left, no chance the ship had enough fuel to pick him up and get back to Earth –that was if they could even find him.

Jnr had a realisation.

"I'm going to die, out here, on my own."

Jnr repositioned himself, pointing away from Mars and towards Jnr-X1.

He fired up the boosters on his jet pack for the last time, heading straight towards the black hole.

Jnr knew where it was supposed to be: after all, it was his discovery.

He could see the event horizon, but only just: the faint rays of light that were trapped on the edge for all eternity, light that stood still.

That meant one thing: Jnr was headed into the gravitational pull of Jnr-X1.

Blood started to run from his mouth and breathing suddenly became difficult.

Panic kicked in.

Tears rolled down Jnr's face: the last thing he wanted was this. There was so much more he wanted to do, so much more he wanted to see, to be with his family again.

Jnr knew it was the end but, if so, he intended to go where no man had gone before, dead or alive: he had to make it to Jnr-X1.

He started to gasp for air, frantically trying to force air into his lungs.

None left, that's it: the tank's empty!

Jnr's eyes started to bulge, and his body started to thrash around with violent jerks, his veins sticking out of his skin like they were going to burst.

He stared at the huge black hole he was approaching, his black hole. Just before his brain gave up and died through lack of oxygen, Jnr managed to say to himself: *I Went In.*

Chapter 13 – The Resurrection Of Jnr

"Sir, one of the drones has picked up something that was emitted from the passage."

"Something? Be more specific."

"It's a human, sir!"

"Have it collected and brought here immediately. Use the tracking beam and have it sent to quarantine first."

"Yes, sir."

He did as requested and Jnr was brought aboard the ship.

He was placed on a table and left to defrost.

The temperature had to be upped a few degrees at a time; too quickly and Jnr's organs would turn to mush.

As he exited the exhaust of the black hole, known as the white hole he was floating along in space at around -270 C.

Jnr was literally rock-hard!

It took over two Earth days to defrost him.

A robotic arm appeared above him and cut off the spacesuit with a laser, precise to a millionth of a millimetre.

There was no colour to Jnr because, after all, he was dead!

Once contamination had been ruled out, doctors took a look at him.

Diagnostics from their computers told them that Jnr was indeed broken.

The fact that Jnr had been frozen didn't matter because it actually kept his body in amazing condition: it preserved him.

"I'm going to start the procedure with the first injection of nanomites," said one of the surgeons.

Jnr was injected straight into his bloodstream through his jugular vein.

"Second injection commencing into the cerebral cortex."

"30 minutes for nano distribution," added the doctor.

As the nanomites got to workon Jnr's body, his temperature started its comeback.

The commander of the ship reported back to his council on this historic event.

"Council, I report to you that a human has been collected aboard my ship. It has passed quarantine and now efforts to revive it are underway. I'll report back as soon as I have more details."

"How is this possible?" asked the council.

"It is believed it must have passed through the passage. It's the only possible scenario," replied the commander.

"Please proceed with caution on this matter," replied the council member.

"Until the facts are collated this information must be kept silent."

"Yes, council, I understand."

With the nanomites now in place, the surgeon commenced with shock treatment to Jnr's body.

First shock, nothing.

Second shock and Jnr jolted: a flicker appeared onscreen.

Third jolt. Jnr's body arced and responded.

A heartbeat!

At first it appeared erratic, then after a few seconds it steadied to normal.

The surgeons looked at one another and nodded in agreement: they'd brought the human back to life.

The commander is summoned down to the lab to witness history.

"What's its condition?"

"It seems to be stable but until the nanomites have finished we won't be able to know if it will be fully functional," replied the doc.

"Very well, keep me informed."

The nanomites surged through Jnr's body, each one had a specific function: cell repair, muscle tissue and bone structure will be rebuilt first.

Then onto Jnr's brain: any damaged cells would be eliminated and replaced.

Jnr was in a coma but all his vitals appeared to function very well considering what he had been through.

The surgeons now left him to rest, to gradually break free of his deep sleep.

Meanwhile, the ship had docked and preparations were being made to move Jnr to a more secure location.

The council members had made their way there to see the human, the very first contact of intelligent life found in their history.

The council stood around the room peering in through the windows at the human laid in front of them. One person accompanied them: his name was Zult, one of their lead scientists.

"Will the human be fully capable, Zult?" asked the council.

"That we cannot determine until a full examination of the body is complete. The nanomites are rebuilding structural integrity as expected. Once the human is alert then we may proceed," replied Zult.

"Very well, please keep the council updated on your progress," stated one of its members.

They move off and leave Zult with the ship's commander.

"What do you want with this human?" asked the commander. It is primitive, and we cannot possibly learn anything to our advantage from this creature."

"That's not of our concern. The council need it alive: that's all we are required to know at this stage," replied Zult.

"The human will be moved with immediate effect to your department. Now, if you will excuse me."

With that, the commander walked away.

Jnr was taken to the science laboratories to where a team of scientists headed by Zult would be responsible for his recovery. The room was moved with Jnr inside, still on intravenous and wired up to strange-looking apparatus.

One week had passed and Jnr was still in a deep sleep. The nanomites had rebuilt any damaged tissues and cells inside Jnr's body: his breathing was normal, his blood pressure normal, his heart rate normal. It was his brain that needed the most attention.

Jnr coughed out loud! He started to open his eyes: it was hazy, he couldn't make anything out. Jnr started to panic. Thoughts rushing through his mind: the last thing he could remember was that he couldn't breathe! He started to scream, all the while struggling to take a breath.

Jnr noticed his hands and feet were strapped tight, which made him panic even more!

Zult made his way over to the window. "Take deep breaths, try not to panic, David Jnr," said Zult.

Jnr looked at the window but couldn't quite make out who was there. "I cannot breathe."

"You can breathe, take your time, breathe slowly."

Jnr concentrated on his breathing and started to calm down a little.

"Where am I? Why am I strapped to this table?" he asked.

"It's for your safety, David Jnr. You have been through quite an experience. You have been in a coma, so we expected you to panic once awakened, as soon as your vitals are normal you may be released of the straps," added Zult.

"Who are you?" asked Jnr.

"My name is Dr Zult. I am lead scientist here and I've been appointed the responsibility of your care until you are restored to full health. Now, how's your breathing?"

"It's better, thank you, but I cannot focus my eyes, they are cloudy and my ears, I dunno, something's not right. I think."

"Your eyes will focus naturally but this may take a little time. As for your ears, can you elaborate please?"

"Yes, well, I can hear you but not in a normal sense, it's like I hear you but without the voice coming into my ears. I cannot explain at the moment," added Jnr.

"Very well, David Jnr. Please relax and we will get to work on your sight. I'm hoping to have it fully functional very soon. If all is well in the next day, then we may proceed in taking you off life support."

"Ok, Doc, and thanks, by the way."

Jnr noticed the doc move away from the window. He could barely make out his outline; still, his vision was quite fuzzy. He could see the machines surrounding him and hear the bleeps of his heartbeat, but that made him question again his hearing. He could clearly hear the bleeps but the doc's voice was completely different to normal. It was like he heard him in his mind but not through his ears! *Maybe it is because he is outside the room,* wondered Jnr.

As he lay on the bed Jnr started to try and picture what had happened to him. His memory was faded somewhat. The mission he could remember but only fragments remained thereafter.

All night Jnr lay mostly awake thinking of his family and friends. Hopefully they would be able to see him today: he needed to make sense of what had happened to him after all. Jnr also couldn't wait to get the damn straps off, too. He needed to move now, he was feeling quite agitated and restless.

Jnr noticed someone at the window: Dr Zult, he presumed.

"Good morning, Dr Zult."

"Good morning, David Jnr. How do you feel?"

"I feel very good actually. I need to sit up: could I please have these straps removed?"

"Certainly," said Zult.

The straps came loose all at the same time.

Hmm, thought Jnr. *Impressive, automated even.*

Jnr sat upright.

"My vision is still a little hazy, Doc, but it's getting better."

"Very good, David Jnr. When looking at me, what do you see?"

"I can see more than just your outline now. You are coming into focus better. Still, it's not quite right."

"I'm a little confused about my hearing, though. I hear you crystal-clear, but it seems like your voice isn't coming into my ears. I know that might sound strange but it's the only way I can explain it. Where am I, Dr Zult? NASA?"

"No, David Jnr, you're a long way from NASA but do not worry, we have all the technical skills needed to help you. You are very safe and most welcome here, David Jnr."

"Will you please call me Jnr? It's easier."

"Very well, Jnr, as you wish."

"So, Dr Zult, you haven't answered my question. Where am I?"

"Jnr, what are the last thoughts you remember before waking?"

"Well, I remember our mission to Mars, to place a telescope in orbit around Mars, and to deliver some equipment to the surface. I also remember something going wrong and not being able to breathe properly. After that, nothing."

"What I'm about to tell you will sound totally bizarre, but please, Jnr, try to listen and understand without interrupting," asked Zult.

Zult proceeded to reveal to Jnr what had happened to him after the fatal Mars mission, how Jnr had died and drifted into the black hole he himself had discovered, and how he had passed through to another part of the universe, how he had been detected ,and indeed rescued from eternal death.

"It's impossible what you are telling me, Dr Zult. I don't believe a word of it! Firstly, we know it's impossible to survive a black hole. Secondly, you cannot come back from death. And thirdly, that makes you another being which we would have knowledge of in our solar system. I would think myself insane to believe what you have just told me, Dr Zult."

"Jnr, what I've told you is the truth. You mention your hearing: it is still the same, yes?"

"Yes it is. Why do you ask?"

"You are hearing my thoughts, Jnr, not a voice. That's why you are confused!"

Jnr thought for a moment. "That makes sense. That's why I hear the machines through my ears and not your voice. That's what was different, but how is that possible?"

"Jnr, try to stand, please, if you can."

Jnr sat himself up and swung his legs over. He slowly lowered himself from the bed. His feet touched down on the cold floor, but his knees started to buckle, and he lifted himself back onto the bed.

"I don't think I can: my legs feel weak."

"Jnr, please relax for one more day. Tomorrow I will help you stand. Then we will talk more in depth about what has happened to you: you are not quite strong enough yet. I will leave you now. Call out for me if you need my help," added Zult.

Jnr layback down upon his bed. His mind was racing with questions. *Is he in a dream? Has he gone mad? Is this Heaven? Did he actually die?*

Dr Zult instructed the nanomites to induce sleep so the team could take him off the life support system, as Jnr no longer needed it.

He slept extremely well and upon awakening realised the tubes and machinery had gone; he was now able to move freely, if only he could stand.

While no one was watching, Jnr tried to stand. He slowly lowered himself yet again: his knees trembled but this time he stood, if slightly wobbly. For a minute or so Jnr stood still, trying to bend his knees. Then he started to move one foot in front of the other.

It was an ungainly sight but he made it across the room. He turned around and started the process again: after a few laps his posture corrected and it became more natural.

It was a weird feeling because inside he felt brand new, but his joints were pretty stiff.

Just then, he heard Dr Zult ask if he was ok, but Jnr couldn't see him or anyone else for that matter.

"Yes, Dr Zult, I feel good, a little stiff but I'm able to walk again. Where are you?"

"I'm in an adjoining room, Jnr. I will be along shortly: keep exercising, it will help."

Dr Zult was with colleagues, deciding whether the time was right to show himself to Jnr. It would be a shock, but after much deliberation they decided the time was right: Jnr needed to know the truth!

Chapter 14 – Type II Civilisation

By now, the enormity of what had happened to Jnr had started to sink in. He felt much better: his movement was improving but inside and especially his mind were spot on. But his head was full of questions to which he needed answers.

If all of this is real, then where the hell am I? Jnr thought to himself.

He didn't feel afraid about the situation. After all, if it was true, then why had they taken care of him?

The door opened and in came Dr Zult.

"Hello, David Jnr, how are you today?"

Jnr stood silently. His focus was nearly back to normal and now he could see who he had been speaking to.

Dr Zult smiled – well, more like a grin with that little mouth of his. It reminded him of Sheldon from *The Big Bang Theory*: you know that smile.

"It's a pleasure to meet you face to face at last, Jnr, and yes, your thoughts are correct. I suppose I do look unusual to you, but in a good way, I hope."

"Oh yes. You can read my mind, I forgot. I cannot therefore hide in my thoughts, can I?"

"No, I'm afraid not."

"Nice to meet you, too, Dr Zult. By the way, I wouldn't say unusual, I would, however, say, different."

Zult nodded.

"I see in your mind you have many doubts. You are confused and you need answers which we will provide. We must take our time, though: too much too quickly is not good for you," stated Zult.

"Ok, I understand, but may I ask one question please?"

"Yes, Jnr, you may ofcourse."

"Where am I?"

"You, Jnr, are on my home planet of Vicron. It is a planet very similar to your own in terms of water, atmospheric composition and land, but the mass is slightly larger than that of your planet. We breathe 72% nitrogen to 28% oxygen, so slightly different to what you're used to, but you should adjust comfortably."

Jnr stood and thought for a second, taking in the unbelievable truth of what he had just learned.

"Jnr, I have been assigned to your well-being and training while here on my planet. We will meet with my council who will tell you much more about what they expect of you in the coming years."

"Years!? What about getting me home? Surely we are not that far from Earth that you couldn't send me home?"

"Vicron is over 20 million light years away from Earth, Jnr. Once you have spoken to the council, only then you will get the answers you seek. Jnr, do you feel up to a little walk?"

"Yes ok, Doc, I'll try."

Dr Zult walked Jnr through the main corridors to the outside the facility.

As soon as he hit the outside air he inhaled loudly: the extra oxygen made him slightly dizzy, so he had to lean against a wall.

"Take a few deep breaths, you will acclimatise quickly."

Jnr was amazed at the scenery in front of him.

There were mountains surrounding the complex. He could see greenery everywhere: it was pretty much similar to Earth. There were insects zig zagging around, birds flying up high up in the sky, little creatures scurrying around on the ground.

It's like home from home, thought Jnr.

The sky was different, though. It was a richer, darker blue than our own sky: the clouds were really thin and wispy-looking, and the sun was pretty bright and seemed huge, but it wasn't too hot.

"It's beautiful, Dr Zult, very much like my own planet."

"Jnr, Vicron is the closest relative of Earth in the universe found up to present, we have searched millions of planets but not many qualify for life, especially intelligent life," replied Zult.

"How long has Vicron existed?"

"We believe it was formed a little over 12 billion years ago. Life began to evolve around 9 billion years ago in the form of microscopic bacteria."

"Right, that's incredible. How long then has your species been around?"

"We have found evidence from our early history at around twenty million years ago, but our time period started after the great war, so it stands at 5,525 years, Jnr."

"That's a long time. On Earth we would term you as a type II civilisation, Dr Zult. Do you understand that?"

"Of course, we have estimated that we will become type III within 500 years from now."

"One of our scientists, Dr Michio Kaku, states that within the next 100 years we should progress into a type I civilisation ourselves," remarked Jnr.

"Well, Jnr, this scientist is correct. Our calculations predict this too, plus it seems you humans are evolving at a faster rate than ourselves for your time in existence."

"How do you know this, Dr Zult, if we are so far from each other in space?"

"Around the immediate vicinity of Earth we have drones which are totally invisible to you, due to our cloaking technology. They have been in operation around your planet for over a thousand years. These drones report back everything we need to know about both the planet and human beings."

"How do they relay information over such a huge distance of space, Dr Zult?"

"Jnr, enough questions for now. Tomorrow we meet with my council: everything you need to know will be answered then."

"'Council': what does that mean?"

"The council are the decision-makers for our species. It contains sixteen members, who are the oldest living generation of our people. Once,a long time ago, Jnr, we were much like yourselves on Earth, and much like yourselves we had to change in order to make progress. The council will explain further upon this matter, I'm sure."

"Now please, Jnr, can we make our way back to your room, it's time for you eat. We need to try you on solid food."

Jnr chuckles, "do you have a McDonald's on Vicron?"

"Afraid not, Jnr. We gave up eating meat many years ago. My species needs lots of energy to function. We get a lot from food sources that contain all the essential vitamins and minerals, but over 60% comes directly from our sun. So meat was banished as food: it takes too much energy to process," explained Zult.

"Ok, I understand, so how do you process the sun's energy?"

"It will be explained shortly, Jnr. Now please, let's return to your room."

Jnr was taken back and seated at a table: food was presented on a plate and a drink that looked awful sat by its side. Dr Zult explained that his dinner consisted of fresh vegetables, a kind of rice, and the drink was a blend of much of the same, but with added vitamins and minerals essential in helping with Jnr's healing process.

A few others watched Jnr but never attempted communication with him. He could tell with the way they looked at each other that thoughts were being passed from one to another, which Jnr wasn't let in on.

"Are you and your team discussing me?"

"Yes, Jnr. You must understand, even though we know all about humans and their history, actually meeting another species is quite something, even though you are quite primitive compared to ourselves."

"Fair point, Dr Zult. What are they asking?"

"They are not asking questions, Jnr, they are making observations."

"Try to eat now please, you need your strength: tomorrow morning we will meet the council together," said Zult as he made his way out of the room.

Jnr made a start on his meal: it didn't look too appetising really, but Jnr longed for real food. His stomach was so empty that cramps were setting in: so no matter what this food tasted like, Jnr was going to eat it.

He decided to try and get some sleep. It wasn't easy, though: he tossed and turned for hours.

His stomach felt queasy, like when you eat a foreign meal that you don't like the look of, and afterwards any movement in your tummy feels wrong – you know, that sickly feeling, like you're going to throw up at any minute.

His mind was struggling with all the information he had learned: it was like a dream for Jnr, not a bad one, but one that he thought he would eventually wake up from.

Did I actually die? Jnr asked himself. If that was true, then these beings must be so far advanced that Jnr must seem primordial to them.

What about the black hole? he thought.

According to our theoretical physicists, Jnr should have been stretched like spaghetti in the turmoil of the black hole: Dr Hawking himself predicts this event.

The upcoming meeting with the council was foremost on Jnr's mind: if they are the leaders of this planet then surely Jnr would get the answers he so desperately needed.

He was feeling a little apprehensive about the council, though. What if he didn't like what they had to tell him? There would be nothing he could do about it.

Was Jnr bound to live the rest of his life on another planet?

After the initial early years, life would become a solitary one for Jnr. No one on Earth would know what happened to him after the Mars mission: they probably thought Jnr was floating around in space forever!

The saddest thought for Jnr was that of his family and friends. Tears ran down his cheeks: it was an immensely sad and empty feeling.

Jnr decided upon himself that the importance of returning him back to Earth was the number one priority: surely with how advanced they seemed to be, they must know a way to return him home.

Jnr finally dropped off to sleep.

"Morning, David Jnr," announced Zult.

Jnr opened one eye and stretched out his body with a huge yawn. "Good morning, Dr Zult."

"How do you feel today, Jnr?"

"I feel a little tired: didn't sleep too well. Apart from that, I feel better than ever really."

"Good. How did you find the food?"

"It was ok. Actually, my stomach felt a little jumpy afterwards, but other than that it was alright for my first intergalactic meal." Jnr smiled.

"We are very happy, Jnr. Obviously we knew your body might try to reject it, but amazingly it didn't. That's a positive start to your recovery."

"While on the subject, your breakfast will be here shortly, which is very similar to what you call oats. Also we have another vitamin-packed drink for you."

"Oh, how lucky am I?" Jnr laughed.

Zult managed a little smile again.

They obviously have a sense of humour, thought Jnr.

"I will return shortly, so we can proceed to our meeting," remarked Dr Zult.

Jnr ate his breakfast which, to be honest, was really nice; the drink wasn't up to much, though.

Zult returned and they headed off to the meeting. They boarded a small vehicle with no driver. Zult moved his hand over what seemed like an instrument panel: a few lights lit up and away they went. The vehicle glided along very smoothly about a couple of feet off the ground.

Jnr noticed that there weren't any more vehicles around at all, really, upon the ground, but it seemed that there was more movement up higher in the sky, but still not many at all, a bit like a ghost town.

Jnr wondered if it was down to the fact that the planet was larger than Earth and maybe it was sparsely populated.

The vehicle slowed up against a glass-looking building. It stopped and out they got. Zult told Jnr to follow.

"The council are awaiting us, Jnr," said Zult.

"How can you know that? We are not in the building yet."

"They have spoken to me."

"So your thoughts can travel distances?"

"We can transmit our thoughts across our planet. Our minds work as one: you will come to know this, Jnr."

Jnr followed Zult into the building. Now he could see more individuals who obviously worked there. They all stopped and looked at Jnr as he walked by – only for a fraction, though, then they simply returned to what they were doing.

Jnr compared it to something like back home: a person walks past with a dog, you look at the dog and smile, then simply carry on without another thought!

Is that what I look like to them, a dog? thought Jnr.

"Jnr, we have arrived. Please try to listen, but not to ask too many questions until you have been spoken to," said Zult.

Jnr nodded.

The huge glass doors opened automatically and there sat the sixteen members of the council.

They approached and stood in front of them.

Dr Zult walked forward and to Jnr it seemed as they were communicating with one another: he didn't hear anything so obviously he wasn't meant to.

"David Jnr, my name is Kandok. We are pleased to make your acquaintance."

"Hello, you already know my name, and the pleasure is all mine," replied Jnr.

"I alone will speak to you throughout this meeting."

Kandok gestured towards a seat. "Would you prefer to be seated, David Jnr?"

"Thank you, yes, I would."

Suddenly the seat moved to Jnr's side, all by itself!

"How did you do that?"

"In time, David Jnr, you will learn, but for now we must talk: please take your seat."

Kandok explained to Jnr what had happened to him and exactly how he came to this point in time. Jnr sat still, taking in the information, passed from the elders of this fantastic race of beings.

He explained that the passage, as they called it, was indeed the black hole Jnr had discovered, and had been created by the Vicrons. The passage was put within Earth's reach very recently with the hope of future contact, only now it had happened rather prematurely.

Jnr jumped in. "How can you just manifest a black hole? What was the purpose of contact?"

"David Jnr, please listen. I have much to tell you: questions can be answered later," said Kandok.

"We have observed Earth and, more importantly, the impact of humans living upon the planet. Over the last 300 years your species has made impressive increases in technology, but this has come at a great price.

"There are many problems that your species must overcome in order to survive. The one thing you have neglected is the fact that humans need the Earth, the Earth does not need humans!

"In fact with every year that passes you are slowly killing the planet. Apart from the effect of global warming brought on through the burning of fossil fuels, which is affecting your atmosphere, wars rage across the planet mainly due to religion, and the threat of a nuclear war is becoming more like an inevitable reality."

"Greed, religion and war will be humans' downfall," continued Kandok. "Once, many years ago, we as a species were in the same position. We continued on the wrong path and we nearly wiped out our own existence. Only after the great war did we realise what we had to live for: only then did we come together as one people. Religion was denounced, for it had no relevance, no reason to exist: it only created hatred. War, with all its madness, death and enormous costs, was scrapped for a more peaceful existence. United as one was the only solution. As we developed as a species we created a new energy source which was plentiful, with very little effect on our planet."

"In short, we put aside petty differences for the future of our people. Now we have peace, no one is poor in our society, no one starves, there is no need for greed, we are now united as one, and now you have come to us, David Jnr. We did not perceive this event, but it might be of advantage to your species and more importantly, planet Earth."

"How?" asked Jnr.

"We would like to teach you our ways and, more importantly, our very history, so that you may return to Earth and explain to your world how change must come into effect in order for your species and planet Earth to survive."

"David Jnr, do you accept our proposal?" asked Kandok.

"Yes, sir, I do accept!"

"Very well, let the training begin!"

Chapter 15 – Augmentation

Jnr had been assigned a team of specialists to work with, to help him understand everything about this planet and its people.

Dr Zult was to be Jnr's guardian.

His job was to explain the science behind his species, from their genetic make-up to the events discovered so far in space exploration.

He was to live with Dr Zult and his family.

Jnr had its own medical officer, Raki: her job was his immediate health and well-being, plus the upcoming medical advances that Jnr had no knowledge of yet!

The last one, Jada, was a neurologist.

He would need to learn from Jada how to use his mind much more efficiently if he was expected to gain the knowledge needed to complete his task.

"Come, Jnr, we have our first meeting to attend. Today you will embark on quite an amazing journey," said Zult.

Dr Zult had a wife called Sameri, a son called Thul, and a daughter, Varna. They all welcomed Jnr to their home, but he could tell they were not really pleased to have a Neanderthal moving in.

Their home was all on one floor, like a bungalow, nice and compact and very clean and tidy – even the kids' room!

Jnr thanked them for their hospitality and followed Dr Zult out. The guys jumped in the vehicle and set off to the office.

On the way, Zult was quiet as he was concentrating on Jnr's thoughts. He could sense every single thought-process that Jnr made, but the one thing that pleased him the most was that Jnr trusted him, liked him even.

Zult thought Jnr was very brave. *How would he cope if the situation were reversed?* he wondered.

"Here we are, Jnr. You will come to like this building: lots of interesting experiments are carried out here."

"Dr Zult, I've noticed that all around I only see ground-floor buildings, like your home. Why is that?"

"We have no need to build upwards, unlike your home, Jnr. We are not overpopulated like Earth."

"Cool," said Jnr.

"We will sit together Jnr as a team and we will discuss what you are going to learn and in what order. There is a lot to go over, so please try to concentrate, especially today."

"Okey-dokey, Doc, whatever you say."

Raki and Jada were already in the room waiting for them to arrive.

After the introductions, Dr Raki asked Jnr to sit.

All three of the Vicrons seemed to be in conversation.

How come I cannot hear or sense any sounds? wondered Jnr.

"We only project thoughts, David Jnr, that we need you to hear," said Jada. "For us, this is an automatic thought-process. We do not therefore waste energy; also it allows us to communicate within a group of people without being distracted. Jnr, you are using your mind already to communicate, I don't think you've realised that. We hope soon you will manage your thoughts the same way we do."

"Right, so I will be able to single out people and direct thoughts to them at a distance or within a group of people having a multiple conversation?"

"Exactly. This is theoretical at the moment but if we succeed, the possibilities are endless for you."

"I've noticed that energy conservation plays a big part for your species," said Jnr.

"As we use our minds much more efficiently than humans, for example, we need more energy consumption. We cannot get this from food alone, so we get the majority directly from sunlight. Let me demonstrate," explained Jada.

"Would you mind, Dr Zult?" asked Jada.

"No, the council have given permission, and I think now would be a good time to reveal ourselves to Jnr."

Jada stood in front of Jnr and within a split second his clothing and skin had disappeared!

He had become totally transparent.

Jnr looked on in amazement.

"How come I haven't seen you like this before now?" asked Jnr.

"The council asked for us to be covered until it was explained to you, Jnr," replied Raki.

He could see the outline of Jada's body, but also he could see his skeletal structure, his heart, brain, blood pumping throughout his veins, muscle movements, everything!

Raki moved forward. "We use the pigment within our skin to our advantage. With this ability the sunlight is directly absorbed to where we need it most at any given time."

"We use this process throughout the daylight to keep our energy levels at their most productive. As sunlight goes down we return our pigments to normal, which in turn prevents energy loss."

"Unbelievable," said Jnr. "So what process causes pigmentation?"

"That's where the nanomites come in," said Raki.

"Ok, I understand, but when you are in the sunlight with your body exposed, what about radiation? Do the levels not increase?"

"Again, Jnr, the nanomites take care of any kind of sickness. They consume radiation particles before they cause any damage to us. So is it this extra energy consumption that allows you to use your brains to communicate with telepathy?" asked Jnr.

"Yes and no. The extra energy is needed for billions more neural connections to be made. Our brains are not much bigger than humans', but we use around twice the amount of neural connections than you," explained Jada.

"Telepathy took many years to develop," said Zult.

"Jnr, years ago we developed augmentation. We used this for many years but eventually, due to evolution, our minds overtook any advantage that augmentation could give us. We became type II, as we have already discussed. There was no more need for augmentation."

"Our scientists have been working on that very subject, too," replied Jnr.

"We believe it is a natural progression for intelligent life to use this technology: it worked very well for us."

"Jnr, we need to ask you a question," said Raki.

"Fire away."

"We believe that for you to advance with the project, you will need augmentation fitted yourself!"

"How will that work and benefit me?"

"What we need to teach you, Jnr, would take hundreds if not thousands of years – that Earth does not have. Having an aug fitted will enhance your mind in ways you cannot imagine. You will learn at an incredible rate. It is the only way to move forward," said Zult.

"Then you know my answer already."

"Good, Jnr. Raki will do the procedure. You will feel nothing as the nanomites will automatically connect with the aug. Pain and illness will be a thing of the past for you, my friend."

"Nanomites in me?" asked Jnr.

"When you were first brought upon our vessel you were given two injections of nanomites: they took care of your body from within, and without this you would not have survived," stated Raki.

"How do they work?"

"They are preprogrammed to repair and strengthen bone structure, blood cells, muscle and neural activity. Also they are self-replicating: they live and die without any input from yourself!" said Jada. "Jnr, we hope you, like ourselves, will soon be able to communicate and direct the nanomites with your mind."

"Well, Dr Raki, you'd better get to work, then."

Dr Zult sent the message to the council of Jnr's decision and the go-ahead was given.

Jnr was taken to the operating wing of the building and laid upon a bed.

While waiting he pondered his situation. *I have died, been taken aboard an alien planet. I have little tiny robots running around in my body. I'm about to have an operation on an alien planet conducted by aliens. Could this still turn out to be a dream?*

Raki and her team entered the room.

Again Jnr could sense the Vicrons were passing silent thoughts about him, how he hoped this all went well and one day soon he could use his mind in the same manner.

"Ok, Jnr, I'm going to instruct the nanomites to induce sleep. You won't feel any pain and the aug will be fitted in around an hour," said Raki.

"Please do not worry, everything will be fine."

The implementation of the aug went according to plan. Raki was pleased with her procedure which, for the Vicrons, was the first of its kind – surgery on an alien being!

They allowed Jnr to come around naturally, no help from the nanos.

As Jnr stirred, his eyes were producing bright flashes of light: it hurt a little.

"What you are experiencing is normal, it will subside shortly. It is a natural occurrence of the collaboration between the aug and the brain," explained Dr Raki.

"Those flashes you're observing are new neural networks being created, the aug and brain are converging."

"The way you view things around you is going to drastically change from now on, Jnr," said Raki.

"Now lie still, rest, this will pass, we are right here."

Jnr could already feel the aug's power.

He could sense the nanomites within his body. He could feel their presence: that's why his body felt stronger than ever.

I don't feel like my IQ has increased yet, thought Jnr.

"That, Jnr, will come with time and practice, plus many hours of education, which will commence shortly," said Jada. "For now you have to heal. We will start in seven days' time if all is well."

Jnr rested as the team moved off into another office to discuss with the council about the progress so far, plus the plans they have for Jnr's future.

Once he felt strong enough, both Dr Zult and Jnr headed off back home.

The next week was to be used for Jnr to get to know family life on Vicron, to see how complex family relationships were carried out on this planet, so that Jnr could fully understand their history.

Sameri, Dr Zult's wife, was a schoolteacher at the same school where her daughter Varna presided: she taught neurology, the same as Jada.

Thul had left school and taken on a position in engineering: he wanted to help with the future development of his planet.

As both Jnr and Zult walked in, they noticed the sweet smell of cooking.

"Hello, everyone," said Jnr.

They all return the greeting, except for Thul.

Thul was a little annoyed that the human had to move in with them. It created a bit of a situation for Thul: he didn't like disruption and this was a major disruption.

Jnr could tell there was a discussion going on: how he longed to be able to communicate like them.

"Hello," said Thul rather reluctantly.

"So you have had augmentation implantation. Let's hope you will progress quickly so intelligence may grace you."

"Enough: that's not how we treat guests," said Zult.

Thul looked away.

"Thul, I'm sorry if I offended you in anyway: that was not my intention. For me this is difficult, too: try to imagine how this all seems for me."

"The problem I have is not directly with you. Now all my colleagues talk about is you, the human, not about me, my work. It's all about you. I know this is not your fault but my life has changed dramatically since your arrival. I'm sorry with the way I've treated you, but this is hard for us, too, Jnr," replied Thul.

"Ok, I understand," answered Jnr, "I would like us to be friends, and if there is anything you need to tell me that will benefit our relationship, then please offer your opinion."

Thul nodded.

"The food is ready," said Sameri.

Dr Zult walked towards the wall and out of nowhere a table top with no legs appeared from the wall, and four seats sprang up from the floor. Jnr was gobsmacked!

"This is nanotechnology," said Jnr.

"Well done, Jnr, you are correct. What made you come to that conclusion?"

"The way it assembled, fluid but solid, orderly. I dunno, that's just what I perceived."

"This is what I work on, Jnr," said Thul. "To you this may look impressive but to us this type of nanotechnology is outdated. This is my area of work. Later I'll show you something really impressive, if that's ok with you, Father?" asked Thul.

"Very well, let's eat now please," replied Dr Zult.

Jnr sat quietly eating his meal. He knew some chit-chat was going on, but he was starting to get used to it now. He knew that if he couldn't hear it, then he wasn't meant to.

The Vicrons ate their food in small pieces, very slowly, plus they didn't seem to eat much at all.

Jnr was starting to miss the taste of meat already.

He thought it probably wouldn't have bothered him but it was!

"It's barbaric to kill for meat," said Varna. This was the first time she had spoken to Jnr.

Obviously Jnr's thoughts were open to everyone: until he'd mastered his mind and learned how to control his thoughts, his mind was like an open book.

"I'm sorry, Varna, if my thoughts upset you. Back home, it's what we do: cattle are bred for food."

"Jnr we, too, did the same in our past but now all life on our planet is treated as equal. We haven't eaten animal flesh for over 4000 years," said Zult.

"Was that after the war you mentioned?"

"Yes, because crops were destroyed, Vicrons survived any way they could, many species of animals were made extinct because they were killed for food. Only when our ancestors grouped together, crops were once again made plentiful, so food was once again available to everyone. The killing of the few remaining animals was banned by law."

"Has the animal population increased since the war?" asked Jnr.

"Yes, in fact it flourished, we have a large population living freely on our lands now."

"That's good," said Jnr.

"Come, I want to show you the project I'm working on," said Thul.

"Do you mind if I leave the table?" asked Jnr.

Sameri nodded.

"Thank you for the food, it was very nice."

"You're welcome, Jnr," replied Sameri.

Jnr followed Thul to his room.

As they entered the room Jnr noticed that the walls seemed to move, only slightly but still: there was something about the building he couldn't quite put his finger on.

"There Jnr, you sit there," said Thul.

Thul sat next to Jnr and all of a sudden, out of a box came a silver, tennis ball-sized sphere, controlled by Thul's mind. It floated in mid-air right in front of Jnr.

He looked at the object and then at Thul. "What is it?"

"That, Jnr, is the future of nanotechnology: they are nanomites at an atomic level."

"What does that mean?" asked Jnr.

"You yourself were given an injection of nanomites. We ourselves have a nano injection to maintain effectiveness within our bodies. This fights off illness and infections, plus the rebuilding of damaged cells or tissues. In just one injection there are five million nanomites."

"Wow that's impressive, Thul."

"To you yes, for us no: now with this new technology we are able to inject a trillion nanomites because of the reduction to a quantum size."

"But that's only a fraction of what can be achieved. Think of a shape or creature or any image that comes into your mind, Jnr?"

Jnr thought: he went through all sorts and came up with a dog.

Thul smiled and looked at the sphere.

It started to move, increasing its mass, and before Jnr had time to guess what was happening, the sphere turned into a silver puppy!

"My God," said Jnr. "That's remarkable."

"Can I think of another item?"

"Yes, Jnr, go ahead."

This time, Jnr went for a laptop, and again the sphere changed shape and, within a second, there it was!

Thul moved the laptop with his mind and placed it on Jnr's lap.

"It feels real, it's solid," said Jnr.

"Yes, Jnr, it is. These new nanomites can morph from fluid to solid or change size at my request. The possibilities are endless," said Thul.

"That's fantastic, so is this your work or are you a part in its creation?"

"We have a team working together on this and yes, I am part of that team. This is one of the greatest achievements of my era, Jnr: this is what I do."

"I bet your parents are really proud of you, Thul."

"Yes, I think they are."

Thul sat with Jnr for awhile explaining the future with this new nanotechnology.

"The project will be put forward to the council soon. If accepted, then mass production will begin and this will benefit all Vicrons in the future."

"Fantastic, Thul. If our scientists could see this, they would be amazed."

"One day in your future this technology will come to the humans and you, Jnr, will show them how."

"Wow, how good would that be!" replied Jnr excitedly.

"Thank you, Thul. I enjoyed our conversation very much but now I feel I must rest. If possible, I would like to learn more from you and I hope we can do this again."

"Yes, Jnr, we may, and I wish you a goodnight," said Thul.

Jnr walked back into the main room and said his goodnights to the rest of the family, using his thoughts! They all answered back, "Goodnight, Jnr."

"Jnr," said Sameri, "try to use your thoughts to induce sleep with the help of the nanomites tonight. I know it's not been long since the surgery but please, give it a try."

"Ok, Sameri, I'll try. Goodnight."

Jnr headed off to his room. He was very excited with the events so far, and to get to sleep on his own would take a miracle. Let's hope he would connect with his new found nanotechnology.

Chapter 16 – Training On Vicron

Over the next week Jnr stayed around the home, studying. Dr Zult had given him a list of subjects that he needed Jnr to get to grips with, which included Vicron historical records, the present way of life, scientific discoveries, medical advances, etc.

Jnr had taken to the aug technology like a duck to water, and he had started to bond with his new found on-board friends.

Internet, like electricity, flowed all around. The walls were the monitor –that's right, walls! The wallpaper was basically a thin, flexible screen; Jnr used his aug to interface with the wall. Imagine: everywhere in your home the walls are like a giant monitor.

That's why he thought it moved when entering Thul's room – it did.

Vicrons' early ancestry was as Dr Zult had already explained it. The time just before the great war was similar to Earth's present day. Nuclear war was a major threat: more than a threat, a near-certain possibility.

Religion caused many problems throughout their world at that time. Again we only have to look at the state of religion today in our societies. Christianity is dying out and Islam is set to take over, not because everyone is converting, but the fact is that young people are not taken to church anymore, so Christianity is a life choice now, and that's why numbers are falling within this religion.

Islam, on the other hand, continues to grow in large numbers due to the fact that Muslim families practise their religion with their children; therefore it is instilled in them from an early age.

Obviously the scientific discoveries were what Jnr was interested in. He learned that the vehicles that he had been driven around in ran on antigravity: they simply hovered a couple of feet off the ground. It was an inexpensive form of travel with no damage to the atmosphere. The costs involved of turning roads from asphalt to superconductors must have been astronomical but worth it.

The ones in the sky used antimatter for their propulsion. Now this was a whole different ball game and right up Jnr's street.

As Jnr previewed the development of antimatter propulsion upon the wall, he realised that on Earth our scientists have been working on this theory, too, and they were not far off reaching this technology. The main problem was antimatter itself: it cost too much money at present to create antimatter back on Earth, but the Vicrons had solved this problem.

Antimatter is harvested from space. Pockets of it appear in space naturally: they simply fly through the area, sifting it out with huge, electromagnetic filters, storing it for later use.

Antimatter has a particle called a positron which has a positive charge and will annihilate when it comes into contact with normal matter. By simply colliding antimatter with normal matter the energy released is a billion times more powerful than what we have today. Just a teaspoon is enough to create a bomb which could in turn take out a place the size of New York; just 4 milligrams of the stuff could power a trip to Mars!

Jnr would spend hours everyday learning as quickly as the information could muster itself. His aug was working perfectly: with just a quick thought, the subject appeared within a millisecond upon the wall.

Nanotechnology is fascinating: nanos placed within the body attack any foreign object that enters, so no more illness, premature deaths, suffering, etc.

In the past the Vicrons simply grew new organs to order: if your heart packed up you popped in a new one.

Our planet's scientists are doing this today.

But now Vicrons had advanced nanotechnology within their bodies: no more transplants needed, and repairs on any part of the body were carried out the instant they occurred.

Every disease known to man would be annihilated the minute it tried to take hold. Can you imagine? No cancer, heart attacks, Alzheimer's, AIDS. Even the common cold for which we have no cure to date would be eradicated. Every single disease gone.

Nanos will also enhance the body's functions, and we would feel strong our entire lives.

It doesn't stop there. Nanotechnology will be used everywhere and anywhere it can be applied –buildings, cars, computers, spacecraft, homes, pavements, clothing, machinery, etc. You get my point.

A quick example. You take an item of clothing. You put it on but you decide you don't like the colour, so you change it. It doesn't quite fit right across the shoulders: you alter it. You want to change it to a different type of outfit, then change it. All you need to do is ask and it shall be done!

It works the same way with your home and everything in it. If you fancy a change then go ahead and tell it to change, using your mind, of course.

A Vicron's home contained literally trillions upon trillions of nanomites. If Sameri decided she wanted to change her home around, she simply directed the nanos and the job was done. Imagine that: she could have a new home anytime she wanted. Nice.

The next subject Jnr came across tantalised him: telekinesis. He sat for hours putting all his newfound IQ into learning this subject, until he had it down to a T.

"Hi, Jnr," said Dr Zult as he entered his home.

"Hello, Dr Zult. Have you had a good day?"

"Yes, Jnr, what about you?"

"Yes, I've had a great day. I have questions for you if I may?"

"Ah, telekinesis. I thought that would intrigue you, Jnr."

"Am I able to do this?"

"Have you tried?" asked Zult.

"Er no, I haven't."

"The answer will be not yet: it took thousands of years for us to develop. I think it's a bit premature to suggest you entertain this idea, Jnr."

"What about teleportation?"

"Again, that took even longer to master. You will need to be at one with your mind to contemplate these subjects. Maybe in the not too distant future, Jnr, you might attain these abilities, but for now there are more important questions for you to consider."

"Like what, Dr Zult?"

"Earth and its future: this is the most important subject at present, Jnr."

"We are in the process of debate on how and when we deem it practical to send you back to Earth."

"Not yet, I've so much to learn, Dr Zult."

"Come, Jnr, let's prepare dinner for the family: we can talk and work at the same time."

The guys got on with food prep and all the while Jnr fired questions about these new ideas he'd come across. Dr Zult could understand Jnr's need for knowledge, but 'walk before you can run' was his favourite term at present.

The rest of the family came home and they all ate their meal in silence, cooked with the help of an Earthling.

Later they all sat talking about their day. When Jnr piped up again, this time he used his mind.

"Sameri, may I ask you a question please?"

"Yes, you may, but please try to direct your thoughts to me only," replied Sameri.

"How long before you think I could use my mind for telekinesis?" asked Jnr.

"That's a difficult question. We know that you are proceeding better than our expectations, but there's a lot to take into consideration with telekinesis. I will give you a simple exercise that you can attempt at your will."

"Start with a small object, try to visualise the energy that makes up that object, look into it, down to the quantum level, see the particles that make up the object, take control of the energy, then simply will it to move from one place to another," explained Sameri.

"So, do I start with an object that doesn't contain nanomites?"

"Yes, Jnr, like a piece of fruit, for example, or an insect. Now would you do something for me?" asked Sameri.

"Yes of course."

"As we speak with one another tonight, please try to concentrate your mind's power on blocking certain sections of your conversation out to all but one person," she asked.

"Is there an exercise for this?"

"Yes, try to concentrate on one person and direct your thoughts to them alone. Imagine you're at one end of a corridor. I'm at the other end, and in between there are doors. The doors are open so people can hear us. Close the doors and project your thoughts to me alone, so the others may not hear. Try to forget that the others are present."

"Ok, Sameri, I'll try, thank you."

The family sat for hours explaining to Jnr how they felt when using their minds, how for them no thought-process was needed for it to take place: it was like breathing to the Vicrons, second nature.

Jnr explained that what he saw in their history was exactly the way humans were progressing in their world today.

"You're right, Jnr. Once we thought the future was robotics, much like you think in the present on Earth but, because we had banished all the problems Vicrons faced, like lack of food, war, religion, hate, poverty, etc, there wasn't much for people to do. Robots had taken over our workload and we decided as a collective that robots had to go, we only needed nanotechnology," said Zult.

"So you work for the fun of it, then?"

"Everyone works on Vicron Jnr but not for financial gain: we have that. We work to progress, to become more efficient, to become more knowledgeable. That's the real wealth, Jnr, knowledge!" said Thul.

"Ah I see, that makes sense to me," said Jnr.

After some great conversation Jnr headed off to his room.

He sat upon his bed and looked for something to use for his first experiment with telekinesis. He scoured the room but nothing looked usable. Everything contained nanos in his room: what could he use?

Aha, a nut: he'd been given a few for snacks, he reminded himself.

He placed it upon his dresser. Taking a seat, he stared at the nut, concentrating his mind to block everything else out, nothing, no movement. This time he remembered what Sameri had said, to see the energy within the nut. This time he tried to see the energy, right down to the quarks, but alas, nothing.

For a while he persisted with his attempts: he looked at the nut in every possible way he could imagine but still the nut refused to move. *Maybe it's not for us humans, not yet anyway*, he said to himself.

After what seemed like an eternity, Jnr decided to call it a night. He'd try again tomorrow.

Before allowing the nanos to turn his lights out, Jnr lay awake thinking about what he'd learned so far. Vicron was an amazing world and its people were very happy with their existence: they wanted only for knowledge and peace. Everything they did was in an attempt to create more intelligence: even within their sports, knowledge was the only winner.

Vicrons played a game called Flyball: two teams of eight have to score a goal on a circular pitch. The goal was achieved when the ball was passed through a hole at either end. The team consisted of two defenders, two attackers and four midfielders. Each player used his mind to control the ball, which couldn't touch the ground or it would be a foul. The four midfielders would continually move the ball from one to another until an attacker had made a break. The ball was then passed, and the attacker had to manoeuvre the ball past the defenders who would be in front of goal trying to repel it.

It was a really fast-paced game which again enriched the mind of the players: that was the main objective of flyball.

Another game called Boff was fought between two players only: this was the ultimate game of minds for the Vicrons. To play you had to be over 750 years old: this was a wise man's game, very similar to chess.

Both games were conducted yearly, it was a major event for the Vicrons. During the year regional games were played and each winner moved closer to the final with every win. Of course not everyone on the planet could attend and watch: the spectators were picked at random, and it was a fair system. Everyone else would tap into their thoughts so, in effect, it was like being there anyway.

Jnr dropped off to sleep without any input from his nanos; because he was tired, he had used so much energy with all his learning that help wasn't needed.

Next morning Jnr woke with a huge yawn and a stretch. He turned onto his side and gazed over towards his dresser and looked at the nut. *It moved!* He sprang out of bed and walked over to it. He tried again: nothing.

"It moved, I saw it move!" he shouted as he ran through to the living room.

There was no one there: they'd all left already.

"Sameri, I did it!" thought Jnr.

"Well done, Jnr," replied Sameri.

"You projected that thought to me alone, too, Jnr, that's remarkable!"

For the next month Jnr spent most of his time with his team back at headquarters, honing his new skills. Experiments were carried out with the results of each one being recorded. It was amazing the pace Jnr was progressing at.

The results were so impressive that the council decided it was time for a visit.

Chapter 17 – The Passage

The council were due soon and Jnr had so many questions for them. Why were they planning his return so soon? How was it going to happen? Jnr had so much more he needed to learn for himself, not just for Earth's sake.

Dr Zult asked Jnr to follow him to the main room to where the council would soon show up.

"The council will test you today, Jnr. Try your best to utilise your mind's thoughts when speaking to Kandok."

"Ok, Doc, but I want to ask questions of the council: would that be allowed?"

"I will ask, but I cannot promise," replied Zult.

Just then the whole council appeared before them. There was a very faint flash of light behind each member as they materialised.

"Welcome, council," said Zult.

For a minute or two the Vicrons exchanged conversations in which Jnr was not included.

"Hello, I'm right here. I think I should be allowed into the talks now, don't you, Kandok?" asked Jnr.

"Very well," replied Kandok.

"Dr Zult has explained your progress so far, and it seems you are learning well. You seem to be very interested in our technologies, but this is not the main goal, David Jnr, we need you to understand the importance of returning you to Earth with the knowledge of our past, which could be Earth's future. We cannot simply stand back and watch an intelligent civilisation collapse taking the Earth with it. That's what is important to us."

"Why is our planet so important to you?" asked Jnr.

"We have searched the universe for thousands of years in the hope of finding other intelligent life forms. There are literally billions of planets within our solar system, the same as yours, where we have found life on many of the planets, but only your planet and our own contain advanced intelligent life," explained Kandok.

"So you're saying there's more life out there: what are they like?" asked Jnr excitedly.

"Nearly all of them are primordial, bacterial-based life forms. Some have evolved to small creatures, but we thought we would never find intelligent life. We thought we were on our own in the universe, until we found Earth. It seems that for intelligent life to exist there had to be perfect conditions: the odds are really high for life to exist anywhere in the universe. We never wanted to make contact with your species: we had no reason to. As a species you're not very well developed compared to ourselves. What point would we have in contacting you? At the same time, we would like to see you progress. Life is fragile, and your planet is fragile: without our help it may not survive."

"So how were you planning on letting us know this news, then, if you didn't want to contact us?"

"We created the passage which you came through. We hoped one day you would send a satellite through the passage to explore further into space. This satellite would have been captured and we would have uploaded information upon it, which we have explained, hoping that you would indeed change your ways for the better, both for the planet and for your species. That all changed when you appeared, Jnr."

"You say that you simply create a passage, as you call it. How? I have not been able to access information on the subject," said Jnr.

"We decided that the technology needed is far too advanced for you: it was deleted on purpose. To open a passage, dark energy is needed. As a species you must learn this in time by yourselves, that it would be dangerous for humans to mess with nature in this way at the present time."

"We know or assume that dark energy exists, only we haven't found it yet."

"Why would it be dangerous?"

"It will take years for you to realise this, Jnr. Dark energy exists in our universe but it belongs to the larger scheme of things that you've yet to discover."

"How, Kandok? Please explain to me how."

"Jnr, we have discovered that our universe is only one of trillions upon trillions of universes: string theory tells you this."

"M-theory?"

"Yes, Jnr. You see, our universe lives on a membrane, a two-dimensional membrane from which we cannot escape. We have found that we live alongside others, containing other universes, connected by strings. Each brane is connected to a super string, which holds the branes in place, but they slightly overlap each other in a spiral pattern. They cannot come into contact with each other because both gravity and dark matter keep them at bay."

"Is that why we observe gravity as a week force?"

"Yes, gravity, dark matter and dark energy exist within the branes on all dimensions. Gravitons are the only matter particles that flow through all dimensions and the multiverse," replied Kandok.

"You say 'multiverse': are you certain about this? How can you know for sure?"

"We have been able to obtain information carried by gravitons. It seems they record information as they pass through each brane. We know that most branes contain a universe very much like our own, but there are differences in some. Life has been detected in some of our tests from other branes, Jnr. We hope one day to visit these other life forms."

"How would that be possible?" asked Jnr.

"Our scientists believe it's possibleto connect to another brane using a controlled passage. Tests are underway as we speak," replied Kandok.

"That's unbelievable."

"Is that how I'm going to be sent back to Earth?"

"Exactly. You will cover twenty million light years of space in the blink of an eye."

"How do you know that travelling this way is safe? Have you been through one?"

"We have used passages to travel to our closest planets for years with no fatalities so far. The science behind creating a passage is nothing new for us, Jnr, but for humans the technology is too early for you to comprehend. That's one of the reasons we have omitted it from your viewing," replied Kandok.

"One of the reasons? What are the other reasons?"

"Once you have been returned, Jnr, we want no chance of your people ever coming to our planet again. An intelligent species would want to communicate and also visit other planets. Communicating is one thing but visiting in mass numbers would spell disaster, we believe. That is the main reason we never wanted to make contact with Earth."

"The passage as you call it, we call them black holes, they occur naturally throughout our universe as we now know, but what we don't understand is where they lead –if in fact they lead anywhere at all, or just collapse. Our science tells us that at the centre of a black hole there is a singularity; when the hole collapses it does so at this point. After that we have no idea," said Jnr.

"You are correct, Jnr. The controlled passage we create contains two exits. One exit is small and bent outwards, containing the singularity; the other is the larger exit which we use for travel. We create a field of energy which pulls an object away from the singularity when passing through the passage. This makes it safe for travel, which is why you weren't torn apart as you exited," explained Kandok.

"So what happens to the singularity once the passage's energy has been used up?"

"A singularity creates life, Jnr. Our universe was created in this way and so was every other universe within the ever-expanding multiverse. What you call the BigBang was indeed this very process."

"How, Kandok, how?"

"A natural passage is connected to a new membrane at its exit: an empty brane, void of everything. Once the passage has consumed everything within its vicinity, it collapses into the singularity. Also, your scientists will learn that information is not lost, it remains contained within the singularity. As this singularity becomes ever denser and hotter, it heats up until eventually the energy cannot be contained."

Jnr listened to every word Kandok was spilling out. This was the answer to our biggest question: how did our universe begin?

"Finally, the singularity explodes outwards at beyond the speed of light for a few millionths of a millisecond. A new universe is created with the ingredients contained already proven to produce life," continued Kandok.

"So that's why we assume there is life in other universes. Fantastic!"

The council were happy with Jnr's progress and it was decided that Jnr would leave Vicron in just three months. In that time the council wanted Jnr to concentrate on their proposed plan of action for Earth's future.

What would happen when he returned home?

Who did he need to speak to?

What needed to be said? No matter who it upset.

Earth's future depended on Jnr getting it right!

Chapter 18 – The Return Of Dr Archer

Jnr decided that he must put all his efforts into the learning of his newly acquired mental abilities, telepathy and telekinesis. With only three months remaining on Vicron before his return journey to Earth, he didn't want to waste a second knowing that he would never return to this exciting, beautiful planet.

Most of his time was spent with Dr Zult and his family, especially his wife, Sameri.

Jnr was able to fully communicate with anyone on planet Vicron in every way possible, whether it was a single conversation or within a gathering of people. It seems that the human mind is capable of much more than humans thought possible, even within a short time frame. Of course Jnr had a little help with his aug.

From now until leaving for home, Jnr had made the decision not to use his voice for communication. Three months with not a word spoken: imagine that!

Telekinesis proved to be much harder for Jnr to master.

Yes, he could control nanomites at will to perform incredible tasks, but the free movement of large objects was proving very hard indeed.

Thul helped Jnr every time he was at home.

Jnr could manage small objects but something the size of a dog, for example, was out of reach at the moment.

Thul and Sameri had an idea. The family were seated to eat a meal when the idea was announced.

"Jnr, you are to attend a game of flyball. Two teams have been assembled which you will be part of. This will help with your learning of mind control – a jump-start if you like," said Sameri.

"But I can move small objects, that's not a problem for me. How will this help?"

"Even though the object is small, the amount of concentration needed to control the ball is multiplied because others will intervene. The ball will have forces pulling it from all directions."

"Ah I see. So in reality I should really suck at it, then," replied Jnr.

"At first, yes, but with practice you will succeed, Jnr, I'm sure of it," Sameri replied.

"Ok, Sameri, if you think it will help, then count me in."

"The game will be 60 days from now so practice with Thul until then."

Jar excused himself and decided to practise in his room.

Thul had given Jnr a spherical metal ball to practice with: it was quite heavy.

Sitting on the floor, Jnr emptied his mind and blocked his thoughts from projecting to the others. He raised the ball quite easily, and slowly he manoeuvred it from one side of the room to the other. It was time to speed things up.

Jnr sped up the ball until it became really hard to think at the speed he needed in order to control the turns without it crashing into the walls. He succeeded, though. *It's time for something bigger,* thought Jnr.

The next morning Jnr asked Thul if he could accompany him to his workplace in order to make better use of the facility's space.

On the way, Jnr explained his intentions to Thul.

"Thul, I think it's time to step up with my training: the ball is not a problem for me now."

"Yes ok, David, if you think you're ready, there are plenty of objects for you to utilise. This could be an interesting day for you, but please don't rush, it may set you back," explained Thul.

"I won't, don't worry, and besides, I want to nail this before I'm sent back to Earth."

"You cannot rush this, David Jnr. You have already come a long way in a short amount of time."

"I know, Thul, and I want to thank you for putting up with me, I know it's been hard for you, but I really do appreciate everything you have done for me."

"To be honest, Jnr, at first it was hard but I've become intrigued by you now. We thought the human mind was too under developed to adopt Vicron abilities, but we were wrong: you have shown us that you have a fantastic ability to learn."

The guys arrived and Jnr immediately headed for the court.

Thul was to join him later so Jnr had time to practise by himself.

He scanned the area looking for potential objects to be used in his quest to master his art.

There was a seating area where people obviously watched others work their magic. In one corner were objects of different sizes and shapes used for this purpose.

Jnr started with small square blocks first.

He commanded them to move across from the right to the left: there were five which he positioned in front of himself.

Right, Jnr thought to himself, *I'm going to stack these blocks one on top of the other.*

He got to work. One after another they stacked up. *That was easy,* Jnr thought. *Ok, a bigger one next.*

Jnr chose the next size up and again he completed the task.

What he didn't notice was that Thul was watching his progress through the main entrance window.

To Thul, this was child's play, but for a human being, this was an amazing task.

"Jnr," said Thul.

"Oh I didn't know you were coming in yet, Thul."

"I've been watching you for a few minutes. I like what you have achieved, but I want you to try something harder."

"Like what?" asked Jnr.

"I would like you to use the spherical balls and to do the same exercise as you've previously managed, please."

"How can you stack balls on top of each other?"

"It can easily be done, Jnr, please try. This time you will need to focus harder to keep all the spheres still as you place them on top of each other. If one moves the stack will collapse," said Thul.

"This will teach you to spread concentration of your mind into controlling multiple objects at the same time – essential for multitasking, Jnr."

"Ok, here goes."

He rolled one ball over and then another. He then placed them upon each other: so far, so good.

As he turned his attention to a third ball, the second ball fell off the first.

"Damn," said Jnr.

Thul jumped in.

"Jnr, I have an exercise which will help. It's still quite hard, but it will help."

"Ok then, Thul, what is it?"

"Place the spheres in a line with a gap in between across the ground, then leave one sphere in the centre and move the other four spheres around the central one, in an orbital-like fashion. Start with one then try to move all four. Keep control of each ball by imprinting your thought of the direction and speed that the sphere is travelling."

Jnr stared at the balls and set one off in a circular motion, so that one was moving around the central sphere. Then he concentrated really hard to command the sphere to keep on its path, onto the second one.

Thul was impressed. Jnr was now in control of two spheres, moving around in opposite directions to each other.

Onto the third: as Jnr started to control the third sphere, the other two crashed into each other.

"Shit, I nearly had it then," said Jnr.

"Don't worry, that was in fact quite good. Try again, please, Jnr, but this time command your thoughts with authority and clarity."

"I will leave you to it as I need to get back to work. Please don't over do it, Jnr. If it gets impossible to manage, then leave it for now. I don't want you to get frustrated as that will not help, it will only hinder," said Thul.

With that, Thul left the court but Jnr was having none of it. "I will get this before I go home today," he mumbled to himself.

For the next couple of hours he tried to complete the said task, but by now Jnr was getting very frustrated.

"It seems such a mundane task, so why can't I do it?" he mumbled to himself.

Thul came through in his mind.

"Jnr, please take a break. I can sense your frustration which will only make the task harder. Your mind must be focused to progress with this task."

"I know, Thul, but if I cannot control a few little balls, how can I even dream of moving, say, a car?"

"Come, Jnr, and eat. I will join you later to explain further," said Thul.

"Ok, I'm on my way."

Jnr reluctantly made his way through to the dining area. How he wanted to master his mind! Nothing less than 100% would be good enough for our Jnr.

While eating lunch, Thul and his colleagues explained in the simplest way how to manoeuvre the balls, which Jnr could understand. He thanked them for their help and set off to the court accompanied by Thul.

"Right, Jnr, I'm going to help with this. I'll show you how I would achieve my goal and try to relate to you the process we Vicrons go through when using our thoughts."

Just then the balls started to move: like a perfectly choreographed dance the balls spun around each other while the central ball remained still.

Thul turned to Jnr and said, "As you can see, Jnr, I'm talking to you and no longer concentrating on the spheres at all. I've set them in motion with clarity of mind and I have no need to waste more energy in achieving my goal. Until I make a change I can concentrate on other tasks at the same time."

"Wow," replied Jnr. "That's what I want to achieve."

"It will come," replied Thul as he left the court.

"It's time to go, Jnr. You can continue tomorrow."

On the way back, Jnr pondered if he would have enough time to learn what he needed to learn before returning home to Earth.

On the subject of home he thought of his family and friends, and also his work colleagues, who of course all thought he was dead. At night he cried at the thought of his parents thinking he was no more. That was the only reason a part of Jnr wanted to return.

Over the next two months Jnr brushed up on his skills. It was the day of the flyball game.

Jnr changed the shape and colour of his clothes to those of his team members.

"Nearly time to go," said Dr Zult.

"Ok, Doc, I'm ready, so let me know when you are ready," replied Jnr.

Jnr was using his last few minutes watching footage upon his wall of past flyball games. It was a very fast-paced game indeed. Jnr wanted to make a good impression for the Vicrons and especially Thul.

"David Jnr, we are ready to leave now."

Jnr headed out of his room and through the doorway to where the family stood waiting to catch a glimpse of him in his team colours.

They all told Jnr he looked the part – even Varna managed a little smirk.

Jnr took his seat and seemed to be chuckling a little.

"You're laughing, Jnr, what is *The Big Bang Theory* you're thinking of?" asked Sameri.

"Oh it's nothing."

"I don'tunderstand. If it's nothing, why does it make you laugh? Who is this person you have in your mind?"

"Ok, Sameri, it's a comedy show I watch, the person I'm thinking of is Sheldon Cooper: he's a quirky character with an even quirkier smile. He has one of the funniest smiles back on Earth. When you people smile it reminds me of him: you would have to see it for yourselves to understand," explained Jnr.

They all looked at Jnr inquisitively for a moment, and then the vehicle went silent for awhile. As they approached the flyball venue, Thul went over with Jnr as to what position he would play and what his objectives were during the game.

"It's ok, Thul, I've been using my spare time wisely. I've watched many matches."

"That's good, Jnr, but this is going to be a hard test for you, my friend."

"Wow, Thul, you said 'friend'," replied Jnr with a smile.

Thul looked at Jnr and one of those little Sheldon smiles of his appeared, too.

The family finally arrived and made their way to the seating area while our two boys headed on down into the players' quarters.

A pre-match talk was given.

Drakor was the team captain: his job was to call the play.

"David Archer, today's game is to test what you've learned so far. The most important thing to remember is to close your thoughts from the other team. We will know nothing of them: no names or the way they will play. This is vital. You must not mention names, as the other team will use this information to confuse our team."

"Ok, Drakor," replied Jnr.

"Also, David Archer, their job is the same as ours which is to break down the mind's defences of the opposite team, then we have control," stated Drakor.

"If your minds are connected, as I know they are, then how come each team doesn't know the other team's names?"

"This is a training game for you, Jnr, the team has been selected randomly and in secret to give you a fair chance of competing. A professional team knows everything about their opponents, their strengths and weaknesses, names etc. This game becomes particularly harder as you improve in the ranks."

"Oh I see."

"Also we are to play with our skins showing today, just for you, otherwise, as we are not going to use names, you wouldn't know who was who," said Drakor.

"Oh right, good."

"You, Jnr, will play upfront with Thul. You are an attacker: the only goal is to score."

Just then the referee called out the teams.

"It's time, let's go," said Drakor. "Good fortune, everyone."

The team assembled themselves into their positions on the court. Jnr moved to the front, facing the two attackers. They both looked at each other and back at Jnr with that silly grin upon their faces.

The referee threw the fly ball up into the air. *That's it, we're away,* thought Jnr.

Jnr propelled the ball backwards to his midfield players and made a run to the front.

He watched as his team passed the ball to one another: they seemed to do it without looking at the ball!

He and Thul were in position waiting for the ball to come down court.

Suddenly one of the opposite team took possession of the ball and started passing to the rear. Jnr watched as Thul sneaked up from behind their midfield and intercepted. He turned and ran – goal!

One nil: Thul had struck first.

Everyone congratulated him, then got back to business.

Over the next ten minutes the opposite side scored twice. Jnr had only a few possessions of the ball. The ref called out half-time, and everyone returned to their team room.

That was quick, thought Jnr, not realising that twenty minutes had passed.

"That was ok, guys," said Drakor.

"It's only 2-1: we just need to work harder for the second half."

"How do you think it went for you, Jnr?"

"Erm, well, it's faster than I thought, actually. No sooner do I have the ball and it's taken away before I have time to think of my next move."

"You need to relax your mind completely: if you panic, you get confused and become open to attack. Remember what I showed you at work with the spheres: control with confidence and clarity," said Thul.

Drakor stood up. "Ok, let's play harder this half."

With that, the whole team rose and made their way out to the opposite side of the pitch.

This time, Jnr played with more authority and it showed: he set up two further goals.

The ref called it over. The game had come to an end: they had lost 8-5.

Thul scored three, and one of the midfielders scored a screamer from around halfway up the court which caught everyone by surprise: it was like a bullet.

Later, Thul told Jnr that the player was expected to become one of the best flyball players ever.

Our Jnr had scored two!

All the players cheered together and, unbelievably, the team lifted Jnr onto their shoulders. They paraded him around the court for everyone to applaud him: it was a fantastic day for Jnr.

After the match, everyone was invited to a celebration meal in honour of Jnr: the two teams that had played that day, plus the families, of course.

All family and friends ate together and Drakor asked Jnr to join the table with the flyball players: he felt so proud of himself. They all congratulated him and treated him as if he was one of them.

Back at home, Dr Zult explained to Jnr that tomorrow a meeting had been planned with the council, when he would be told what was going to happen with his return journey home. Jnr nodded and excused himself. He was tired and needed sleep: the game had taken a lot out of him, and being a veggie now he felt tired quite often anyway.

The meeting came and went.

Jnr was to receive a final injection of nanomites, the updated version that Thul had worked on: these would complete his body's protection. After that, Jnr would never get injured or contract a disease again, ever.

A ship constructed of trillions upon trillions of nanomites, powered by a small nuclear fusion engine was to take Jnr home.

Jnr was instructed about what he had to do once back on Earth, whom he needed to speak to, and how to show them what he had learned. Also he was warned not to let anyone have control of his ship; as it was under Jnr's command, he was to keep it out of sight until needed.

Kandok made it clear that the humans must not acquire their technology at all costs.

Jnr was also warned that he might be interrogated upon his return.

Until the launch day, Jnr stayed with Dr Zult and his family, and funnily enough, he had a sense of wanting to stay. He liked it there but Vicron didn't need Jnr, Earth did.

It was the last night before Jnr was to leave Vicron. He decided he wanted to cook a thank-you meal for the family. Sameri usually did all the cooking and she was damn good at it, but Jnr insisted, so reluctantly she agreed. On one condition, though, Sameri wanted to supervise.

Jnr did the cooking and Sameri helped him take it to the table: the whole family enjoyed the meal, which surprised them.

"Thank you for my meal, I really enjoyed it," said Varna.

Jnr was surprised. Varna had hardly spoken ten words to Jnr since he had been on the planet. It seemed as though she was taking a shine to Jnr now it was time to go home.

All the family agreed and thanked Jnr.

Everyone stayed up later than usual on this last night. They all talked about what Jnr had learned, and wanted to know more about his own family back on Earth. Jnr told them of his life and his love of his family and friends. Funny – we may be stupid, we humans, in so many ways, but at least we have the capacity of love for each other. So why, then, does the human race continue to squabble with one another?

Jnr just couldn't get to sleep at all: too much going on in his mind. He decided he'd use the nanos to induce sleep because he was going to need it for tomorrow.

The next morning Jnr had to be woken up, he was in such a deep sleep.

They all ate breakfast together and afterwards accompanied Jnr to the launch. As they passed the Vicrons' homes people gathered to watch as Jnr was paraded by: he waved and some even waved back.

Jnr could hear the well-wishes people were offering him. *Have a safe return*, he heard: that was nice. Funny that everyone seemed to look the other way when he first arrived: anyone can change one's perception of another, having understood them more.

The ship was sitting waiting and so were the council, along with the scientific team that Jnr had already met.

A Vicron scientist walked forward to Jnr. He explained that the ship would take him into the passage and on towards Earth; the only time Jnr would have to take control was upon entering our atmosphere and, of course, the landing.

Kandok and the rest of the council approached next. He directed his thoughts to Jnr only and explained what he expected of Jnr.

They then thanked him for everything and wished him a safe journey, and they expressed their hope that the mission would turn out a success.

It was time to go.

Just before climbing into the ship, Jnr turned to Zult and his family and thanked them for their help and persistence with him while he remained in their care.

Tears welled up in his eyes: such lovely peaceful people that he would never set eyes on again. A very sad moment.

He climbed in and strapped himself down into his seat. The cockpit closed down around him.

The dashboard came to life and the engines roared into action.

He took one last look at the whole family and said, "I will miss you and I will never forget you, thank you all."

Everyone waved goodbye as the ship rose into the sky.

Jnr was now on his way home.

Chapter 19 – Destination Earth

The ship was really moving through space, but it was a nice smooth ride for Jnr.

It wouldn't take long to reach the passage. Jnr was apprehensive but elated at the same time: the thought of seeing his family again gave him hope.

It dawned on Jnr that time would have moved on somewhat since he left. *How long?* he wondered.

Could it be hundreds of years, in which case no one alive would know him or know of him? Was it even too late for Earth? It might be that nuclear war could have killed off the human race and the planet could be deserted.

Nah, thought Jnr, *I'm getting ahead of myself here.*

But in the back of his mind he knew that scientists on Earth believed that if you could travel through black holes, time would indeed be affected in some way.

Why didn't I ask this very question back on Vicron? Jnr asked himself.

Too late to go back now: he could see the passage approaching!

For the second time in his short life he panicked a little, with goose bumps appearing on his arms. He felt a little cold sweat run down his cheek. He had been here before – ok, the last time he was dead, but this time he was very much alive.

Jnr tightened the straps that held him in his seat.

The ship started to vibrate a little as it neared the leading edge of the passage.

Jnr was told by the scientist to enter the passage on the right side so as not to get sucked into the singularity and be stretched forever.

Jnr's ship entered exactly where it was supposed to, and straight away it started to shake violently. Everything sped up, and light seemed to stretch as far as the eye could see: colours, lots of colours, bright flashes that made him wince.

To Jnr, he felt like he was travelling along a rainbow at the speed of light: 186,000 miles per second!

Jnr saw a massive flash of light, then darkness.

It took a few seconds for his eyes to adjust, but he made it: he was nearly home, or so he thought.

It turned out that he had materialised just outside of Jupiter!

The Vicrons had worked out that Jupiter was only 350 million miles from Earth at its closest orbit, so that was where they placed the passage, away from prying eyes.

Jnr looked at Jupiter as he flew alongside. *What a sight*, Jnr mumbled to himself.

He had a realisation: he had just spoken. That was the first time in months he'd actually used his vocal cords.

As Jnr was chuckling to himself, he again heard the engine step up a gear,and wham! – he was pinned to his seat as the ship propelled itself into what he could only think was some kind of hyperdrive. It seemed like he was travelling at the speed of light again.

They didn't tell me about that, thought Jnr.

Jnr fought hard to try and look forward: the G-forces were tremendous upon his body. He could see a faint shape, ever-growing, coming towards him. It was Mars. It was still quite away off, but Jnr knew what he could see.

He watched as it grew larger, but still it was so far away it appeared so tiny in the blackness of space.

By now, Jnr was wondering what people back on Earth were going to make of his return. They had obviously presumed him dead, so this was going to be a massive shock for all, especially his family.

He also thought of his friends, Jib and Raph: he couldn't wait to tell them of his adventure.

How he hoped to get to see his fellow astronauts. They must have been devastated to have left him in space: what a decision to have to make.

It was taking so long to move through space, even at the tremendous speed at which he was travelling, that he decided to instruct his nanomites to take him into sleep and alert him on his approach to Earth: he didn't want to miss that.

As Jnr slept, the ship passed Mars: there was a colony now, but alas, Jnr missed it. Jnr suddenly snapped out of his sleep and noticed that the ship was slowing down.

Before him, a sight to behold: Earth!

It looked so beautiful from space, the clouds roaming around the planet. He could make out shapes on the surface. *It won't be long now*, thought Jnr.

It looked exactly the same as when he had left for Mars: perfect.

He could make out the shape of America below, so that was where he headed.

Meanwhile, at NASA, satellites had picked up something on the radar.

One of their technicians noticed a strange anomaly coming towards Earth, it was strange because its speed was slowing.

He contacted his superior, a man named Jackson.

"Sir, I have something I would like you to see: you need to come now."

Jackson slammed down his phone: he hated being interrupted.

He marched his way to the control centre, hoping this wouldn't be a waste of his precious time.

"Ok, what have you got for me that's so important?" barked Jackson.

The young technician was hoping this would turn out to be something, because, if not, he would receive such a roasting. Jackson was of a military-type mentality: he thought he was a sergeant major.

"Sir, look there." He pointed to the huge screen and highlighted it.

"What is it?"

"I don't know, sir."

"You don't know? So why have you bothered me before knowing what it is? Do you realise how busy I am?"

"Yes, sir of course, but whatever this is, it actually slowed down and it looks like it's headed into our atmosphere," replied the nervous young lad.

"How can it slow down?"

"I don't know, sir, I've never seen anything like this before. It came in quite fast then seemed to come to a really slow speed as it got close."

"Ok, are there any ships or satellites in that area, either ours or otherwise?"

"No, sir."

"Ok, keep a tight lid on this for now, I'm going to make some calls," demanded Jackson as he marched off.

Jackson entered his office and on a secure line called the head of defence at the White House.

The man he needed to speak to was Colonel Baxter: he explained to Baxter what he had just seen.

Baxter told him to tell no one and to keep him in the loop as to what the mysterious object was doing.

Baxter then proceeded to call the President.

"Could you please put me through to the President on a secure line? This is Colonel Baxter: this call is of the utmost importance."

"Yes, sir, one moment," the receptionist replied.

"Ah Colonel Baxter, to what do I owe this pleasure?" said President Louis Beevers.

"Sir, please may I speak to you alone? What I have to tell you is of the upmost importance."

"Oh I see. Ok, please make your way to my office. I'll have the room cleared," said Beevers.

There were three of his entourage in the room who quickly grabbed their briefcases and left.

"Thank you," said the President.

Knock knock.

"Enter, Colonel Baxter. Now then, you have my undivided attention. How can I help?"

"Sir, an object as been spotted just outside of our atmosphere. It came in fast and actually slowed down. It looks like it's headed for Earth, sir."

The President looked at the ceiling for a second in thought.

"What could it be? How can an object slow down in space? Do we know the size of this object?" asked Beevers.

"It appears to my technician as a small object, like a craft maybe," Baxter replied.

"How can it be a craft of some sort, Baxter? It might be a rogue satellite, space junk or even a comet," barked out Beevers.

"Excuse me, sir, but neither of those kinds of objects can slow down in space."

"Hmm, what do you propose it is, then, and what should be the course of action?"

"The technician is tracking it as we speak, I suggest that we send up some fighters to take a look at the object if infact it does get through our atmosphere, sir."

"Do we know where it will breach?"

"Not yet, sir. I need to get Jackson into the control room to find out more. Sir, I will keep an open channel directly to you on a secure line if you wish."

"Yes of course, Colonel: please proceed with caution," explained Beevers.

"Yes, sir, thank you."

Baxter left the room to continue his investigation into the mysterious phenomenon.

Jackson approached the technician as requested by Baxter.

"What's your name, son?"

"It's Timmy Carter, sir."

"Ok, Timmy, do you know anymore about this thing that I need to know?"

"Yes, sir, if it makes it through our atmosphere it should appear over Oklahoma."

"You sure about that, son?"

"Absolutely, sir."

"Good work, Timmy, thank you," said Jackson and off he went back to his office. He dialed to call Colonel Baxter.

Jackson relayed the co-ordinates to Baxter as to where this object might enter their skies.

Baxter called Camp Gruber in Braggs, which resides in Oklahoma and is a military training base.

He ordered jets to be scrambled immediately along with a ground team and chopper support. He also stated that it was not a training exercise and was top secret for now.

Captain Dan Long was to head a team of four pilots in Lockheed F-35 fighters: they were to cruise the sky at high altitude and wait to see if this object did actually make it through and to report back their findings.

They took off within minutes of the call.

A team assembled in wagons and drove to the salt plains where they suspected the object would appear. Two Black Hawk choppers also backed up the ground team just in case they were needed.

The pilots cruised at 50,000 feet around the co-ordinates given, waiting in anticipation of the incoming object.

Jnr braced himself as he knew that he was just about to enter Earth's atmosphere: he knew this was going to be a bumpy ride, but hopefully his last one.

The ship entered the atmosphere and all hell broke loose, but Jnr was confident in the Vicron technology: there was no way this ship was going to break up.

The ship once again vibrated and Jnr could see the red glow that looked like fire coming off the nose of the ship. It only took a short amount of time to clear through into the inner atmosphere.

Suddenly there it was: Earth!

Jnr began to giggle with excitement at the very sight of it.

He started to slow the ship down to normal flying speed as he didn't need to be at 20,000 mph now.

"Ground base, this is Captain Long. I've spotted the object around four miles to the south, intercepting now, over."

"Received, Captain. Please proceed with caution and report your findings once acquired, over."

Jnr didn't notice the planes approaching: he was too busy taking in the splendour that lay before him.

There was no communications module on this ship. How he longed to hear human voices and to let them know he had come home safely.

"Ground base, this is Captain Long I'm at a thousand yards off the craft. We will proceed to surround it and try to communicate with its occupants, over."

"Captain Long, you said 'craft', is that correct? Can you repeat? Over."

"Yes, sir, I said 'craft'. I don't recognise it, I don't think it's one of ours. We are going to move in for a closer look, over."

Jnr now noticed that four planes were moving in to intercept. They moved around the ship in a welcoming formation: it looked as though they were escorting him along.

The captain tried to make contact.

"This is Captain Long of the US Air Force, please identify yourself, over."

No answer, so again he asked the same question.

Again, no answer.

Jnr by now was waving frantically with both arms at the captain's plane, at the same time shouting, "Hello!"

"Ground base, this is Captain Long. I've attempted comms twice with no reply but there seems to be a pilot who is waving his arms around. He looks kinda excited, over."

"Ok, Captain, please escort the vehicle down. There are Black Hawks waiting to take over near ground level, over."

"Message received, over."

As Jnr approached the ground he slowed the ship gradually and coasted down to a perfect landing. How relieved he felt now that he had touched down on Mother Earth.

The planes headed back to base and now there were two Black Hawks hovering just above the ground, around one hundred yards away from his ship, one to the left and one to the right.

Jnr could also see an array of Army vehicles heading his way across the salt plains.

Jnr climbed out of the ship and took his first breath, a long deep breath.

It felt a little hard to breathe as Jnr was used to breathing in a higher percentage of oxygen back on Vicron.

Immediately he commanded the ship to go and wait at the very roof of the world for further instruction.

Jnr stood stretching as he awaited the cavalry to turn up: he had been in that seated position for two days straight.

He was told by Kandok not to tell them of his abilities until it was needed, so he had to play this cool.

The choppers had now landed and the convoy surrounded him from all sides. Troops jumped out in an orderly fashion and formed a perimeter around him, all with their guns pointing in his direction. They stopped at around fifty feet and stood silent.

Jnr could sense that they were pretty nervous: after all, he could hear their thoughts.

Jnr shouted out, "There's no need for guns, I'm unarmed!"

A man walked past them to about twenty-five feet away from our Jnr.

"Lower your guns please, gentlemen."

Jnr breathed a sigh of relief.

"My name is General Masters: please state your name."

"My name is Dr David Archer."

The general looked slightly confused. He stood looking at the ground, scratching at his chin.

"Hmm, I remember your name: are you the astronaut that went missing?"

"Yes that's right, General. What year is it?"

"2033. Dr Archer, you have been missing for twelve years!"

"Right," said Jnr. He was stunned.

"Twelve years. I need my family to know I'm ok, General, that's if they are all still alive and well."

"Don't worry, Dr Archer, we will look into that back at the base. Dr Archer, where have you been?"

"I will explain at the right time. First, may I please have some water?"

The general reached down to his hip flask of water and started to walk towards Jnr.

"No, General, throw it to me. I will need to go into quarantine first before I come into contact with anyone," said Jnr.

"Oh yes, of course," Masters replied, then threw the container to Jnr.

Jnr caught the flask and frantically tried to open it before his common sense kicked in. He told himself to take his time, to sip the water, rather than swallow it all down in one go.

He could immediately taste the chemicals in the water, nowhere near as fresh as the water on Vicron.

General Masters got onto his radio and requested a quarantine containment unit be sent over straight away; then he would contact Baxter and explain the situation.

Baxter received the call and together with his team, plus the President, was to set out to the base, to meet and talk with Jnr.

It would take four hours approximately to get there, so plenty of time to have Jnr moved to the base.

A Chinook appeared on the horizon carrying the unit to where Jnr was to be detained.

The chopper pilot landed the unit and released the clamp.

Jnr made his way over, opened the door and sealed it shut from inside.

The unit was self-contained which had an oxygen generator and was obviously sealed to let nothing escape. There were glass windows and a comfortable bed-cum-sofa for Jnr to sit on while he was transferred to the base.

The soldiers hooked up the unit and the chopper lifted it up. They set off with our Jnr sealed inside.

Jnr was now wondering how this situation was to play out: he knew he would be in the unit for at least twenty-four hours, maybe more.

Back at the base he was housed together with the unit in an aeroplane hangar. It would be closed so that no news crews or journalists could catch a glimpse as to what was happening.

This was top secret, for the moment at least.

The lights came on and in walked General Masters with a couple of guards.

"Hi, Dr Archer, I hope you are comfortable in there."

"Yes, General, I'm fine, thank you."

"We are going to plug the external power on for your oxygen now. Can I get you some food and water?"

"Yes please. I'm vegetarian so no meat, but I'm starving so anything veggie will do, and yes, plenty of water please."

Masters ordered Jnr some food and water. "Make sure it's cold bottled water," he added.

"Dr Archer, how the hell did you survive? You must admit it's rather odd that you were lost in space and then turn up as fresh as a daisy twelve years later? It's just not humanly possible."

"General, once the President arrives I will tell all. You will need someone to take notes, too, but I don't want to have to tell my story over and over again at the moment. Trust me, General, it will be worth the wait. What is the President's name by the way?" asked Jnr.

"Beevers, Louis Beevers. It's his second year of his first term. A lot has changed since you've been gone, Dr Archer."

"Jnr. just call me Jnr, General."

"Ok, Jnr, the world has moved on a lot. Beevers is the President of the US, and he is a president of the board of member states," added Masters.

"What does that mean?"

"Since you left there has been a new world order created. There are 40 presidents of the member states, of which President Beevers is a member. They make all the decisions as a collective. 40 countries have joined so far, with more expected in the near future."

"Does it work?" asked Jnr.

"Yes, it does for the countries that are represented, that is."

"And the countries that aren't?"

"Well, they are frozen out of existence as far as we're concerned."

"We have a one-world currency and everyone is free to work or live in any part of the member states if they wish: more individual freedom for all," explained Masters.

"Except those countries that don't fit the bill, I suppose."

"Jnr, it works for most."

Jnr could see in the general's thoughts what happens to the countries not on the list: they are shut down, no imports or exports, no help at all from the state, left to their own devices, no matter how dire!

That sickened Jnr to his core.

Just then, President Beevers turned up with a few of his team.

Here we go: interrogation time, thought Jnr.

Chapter 20 – The Interrogation Starts

"Hello, Dr Archer, my name is Louis Beevers, I'm one of the presidents of the member states, which I believe General Masters has already briefed you about. It's a pleasure to meet you."

"Pleased to make your acquaintance, sir," replied Jnr with his usual respectful manners.

"Right, Dr Archer, I would like you to start at the beginning and tell us where you have been and what you have been doing for the last twelve years please."

"You had better pull up a chair then, sir: this is going to take awhile."

Jnr relaxed and started with his story, from the accident up until this very moment. Everyone in attendance listened to his every word. I swear you could hear a pin drop.

Apart from the President and General Baxter, there were a couple of guards, a lady taking notes and two science officers, all sitting quietly listening to this remarkable story that Jnr was telling.

Jnr then asked if his family had been notified of his return.

"Not at present, Dr Archer, we will need a little of your time first so we can get to grips with what you are telling us. Tell me, Dr Archer, our troops saw your ship fly away from the scene. Who was flying that ship and where has it gone?" asked Beevers.

"The ship is in the uppermost atmosphere and no one was flying it. I programmed it myself: it awaits my command."

"You're telling me that you command your ship? How?"

"I don't want to divulge that information at present but rest assured, sir, it will be made clear once we have met with the presidents of your member states," replied Jnr.

"Why would I allow that, Dr Archer, and for what reason do you want a meeting with the members?" asked Beevers.

"Sir, I agreed to go along with this for the future of humanity and the Earth. I have so much more to show you but I will only do so with the whole of this member state in attendance, as the information I hold is for everyone, not just a select few."

"Very well, I'll see what I can do. Dr Archer, how can we trust you?"

"What do you mean by that statement, sir?"

"Well, look at this from my point of view. You disappear and really should be dead, even though you've told us you did die. It all sounds rather mysterious, Dr Archer."

"I agree, sir, but you have nothing to fear from me. I didn't have to come back and if I chose I could have done so and remained hidden from everyone," stated Jnr.

"Well, technically that's not true. We saw you coming, Dr Archer," replied General Baxter with an 'I'm so clever' smirk across his face.

"Yes, sir, you did, but that's because I wanted you to."

"I've come back to Earth to tell my story and to hope that mankind will take it on-board. I don't have a hidden agenda, so I don't need to hide from anyone."

"Alright, let's end the conversation for now, I'm going to try and arrange a meeting, Jnr."

The whole group said their goodbyes and left the hangar. Jnr was alone now: still, he hadn't been told how long he had to remain in the quarantine unit.

It started to worry Jnr: what if they were to hold him there and not let anyone know of his whereabouts at all!

He thought long and hard as to what his plan would be if that was indeed their intention. Jnr knew it would be a risk coming back to Earth, but he had to do it – ironically for everyone's benefit, not only his.

While explaining where he had been, Jnr noticed that the general was doubting Jnr's story and was intending on getting his hands on Jnr's ship.

His plan was to send up fighters and use radars to find the ship, but what he didn't know was that Jnr had sent it up to the roof of the world:it could not be reached. Also he had instructed the nanotechnology to go into stealth mode, invisible to everyone:it would simply sit out of sight until Jnr needed it.

There were guards ever-present outside the hangar's entrance, but if need be Jnr could get out of there, no problem.

If you remember, Jnr had nanotech running through his body, plus his clothing. All he would need to do was release some nanos onto the glass, which they could eat through in no time at all. Then he would instruct the nanos in his clothing to surround his body, like a skin-tight suit, completely covered and then into stealth mode, he would be invisible. So our Jnr did have options of his own.

For now he would have to remain quiet and hope they would be reasonable and allow him out once the quarantine period was over: he had to trust Beevers!

Speak of the Devil, Jnr thought to himself as Beevers entered the hangar with a scientist accompanying him.

"Hello again, Dr Archer, we require a mouth swab and a urine sample please, if that would be ok with you?"

"Yes, no problem, pass them through the hatch," replied Jnr.

The containers are placed into a hatch and pushed through to Jnr.

Jnr tells the nanos to remove themselves from his mouth and urinal tract areas so as not to be detected.

He turned his back and filled the urine sample first, then he proceeded to turn to the two men facing him and took a swab of saliva from the inside of his mouth.

"Is that ok?"

"Yes, Dr Archer, please put them back into the hatch," said the science officer.

"Sir, may I ask how long I need to be in here for?"

"The doc tells me that once the tests are complete you may be released. Should be tomorrow. We will then contact your family. How does that sound?"

"Sounds good to me, sir, thank you."

"You're welcome, would you like any reading material at all?"

"Oh yes, if possible may I have today's paper?" asked Jnr.

"We don't use papers anymore, Dr Archer. You know, technology and all, I will have a tablet sent for you."

"Thank you, sir."

The two guys turned and walked away from the hangar.

An hour or so later, a tech guy turns up with a strange-looking device.

"Hello, Dr Archer, my name is Juan. Here is the tablet you requested. "He pulled both sides of the device and a screen scrolled out in between the ends.

"Wow, that looks interesting," said Jnr. "What's it made of?"

"Well, the screen is made from silicon: you make it as long as you need it to be by pulling on the side handles. Once you're finished, simply push it back together. Also plug the charger into the wall socket and it will charge wirelessly."

"Good idea, things have moved on somewhat while I've been away," replied Jnr.

The technician put the tablet into the hatch and pushed it through.

Jnr rose from his bed and took the tablet out, then plugged in the charger.

"Dr Archer, you can browse anything at all, but communication of every kind has been disabled at the general's request, I'm sorry to say," said Juan.

"Oh I see. Not to worry, Juan. Thank you for your help."

"My pleasure, Dr Archer, if you need anything else or any help just speak up, as we can hear you ok!"

"Ok, Juan, I will do. Thanks again."

Juan walked off and left Jnr alone again.

Hmm, they can hear me, thought Jnr, *so they are watching and listening to me. I wonder if they think I'm going to turn into an alien or something when no one is around.* He chuckled to himself.

Jnr would first search the web for information following the Mars landing accident involving him. He found what he was looking for, but noticed that it wasn't reported to the media until the return module had landed without him.

A press conference was held and that's when he saw his parents: they were in attendance at the conference. They looked so sad; in fact, so did everyone.

Chai, Simon, Selev, Shaun and Julia were seated next to Jnr's parents,with the mission controller George on the opposite end.

Jnr breathed a sigh of relief knowing his fellow astronauts had made it back in one piece.

He read the whole article, especially the part which involved him.

The crew explained what had happened and obviously they believed Jnr had floated into space, never to be seen again.

My poor mother, thought Jnr. She was looking straight at the camera and that never-ending smile of hers had gone: she looked so tired and blank.

Jnr spent the next two hours researching everything he could find on the Mars mission. He wanted to know if Jib was up on Mars, living on the new colony.

He searched the web for details about Raph, but found nothing.

Jnr lay back on his bed and with his hands behind his head he thought of his friends and family, how he wanted to see everyone.

He started to drift off to sleep: he was very tired and occasionally he would keep waking. It's hard to sleep when something is weighing heavily on your mind. A restless night was to follow.

"Wakey, wakey, Dr Archer."

Jnr rolled over to see who was talking to him: it was the science officer.

"Good morning," mumbled Jnr.

"Would you like some breakfast, Dr Archer?"

"What's your name?"

"My name is Dan," he replied.

"Ok, Dan, please call me Jnr. Could I have some toast and a nice strong coffee please?"

"Certainly Jnr, I'll not be long."

Jnr sat rubbing his eyes on the edge of the bed and started to decide what his plan of attack would be for today: he so wanted out of this box, that was for sure.

His breakfast turned up which he wolfed down. The toast was lovely and, even though he'd not had a cup of coffee for a few years, this wasn't what he expected, it was like rat piss.

Jnr decided to jump on the tablet, but just as he was about to fire it up in walked President Beevers, accompanied once again by the general and Dan.

"Ah hello, guys," said Jnr.

"Hello again, Dr Archer, I've got some great news for you. By 1 o'clock this afternoon you may leave this quarantine chamber!"

"Thank God for that, it's not much fun in here, to be honest," replied Jnr.

"We've prepared a room or more like an apartment within the facility for you with all the mod cons, Jnr."

"Wait, stop there. You mean I'm still to be kept here?"

"Yes, Dr Archer, I'm afraid so, but on the flip side we have your family flying over as we speak. That's what you want, isn't it? To see your family again?"

"Well, yes of course it is, but why do I need to remain here? I'm not under arrest or anything, am I?"

"No, Dr Archer," Beevers said with a chuckle. "We just need to monitor the situation for a short time to see if you can adjust without any complications. We may also need to do a few tests, that's all."

"Do you think I'm dangerous or an alien in disguise, sir?"

"No, certainly not, Dr Archer, but please put yourself in our position for a moment: what would you do in our predicament?" asked General Masters.

"I'm the same person, sir, who launched to Mars. I was hailed a hero back then: I'm no different now."

"Well, after our tests are concluded then you may leave, but until then we must proceed with caution. I'm sure you understand, Dr Archer."

"You're a reasonable man, Dr Archer, and a scientist to boot. If we found a dead alien floating around in space and some how brought it back to life, wouldn't you have questions? Would you want to just let it loose on the world? No, I'm sure you wouldn't. What you have told us sounds unbelievable and I'm sorry, Dr Archer, I do indeed find it unbelievable. Now, if you say these Vicrons were miles ahead of us, type IIs, as you call them, how do we know that you're not one of them? Maybe contained within you could be a device that could wipe us out!" barked out Masters.

"Sir, with all due respect, that sounds more ridiculous than my story," replied Jnr.

"Gentlemen," interrupted Beevers, "let's leave this for now. Later, Dr Archer, your family should be here. After your reunion with your family we could talk more."

They once again left Jnr by himself.

Jnr could sense the general's thoughts which he didn't like. He was aware that the general was very suspicious of him. How was he going to tackle this dilemma?

Chapter 21 – Family Reunion

President Beevers came as he promised and had the guard unlock the quarantine unit. Jnr could now walk amongst men once again.

"Come, Dr Archer, please follow me?" asked Beevers, the guard following with his gun held down.

"I'm sorry if you feel we have treated you unreasonably: it was not our intention."

"That's ok, I suppose you were only following protocol."

"As soon as you are settled in, I'll have some new clothes sent in for you. I bet you can't wait to get that suit of yours off, can you?"

"Sir, it's ok, I like this suit."

"Do you? Ok, we will have it washed and cleaned for you, then, freshen you up."

"No, sir, it's ok, I would like a shower, though."

Just then, President Beevers stopped and turned to Jnr.

"Dr Archer, anyone else would want to change that outfit. You have been in it for days now. Why are you acting so strangely? What's so important about your attire?"

"Sir, please trust me, I'm no threat to you or anyone else. I'm not an alien from outer space, I'm not here to cause chaos. I will reveal all to you, which you will be amazed by and I suppose relieved, too, at the same time. Remember, I have to trust you, too!" replied Jnr.

"Very well, Dr Archer. This way please."

Jnr was listening to the President's thoughts. He didn't trust Jnr. *What's so important about his clothes?* he kept asking in his mind.

Our Jnr knew he was sounding cagey, but he could not reveal anything yet. If he did, he knew that he would never get out of here.

Jnr also realised that if they knew of his aug, nanos and his new abilities, they would take him apart like an animal for military purposes. Imagine if every soldier had Jnr's capabilities:they would be unstoppable!

That was not about to happen.

Kandok had told him exactly how to proceed and Jnr was going to stick to the plan. All he could hope for was that the rest of the presidents of the member states would heed his advice. He knew it wouldn't be an easy task – we are talking about human beings here.

It's a shame really: as a species, we are the most intelligent on planet Earth, so how come we screw everything up? Why are we so self-centred? Why are greed and power over others our main objectives?

Take an ant colony, one of the simplest forms of life: they all work together as one to ensure their survival and, more importantly, their future's survival.

This can be said of nearly every species known to man: they all look after one another in order to keep their species strong.

Not humans, no: we are so clever and at the same time so retarded in the way we behave.

It maybe an evolutionary trait for every race that has or will ever exist in the universe, even the multiverse. Some races will just wipe each other out or, like the Vicrons, realise their mistakes before it's too late.

Jnr knew the task at hand was enormous, but he would give it his best shot.

"Here we are, Dr Archer, all brand new and full of mod cons to keep you amused," said Beevers.

"Very nice, much better than that box."

They both entered Jnr's new pad.

"So you have a kitchen, bedroom, bathroom and a living room – all you need really. Of course, you will still be monitored, I'm afraid. Procedure, you understand."

"Yes, sir, I'm getting used to it," stated Jnr.

"Only precautions, Dr Archer. Oh, I've arranged a meeting in five days' time with the members of the state, so if all goes well, you may then move back into civilian life."

"If all goes well?" asked Jnr.

"There are 40 presidents, Dr Archer, obviously it will depend on what you have to tell them or 'show them', as you put it, in order to proceed."

"Proceed? Proceed with what?"

"If everything goes smoothly and the members are satisfied with your explanation of events, then you may be released to carry on your life," answers Beevers.

"And if not?"

"Dr Archer, let's not worry about it for the moment. I'm sure everything will turn out fine."

"I wasn't worrying, but I am now!"

President Beevers left Jnr alone to explore his new surroundings.

As Jnr was checking out his new pad, Juan turned up at the door.

"Hi, Dr Archer, may I come in?"

"Yes, Juan, come on in."

"I would like to explain how everything works in your apartment, sir."

"Look, Juan, please call me Jnr, ok?"

"Ok, Jnr, if you insist. The system that runs your apartment is voice-activated to your voice alone. Simple commands like 'lights on', 'lights off', 'TV on' etc. Try it, Jnr," explained Juan.

"Technology has moved on. Ok where to start?" mumbled Jnr.

"Living room lights on."

Nothing happened!

"Jnr, you do not need to shout, when commanding lights simply say 'lights on', and they will turn on in the room which you currently occupy. When moving from room to room the lights will turn on and off accordingly, to conserve energy," said Juan.

"Oh I see, ok. Lights on," repeated Jnr, this time much more quietly.

It worked.

"Tv on." Again it worked.

"Right, Jnr, you are always connected to the Internet 24/7, browse on your tablet and once you've found what you're looking for, simply flick the image towards the TV and you can view it there, to control the curser use your finger on the tablet's screen," explained Juan.

"That's cool," Jnr said with a smile.

"I'll leave you to it, Jnr, please let me know if you need anymore assistance."

"I will, Juan, thank you."

Jnr turned on the tablet, stretched the screen out and started to browse.

Jnr learned what became of the team of astronauts that accompanied him to Mars. Both Julia and Shaun were now working at Kennedy as astronaut trainers, while Selev and Chai were to carry on and both had successfully flown a further two missions, to Mars of all places.

George, meanwhile, carried on as mission commander for another five years, but then retired and moved to England. According to press coverage after the accident on Mars, George was never the same again. He felt that it was his fault Jnr had gone missing. Even though he wasn't even there, it put great strain upon him: you could tell from the pictures.

According to sources, George always sat staring at the screen for hours, looking for signs, which never came.

Next Jnr searched for info on his friend Jib.

"Found him," Jnr said to himself with a chuckle of excitement.

There were pictures of an older-looking Jib standing inside what looked like a giant greenhouse full of plants.

After reading everything he could find about his friend's work on Mars, Jnr couldn't be more proud for Jib: he'd spent four years now on Mars and achieved so much.

The Mars colony was a thousand strong now and they had overcome all the challenges that Mars offered. Every three months a supply ship was sent, mainly to bring new recruits and to take anyone back who was too ill to carry on their projects.

Still Jnr could not find any information regarding Raph, which worried him. He couldn't contact anyone yet, so for now at least he would have to wait.

Just then, Jnr sat bolt upright! He had sensed that his mother was close by. *They're here.*

Jnr shot out of the apartment and, sure enough, his whole family were walking towards him in the corridor.

He ran towards them with outstretched arms, crying with joy.

"Mum, Dad!" shouted Jnr.

"Oh Jnr,"replied Anne as she chucked her arms around him.

President Beevers had been true to his word.

They all hugged together, crying and kissing each other.

"Grandma, where's Granddad?" asked Jnr.

Everyone looked sad and Jean had to give Jnr the bad news.

"David, your granddad Roy passed away two years ago. I'm sorry," said Jean.

Jnr grabbed his grandma and hugged her tightly. "I'm so sorry."

The whole family, including Charles, hugged each other for what seemed like an eternity.

Jnr turned to Beevers and shook his hand. "Thank you very much, Mr. President, you've made me so happy."

"It's my pleasure, Dr Archer. Why don't you go and have a good chat: your family have so many questions for you," replied Beevers, "Excuse me, Dr Archer. How did you know they were here? It was meant to be a surprise."

"I thought I heard my mother's voice, that's how," he replied.

As we now know, he could sense they were there.

Jnr beckoned them to follow him into his new home.

First job, kettle on: he knew they would want a proper cup of tea – Yorkshire tea, that is.

With the tea made, they all sat listening to Jnr explain what had happened to him for the last twelve years, his mother holding his hand, still sobbing.

Jnr obviously told them nothing of his abilities, especially because he knew they were being overheard.

Jnr learned that his father, David Snr, still worked in his garage and his granddad Charles and Grandma Sophia had retired – more time to spend in their garden.

Grandma Jean had sold their home and now lived with Jnr's parents: she looked so lost without her husband.

For the next few hours they sat and talked: they told Jnr about everything that had happened since the accident. George kept in contact ever since; he even visited them as he and his family now lived on the outskirts of Mansfield which was only an hour's drive away from Jnr's parents' home.

"What about Raph, Mum? I can't find any news of him."

"Well, Jnr, for a couple of years he would ring us quite regularly, then out of the blue, nothing. We don't know why," replied Anne. "We just thought maybe he got bored of calling."

"No, Mum, I think there's something wrong. Raph is a good lad. It's not like him to simply just stop calling without an explanation."

"I'll find out more once I've got out of here."

"I'm hungry. What about you guys? Have you eaten?" asked Jnr.

None of them had since the flight.

"Juan, can I order some food please!?" shouted Jnr.

"Ooh," said Sophia. "Room service."

Everyone laughed – that is, apart from Jnr.

"What's up, Jnr?" his mother asked.

"Mum, I'm kept here for now: they need to check on me and see if either I'm a threat or I have a disease of any type. That's why I'm here and haven't come home yet. I'm not even allowed to contact anyone at all," explained Jnr.

"Surely it won't be for long, Jnr. I wouldn't worry too much. You'll be home soon, love."

Knock knock: it was Juan.

"Hi Juan, is it ok if we have some food please? My family haven't eaten for hours."

"Yes, Jnr, what would you like?"

Juan gives them the options and they all order.

"Give me about 30 minutes, please, Jnr, ok?"

"Yes, Juan, and thank you again."

"No problem, I'll be back soon."

"So, Jnr, even though you couldn't get meat on that planet and you had to become a veggie, you're sticking to it?" asked Anne.

"Yes, Mum: it makes sense to me now. Earth is no different to Vicron: animals have the right to live, too. Life is important to all species," stated Jnr.

"Oh I see, well, I suppose if you look at it like that, then yes, you're right, but I've ordered beef now, Jnr."

Jnr laughed. "It's a choice you have to make by yourself, Mum, not because I say so."

As the family were talking, Juan turned up with a trolley full of food plus fresh orange juice and some chilled bottled water.

"Here we are, guys. Please enjoy, compliments of the chef," said Juan.

"Jnr, after dinner, President Beevers would like a chat. Is that ok?"

"Yes, no problem: just tell him to come in about an hour, Juan."

"Lovely. Is there anything else I can do for you, Jnr?"

"No, we're fine, thank you."

Juan left and everyone got stuck into dinner. Jnr had ordered the veggie supreme pizza. Apart from a steak, that was the food he had missed the most: pizza and a huge bunch of fries.

After dinner the whole family continued chatting, plus they all filled Jnr in with what they had been up to since he had seen them last.

President Beevers announced his presence."Dr Archer, may I come in?"

"Yes, sir, please come in."

"I'm sorry to disturb you all.I hope you enjoyed your meal," said Beevers, for which everyone thanked him.

"Right, Dr Archer, the meeting has been set. Once the meeting is over I'm pleased to tell you that a flight has been arranged for yourself and your family on the very same day to return you home, back to England!"

"That's fantastic, sir. I can't thank you enough, you have been very good to me and my family, thank you," replied Jnr.

"You're welcome, Dr Archer. Rooms have been made available for your family here. They may come everyday to see you until the day of the meeting, then homeward bound." Beevers smiled.

Jnr stood and shook Beevers' hand. "Again, thank you, sir."

President Beevers turned and wished everyone a pleasant stay and then let himself out. All the while Jnr concentrated on his thoughts. *He seems to be genuine,* thought Jnr.

Over the next few days the family stayed together with Jnr as much as they could. His mum had settled by now: what a shock to find your son is ok after all the time she thought he was no more.

The day of the meeting had arrived. Jnr was hoping the outcome would be what he and, more importantly, Kandok had envisioned.

Two guards turned up to escort our Jnr, and the rest of his family had to remain at the base.

The family had so wanted to attend, but Jnr asked them not to worry: he would be back soon!

Chapter 22 – Presidents of the Member States

Jnr was driven along with President Beevers to the meeting. Neither of them spoke: Jnr was content with listening to the thoughts of Beevers.

Beevers had already wondered how Jnr's information would be received by the rest of the members. Would they take on his advice? This could not be done overnight, even if everyone agreed on the outcome. Who would be in charge? How would the member states feel at having their wealth robbed to share with the poor countries? Why should they?

"Sir, they are not being robbed, it is sharing: that's the key," said Jnr.

"How did you know what I was thinking, Dr Archer? How could you possibly know that?" asked Beevers with a very surprised look upon his face.

"Today I will reveal all, President Beevers: your questions will be answered."

The car came to a halt and the guards surrounded the vehicle, making checks before opening the doors.

Both men were led out of the car and into the building: there were a huge number of guards covering the entrance and the corridors.

"Why all these guards?" asked Jnr.

"There are many rebels who would like to see an end to prosperity, Dr Archer. One can't be too careful."

The two men entered the room and Beevers took to the podium.

He asked Jnr to stand by his side.

President Beevers spoke. "Welcome, ladies and gentlemen, members of the state. Thank you for attending this historic meeting at such short notice. Many of you may recall an accident on Mars twelve years ago in which an English astronaut was lost in space. Well, this is the astronaut in question, Dr David Archer."

Jnr walked forward and raised his hand to acknowledge the leaders.

"He returned to Earth from a planet many thousands of light years away. He will now present his story to you. Please take note of what he has to say, thank you all," explained Beevers.

Beevers gestured for Jnr to take the podium and he took to his seat.

Jnr presented his story. He kept it brief but to the point, emphasising the key points.

The members listened to Jnr, and he could sense a lot of thinking going on from *Wow* to *Lie*. Some wondered if President Beevers had anything to do with this. Jnr could tell that this member state was fragile at best. Even though they had joined forces, each and every member state still had their own agenda.

"I will now take questions," stated Jnr.

Everyone fired questions at him at once.

"Please raise your hands and I'll ask each one in turn."

Jnr picked one.

"How do we know any of this story is true?"

"Think about it: how can someone disappear into the blackness of space and turn up years later? It's obvious that without the Vicrons' help I would indeed still be dead, floating around in space," answered Jnr.

"How do we know this race of beings aren't hostile and maybe one day would attack Earth?" asked another.

"These beings, Vicrons, have been around a lot longer than us. They have watched our progress for thousands of years. Anytime they wanted they could have taken our planet. As I've said already, the Vicrons have been in our situation: they know that war doesn't pay, greed doesn't pay. This is their message for us. Why would they help if their intentions were to take our planet?"

"You say they have cheap energy, nuclear fusion. Why would anyone spend an unimaginable amount of money to create cheap energy to simply give it away? It doesn't make sense, Dr Archer," asked another member.

"That's the problem right there. Cheap energy and cleaner energy which in turn will help the poor and the planet's climate. Yes, you cannot simply give energy for free, but instead of making crazy profits just to keep the shareholders happy maybe it's time to rethink the whole situation. There are many countries that are still underdeveloped: they cannot afford to feed their population, never mind keep them warm. They have nothing to offer and are left to their own devices: why?" asked Jnr.

"There is so much money in this world owned by the few. Why are there families worth over five hundred trillion dollars? What are they going to do with all that wealth? This cannot continue! People are starving in our generation. This cannot continue. Something has to be done now before it's too late: we have to change our ways in order to survive. This is the message the Vicrons are giving us," stated Jnr.

"That's all good and well, Dr Archer, but how do we go about achieving this?" asked Beevers.

"That, sir, is your problem, I can only relate the message given. Let me show you something," replied Jnr.

Jnr stepped forward towards the members.

"As I've told you, the Vicrons communicate through telepathy. I can do the same. Please close your eyes and concentrate on the images I'm about to show you."

Every member closed their eyes.

Jnr showed them images from the planet Vicron.

First he showed the planet and all its splendour, then the images of the Great War, the aftermath and how the Vicrons grouped together, today's society, and the children of Vicron.

All the members looked upon Jnr stunned!

"So now you see the truth of my story. I hope you will take this advice and use it wisely, for all mankind now and in the future."

Another member asked, "Did these beings offer any technological advancement to you, Dr Archer, in order for us to progress with the likes of nuclear fusion?"

"Yes, through me, sir, I have the knowledge to help our scientists with this new energy source. Also I have nanotechnology within myself, my clothing and my ship, but I will not release any technology until I know it will be used for the good of the people, not for any personal gain or for military purposes," stated Jnr.

"You say in you and your clothing, Dr Archer," piped up Beevers.

"Yes, sir, I was injected with nanomites to help with my recovery. On Vicron, its technology is all around: let me show you."

Jnr commanded the nanos in his suit to turn into jeans, trainers and a hoodie!

Everyone in the room gasped at what they had just witnessed, and the room then fell silent.

"President Beevers, may I have a glass of your water, please?" asked Jnr.

"Yes, Dr Archer, of course."

He was just about to get up and fetch Jnr the glass.

"It's ok, sir, I'll get it thank you. Please take your seat."

Jnr raised up the jug full of water using telekinesis. He filled the glass and floated it across the room.

Gasps were heard from everyone!

"How the hell did you do that, Archer?" asked Beevers.

"Sir, this is one of the subjects I was taught on Vicron. In time, many thousands of years from now, everyone will most probably be able to achieve this ability. It's inevitable, as long as the planet is not destroyed first. The mind is enormously powerful indeed."

Beevers stood up and concluded the meeting, thanking everyone for attending. Now the decision needed to be made as to what to do next, explained President Beevers.

Every single president went up to Jnr and shook his hand, extending their thank-yous and hoping Jnr might help in reaching a decision on how to move forward with the first phase of a new future for humanity.

Jnr left once again with Beevers.

"Well, Dr Archer, you certainly kept that quiet. Why didn't you tell me beforehand?" asked Beevers.

"Sir, I did what I was told to do by Kandok: we needed the leaders of the world to hear this as one. The question is now: what's going to be done?"

"I will speak with each president over the next few days to gather their thoughts. I will then ask for another meeting to discuss how to proceed further with the matter."

"Oh right, I see. And me? Am I allowed to go home now?" asked Jnr.

"Yes, Dr Archer, we are on our way to the airport now, where your family awaits. But I must be able to contact you, Dr Archer at anytime, and there will be eyes on you at all times for now. I'm sorry."

"It's ok, sir. Procedure again, I suppose."

Jnr met up with his family and they all boarded the plane heading back to the UK.

Beevers had given Jnr his personal cell number and he was told to call anytime he liked.

The journey home was to be long and tiresome, but very much worth it.

Chapter 23 – Home Sweet Home

On arrival, Jnr noticed his parents' home had been given some alterations: nothing exotic or extravagant, just improvements in general, but it still looked the same house he'd grown up in. The rear garden had now got a lazy spa, outdoor sofa and chairs, plus it had all been decked. Perfect relaxation – if the weather was right, ofcourse.

Inside the home, nothing had changed, except his Grandma Jean slept in the spare room.

Jnr's room remained unchanged. It was as if he had never left at all: the pictures of the planets still adorned his walls.

The family sat and talked for hours. Jnr told them of everything he had encountered and learned on his travels. He explained his concerns about the President's reaction at what the Vicrons had told them: how to change in order to survive. Jnr told his family his thoughts and what he expected was to happen next.

"But, Jnr, if they were suspicious of you, then they wouldn't have let you come home, would they?" asked David Snr.

"Dad, yes, they have allowed me to leave but I'm being watched at all times. I was told this: they are probably listening to us now as we speak."

"And besides," continued Jnr, "at the meeting, I heard their thoughts. They are all sceptical of my story, even though I showed them what I'd seen. They say this new world order was created to help maintain stability and peace, but I see what they think. It's nothing but a scam. The elite now have more power to control the people: they will never leave me alone to live my life the way I want to."

"What do you mean, Jnr?" asked Anne.

"Mum, I have knowledge and technology that they want to use for their own selfish goals, not to empower people as the Vicrons wanted. I was warned about this from Kandok. I will keep my head down and see how it pans out. If they want too much from me, I will simply disappear."

"Where, Jnr? Surely not back to that planet?" asked Charles.

"No, Granddad, I will hide in plain sight:when the time is right I will visit these presidents personally so I can talk to them one by one, and find out exactly what their thoughts are."

"And what happens if nothing changes, Jnr? Then what?" asked Snr.

"I don't know, Dad, to be honest. Hopefully things will change."

"David, do you want to call George? He would love to hear from you," asked Anne.

Jnr answered his mother in her mind.

"I would love to talk to George, Mum, yes, but not on the phone. I will work something out. I know I can trust George, but let's not mention his name aloud, ok? I will surprise him."

Anne nodded.

All the family were tired and hungry so a fish and chip supper was in order.

Jnr and his father set out to the chippy.

Anne had set up the table and put plates in the oven to warm.

The guys returned and handed over the food: everyone loves a steaming hot plate of fish and chips, splattered in salt and vinegar.

After dinner, Jnr decided to retire to his room: he wanted to do some research but he knew he would be monitored, so he would have to be careful.

After checking out the latest developments here on Earth, Jnr decided to get some sleep. He had a little jetlag, ofcourse, but still he could use his nanos if need be.

As he lay upon his old bed for the first time in years he couldn't help but think of George. He had to pay him a visit, but how? He didn't want anyone knowing of his movements, and he certainly didn't want to bring George into the fray.

He thought of a plan: he knew the address which his mother had provided him with.

Jnr used his nanos to cloak himself from sight, at the same time dropping temperature so as not to be detected by thermal imaging. He made his way out of the house and walked to a local playing field which was completely empty at this time of the night.

He called down his ship: silently it obliged. Jnr climbed in and set off into the night sky.

As he made his way to Mansfield, he kept quite low so as not to cross paths with other aircraft that might be flying around with holidaymakers and so on.

Jnr and his ship were invisible and undetectable from everyone: Jnr could go anywhere in the world, undetected.

First things first, thought Jnr. *I need to speak to George: now is as good a time as any.*

He found the house after a bit of ducking and diving.

Jnr landed in his huge garden and commanded his ship to shut down until further notice, and obviously keep out of sight.

George had a lovely, big home which had security cameras everywhere. Luckily for our Jnr, they didn't notice him.

He tried to log into George's mind.

George didn't budge.

Again Jnr tried to communicate through his mind. "George, please wake up, it's me, David Archer."

George started to move: his eyes flickered as his mind heard Jnr.

Suddenly he sat up bolt right with a shocked expression on his face.

I must be dreaming, thought George as he shook his head.

"George, it's me, David. Please don't freak out, it's me talking to you from outside your home."

George shivered and started to panic. He thought he was still in a dream!

"Where are you? Are you real?"

"Yes, George, it really is me talking to you. Don't speak out loud: think and I can hear you," said Jnr.

"But how can this be?"

"George, I need you to come downstairs and unlock your back door. Open it wide and go and put the kettle on. Please, George, I have to speak with you."

George got up and did as he was instructed: why he did it, he didn't know.

"Do it quietly, George: don't wake anyone up."

George opened the door and then made his way into the kitchen.

"Are there cameras operating inside your home, George?"

"'Erm yes," he answered.

"Please turn them off. I don't want to be seen, George. I don't want anyone to know you have spoken to me. Please trust me, George, as I do indeed trust you."

George operated the control panel and shut down the cameras in his house.

"There, the cameras are offline. Where are you, David?"

Jnr made his way through the doors into the kitchen and faced George.

He dropped his cloak and revealed himself.

George gasped and covered his mouth with his hand: at the same time his knees buckled and he started to cry.

"What is happening, David? This is not real. You're dead, you disappeared: there is no possible way this can be real. I must be dreaming," spluttered George through his tears.

Jnr rushed forward and caught him from falling. He cradled George and helped him to stand upright.

"You see, George, it's real. It's me, David, I'm really here."

Both guys wrapped their arms around each other for what seemed like for ever, both crying with excitement.

After a minute or so, George looked Jnr straight in the eye and asked, "How can this be, David?"

"Please sit down, George. I will make us a strong coffee because you're going to need it. I want to tell you everything!"

George took a seat. "How, David, do you know what I'm thinking? How is it possible to communicate in the way you did?"

"Let me finish this coffee first and then I will blow your mind, George."

Jnr, sitting beside George, spoke quietly and told him the whole story from the accident until now, the present day.

"What you're telling me, David, is very hard to comprehend. I have so many questions."

"Yes, George, I know you do, I hear them rattling around in your mind," answered Jnr.

"What you know and have learned can help so much, David."

"Yes, George, but here's the problem: will it be put to good use?"

"I've met the presidents and I know they are already wanting to use me and my new abilities not to help mankind, no. They want it for military purposes, that's not going to happen, George, this is why I needed to speak to you. I need help," replied Jnr.

"But what can I do to help, David?"

"Well, that's a good question. I don't know what to do: all I do know is that you are the one person I feel I can trust, George."

"Ok, so what are your plans?"

"I'm going to meet all the presidents one at a time, the same way as I have contacted you. I need to know their thoughts. I need to try and convince them that my knowledge is more important for the future, rather than today's military applications. Also I need to know who is with me and who is against me," explained Jnr.

"And if you find you're wasting your time, what then?"

"I really don't know. What I do know is you must keep our meeting to yourself for now. You must tell no one, George, until I've figured out the next step."

"Yes, of course, David, I promise."

"I want to use my knowledge for science, which in turn will help everyone on the planet, but I don't think that's going to be allowed to happen, not yet anyway."

"I'm going to keep in touch with you, George. I will let you know what I find out, so if I stop coming for any reason you will know that something has gone wrong!"

"And if that day comes, what do I do?"

"Well, for one, you must be very careful who you talk to: the last thing I want is for you to be silenced, George. Who knows what the member states would do if this became common knowledge?"

"Yes, you're right," replied George.

"You know, David, your fellow astronauts would love to know you're alive."

"Yes, George, I know, but at the moment I have to keep quiet. I'm being watched twenty-four hours a day so for now it's out of the question. I can't wait to see them myself."

"How are your family, George? Is Irene still as good a cook as the last time I met her?"

"Oh yes, Jnr, they are fine. Barry is again into the business world and Stavros is working on quantum computing. Irene likes it here and cooks most days for us – when she isn't gardening, that is," said George rather proudly.

"That's great. What about you, what do you do?"

"Well, I still keep in contact with NASA: every now and then they need my advice. Most of the time I'm writing books which I enjoy: it keeps my mind fresh."

"What do you write about?"

"Space, what else?" George laughed.

"David, after the accident on Mars I stayed on for a further five years, hoping somehow that we would find you, but of course I knew we wouldn't. I blamed myself for losing you," explained George.

"Why, it was completely out of your control, it was my fault alone."

"True, but my astronauts were more like family to me. It was my job to make sure you came back home. I cannot explain to you how it feels to fail when someone's life is at stake, David it's not nice."

"Still, George, there was nothing you could do or anyone else for that matter. Anyway, enough doom and gloom, I'm here now. That's the best outcome, don't you agree?"

"Yes, David, of course."

Jnr set off home and jumped back into bed: he needed sleep.

The next morning Jnr woke to a right racket outside his house. He jumped out of bed and headed over to his window: looking down he could see a crowd gathered outside in the road.

There were TV reporters, plus a crowd of locals lining the pathway to the front of his house.

How do they know I'm back? wondered Jnr.

He ran downstairs to find his family sitting at the breakfast table looking glum.

"What's going on, Dad?"

"Well, what do you think, Jnr? Obviously they have been tipped off: by who is the question. I can't even get out of the gate to go to work without being pestered," explained Snr.

Jnr immediately thought of the meeting with George, but he knew George wouldn't have done this. *If it wasn't George, then who?* pondered Jnr.

"I'm going to call President Beevers, he needs to know."

Jnr made the call from the house phone.

"Hello, President Beevers, it's David here."

"Hi, David. How are you? Well, I hope."

"Yes, I'm well, thank you, but I'm afraid the word is out. I have reporters outside my house. How could they know already?"

"Ok, David, calm down, it could be a number of people, probably one of mine but it doesn't really matter. Something of this magnitude cannot remain covered for long," answered Beevers.

"So what do I do about it?"

"Nothing. Don't go outside and certainly do not talk to the press until I've figured something out. Stay indoors. I'll have some guards sent over to make sure they keep their distance. Don't worry, I'll be in touch soon."

Click: the receiver went dead.

Jnr joined the family in the kitchen and told them of the conversation he'd just had.

"What does it mean, Jnr? Why do we need guards?" asked Anne.

"Don't worry, Mum, it just a precaution. Those reporters won't stay out there all day without me making a press conference. Soon they will be knocking on the door: the guards will keep them put until we have a solution," Jnr hoped.

"Well, I'm off to work," said Snr. "I've got people relying on me. I'm just going to have to drive over them." He laughed.

"Dad, don't say anything, if they manage to get a question in, tell them you have no comment. It works on TV."

Snr quickly jumped into his car and drove slowly out of his drive: the reporters swarmed around his car, barking questions at him, but he kept going, totally ignoring them.

"Lock the door, David," said Anne with a worried look about her.

"We might as well have some breakfast," said Jean. "Looks like we're going nowhere soon."

"That's a good idea, I'm starving," piped up Jnr.

"It's going to have to be beans on toast, unless one of you wants to risk going to the butcher's," said Anne.

"Beans on toast is fine, Mum. I can't go out and I don't think Grandma fancies her chances," chuckled Jnr.

Just as Jnr had started into his breakfast, the phone rang.

"I'll get it, Mum," said Jnr.

"Hello, David speaking."

"Hi David, President Beevers here. I'm talking to an official at a nearby base. We will work something out, David, I'm sure. Don't go anywhere: await my next call!"

Jnr didn't like the sound of that.

So he wants to lock me away again?

Chapter 24 – Shock To The World

Catterick Garrison is a major garrison and town located three miles south of Richmond in the district of North Yorkshire: this is where Jnr would stay for awhile, according to Beevers.

A press conference would be held so that the world would learn of Jnr's return from Vicron.

Our Jnr didn't like the idea, but on the flip side it would be better for his family if he was out of the way for now.

Sergeant Gordon Reed was to take Jnr under his wing while at the barracks.

He had a small room with all the basics: bed, toilet, TV, phone, laptop, etc. It was ok, plus he knew he wouldn't be there for too long.

A knock at the door.

"Come in!" shouted Jnr.

It was Gordon.

"Hi, Dr Archer, how are you settling in?"

"Good thanks, Sergeant Reed."

"That title is held for Army personnel only: you may call me Gordy."

"Ok, Gordy, you may call me Jnr, then, from now on."

"Ok, Jnr, I have some info for you. This is a site map, the cafeteria is located here and the mealtimes are here," said Gordy, pointing to the relevant spots.

"If you prefer, you may eat in your room, or you can eat with myself in the main dining area: your choice."

"Oh thank you, very kind of you. By the way, the answer to your question is yes, I am the one who's come from space!"

Gordy looked at Jnr with a blank expression.

"I can hear your thoughts, Gordy, but please keep this to yourself for now until the grand unveiling at the upcoming press conference, ok?"

"Yes sure," Gordy mumbled, still looking confused.

Gordy asked Jnr to join him at six for dinner and left the room.

Jnr unpacked his few belongings and decided to watch some news for awhile to see what was happening in the world today. He noticed that in reality, even though they have this precious NWO, it still seemed like the same old doom and gloom he saw before leaving Earth twelve years ago.

The world now had a single currency and a one world police force, apart from the exclusion of the few really poor remaining countries who had nothing to offer, and so are not allowed to join the party.

These few countries were much worse off now than ever before in human history.

Why is this happening? thought Jnr.

There were literally millions of people living in squabble, no food, money or decent shelter for that matter. Medicines were thin on the ground, so disease spread like wild fire: maybe that's what the elite want! With a general population in decline it's easier to control the remaining sheep.

He used the word 'sheep' because humans were now tagged in the form of an identity chip. This little chip is implanted within a person so as to monitor their health, whereabouts, identity and, more importantly, account details.

This was for the benefit of the people, they were told, and they took the bait.

Now, each and every person is monitored twenty-four hours per day, and every transaction noted – they are now slaves to the system!

No one could now disagree with the establishment. No more demonstrations to standup for their rights. You demonstrate against the powers that be and they simply turn your chip off: no more money, no food, no way to pay bills. Now what are you going to do? That's right: comply!

6 o'clock was fast approaching so Jnr checked out his map and made his way to the dining room.

Gordy was waiting at the entrance: he waved to Jnr.

"Hi, Gordy. Am I allowed to call you that in front of other officers?" asked Jnr.

"Yes, Jnr, no problem. You're a civilian so it's irrelevant. Come, let's see what's on offer."

As the guys eyed up the menu Jnr noticed that there wasn't much in the way of a vegetarian menu, just a few usual dishes to choose from.

Gordy opted for liver and onions with mash; Jnr took the fish option with parsley sauce, mashed spud and petits pois.

Gordy took them to a table for two: he didn't want anyone joining them as he had got questions for Jnr.

Of course Jnr knew this: after all, he heard everything but he didn't detect a master plan behind Gordy's thoughts. It was his own curiosity that was getting the better of him.

While tucking into his food, Jnr was listening to the questions bouncing around in Gordy's head: he gathered that they hadn't been given much information about Jnr, and whispers were circulating around the base.

"Don't worry, Gordy, after our meal I will answer some of your questions, but for now, enjoy your meal," said Jnr.

Gordy looked across the table with that gormless surprised look that Jnr was now getting used to.

"I'm sorry, Jnr. For you, this gift you have been granted must be a bit of a curse at times. I can't help but think about the situation, as our superiors have given very little away about you. I do apologise," said Gordy with sincerity.

"No need, it's hardly your fault. I see it as advantageous most of the time, and besides, I can simply ignore thoughts that are not relevant to me."

"Oh right, that's ok, then." Gordy smiled.

After dinner Jnr answered Gordy's questions to put him at ease. He obviously deflected some: they would have to wait until the announcement.

The next morning Jnr was promised a guided tour of the base from Sergeant Reed. Ofcourse, Jnr was really interested in the science department: what new advances were the Army working on?

Both guys jumped in a jeep and set off. It was a huge base: it even had its own little town.

"I'm particularly interested in the science department, Gordy. Can we go there?"

"Yes, why not? Only you won't be able to talk about present studies, as they are military-based and confidential, of course, but I think you will find our department quite exhilarating."

Sergeant Reed took Jnr through the main entrance to where Dr Sheila Childerley stood talking to a group of school children there on a visit. She waved at Gordy and Jnr.

"That is Dr Childerley. She's a lovely person, as well as a great scientist: good with the kids, as you can see. She is the lead scientist here and has worked on some amazing technologies, some of which involve nanotechnology," said Gordy.

"Oh, that's interesting. I hope to chat more with her, then."

"You will, but later. Let me walk you around the department."

Off the two guys went and Jnr noticed that it reminded him of the science lab back in the States where Dr Seabank was the main man, but without the amazing coffee machine.

After the tour Gordy took Jnr to meet with Dr Childerley.

"Hi, Sheila, I would like you to meet Dr Archer. Dr Archer may I present Dr Childerley?"

Both scientists shook hands. Sheila looked quite puzzled as she gripped Jnr's hand.

"Weren't you the scientist that disappeared on the first Mars landing?"

"Yes, Dr Childerley, that was me."

"That was years ago. I've heard a little on the science grapevine about you, but I thought it was all poppycock – your return, I mean. Rumours are spreading," explained Sheila.

"I'm sorry, Sheila, Jnr cannot comment yet about the subject – top secret until the press conference – so direct questions on the subject are out of bounds," stated Gordy.

"Oh I see. Ok, indirect questions from now on, then, I suppose."

Jnr smiled and asked Sheila what she was working on.

"I'm sorry, Jnr, I cannot talk about my work either." Sheila smiled. "Top secret, too."

"What I can tell you is that my work involves nanotechnology: are you familiar with it, Jnr?"

"Yes, Sheila, I know a little about the subject. What are your objectives with nanos?"

"My role is to combine nanotechnology within military machinery in one form or another: medicines involving nanos are an interesting concept."

"Yes, I could see it being a great advantage for, say, treatment of cancer," replied Jnr.

"Yes, Jnr, there's an endless list of the benefits with nanos. We have the technology already but we need more advances in this area."

"Ok, we have to go. We have to finish our tour soon because I have prior engagements, I'm sure you two will speak again," explained Gordy.

The scientists shake hands before departing.

Jnr is whisked around the base at breakneck speed, not stopping to see anything else, but in all fairness it didn't float Jnr's boat anyway.

Back in his room he decided to call his parents to let them know all was well, even though the very next day they would be there for the press conference.

Jnr was looking forward to his announcement: he could then live his life without having to keep hush-hush about the last twelve years that he'd been missing.

After this he could visit his fellow astronauts: there was so much he wanted to do for himself, never mind the member states.

The next morning, Jnr decided to have breakfast in his room as he awaited the arrival of his family. He was excited to say the least. No more hiding, no more silence, and hopefully, after this, the press should back off if only slightly. His mother hated the attention they were receiving.

Knock knock.

Jnr opened the door, Gordy was there plus his family: he hugged each and everyone and thanked Gordy before asking everyone to come in.

"Anyone want a cuppa?"

"I'll make it," said Anne.

"Mum, I'm quite capable of making a brew, you know, plus I bet you would like to sit for awhile."

"Oh Jnr, I know you are, but I don't mind: mine tastes better than yours, son." Anne laughed.

"Tell you what, Mum – we'll do it together."

"Jnr, are you ok? I mean with all this going on you haven't really had time to yourself."

"Yes, Mum, I'm fine. To be honest, I cannot wait to get it out in the open: it will feel like a weight has been lifted from me. Hopefully I can get back to some kind of normality after this," replied Jnr.

"I hope so, son. I worry about you."

"Don't worry, Mum. Everything will be good from now on, I will be in demand for awhile, I imagine, but one day it will all calm down."

"Well, alright, as long as you're ok, Jnr, that's all that matters to me," said Anne with that lovely smile of hers.

Jnr hugged her and told her how much he loved her and how much he had missed her: both shed a tear.

"Come on, Mum, let's take this tea through."

The next couple of hours flew by as the family talked small talk. Jnr explained that Gordy would fetch them at about four, so they would remain in Jnr's dwellings until dinner, which would be earlier today: there will not be time to eat afterwards, because Jnr would be too busy.

As Jean lay asleep, Charles plucked up the courage to ask Jnr a few questions. Jnr knew this was coming, of course; he also knew the questions were from his colleagues at university. I suppose they wanted a scoop.

"Jnr, may I ask you something that's puzzling me?" asked Charles.

"Yes, Granddad, what is it?"

"What does this all mean for us – as a species, I mean?"

"That depends on who you ask, Granddad," replied Jnr.

"What do you mean by that, Jnr?"

"For one, we now know we are not alone: there could be thousands or millions of other life forms out there in space. It will only benefit us in knowledge, Granddad."

"Why?" asked Charles.

"Well, we're not alone but it will not make a difference to us. We will never be able to visit other life forms anyway: they're simply too far away, and as we speak they are moving away from us at the speed of light. We cannot hope to reach them."

"Unless we, too, learn how to create wormholes or passages as you call them?"

"Well, yes, Granddad, but let's say it takes a thousand years to gather the required knowledge. By that time they will be even further away that you would have to guess where to put the passage. We could not possibly see that far with even the greatest telescopes, so it would be pot luck. Would you take that chance?"

"No, Jnr, I suppose I wouldn't."

"Ok, guys, are you hungry?" Jnr asked.

Everyone replied yes, so off to the food hall they went, accompanied by Gordy.

"After we've eaten, we are to head to the main hall for the conference. I'll take you all together to where you will be seated with myself in the front row. Is that ok with everyone?" asked Gordy. The whole family agreed.

The time had come, so off they all went.

Jnr's family took their seats at the front, and Jnr went backstage to await his turn to take to the stage.

The place was packed to the rafters: reporters from all around the world were there. Scientists, too.

President Beevers had flown in, which Jnr had no knowledge of. He alone would announce Jnr to the stage, after he had bragged to the rest of the world that it was he who had arranged this announcement: Beevers loved the attention.

One of the organisers sat next to Jnr and explained the proceedings and when he would need to go out in front of the world's press.

Jnr felt quite relaxed: no nerves. He couldn't wait to get this monkey off his back so he could get on with his life.

In came Beevers.

"Hello again, Dr Archer. How are you feeling, nervous?"

"Hello, sir? Nice to see you again. No, I'm not nervous at all – quite excited actually," replied Jnr.

"That's great, I will announce you, Dr Archer. Just follow my signal: you will be sitting behind me during my part in the presentation."

"Yes, sir, no problem. President Beevers, may I ask you a question?"

"Certainly, what is it?"

"Have you had a chance to speak with the rest of your fellow members about what the Vicrons told them?"

"Yes, I've spoken to most of the members up to present. There are a few away at the moment, but don't worry, Dr Archer, I will speak to each and everyone in turn, as promised," he replied.

"And the general consensus amongst them?"

"That we will talk about later, Dr Archer. Now if you'll excuse me, I have an announcement to make."

Beevers trotted off to the podium. Jnr followed and took his seat.

So many people in such a small venue, thought Jnr.

The press had the front covered, and, sitting patiently behind were the scientists.

As Jnr looked out at the crowd he suddenly felt a little sad. Both Dr Hawking and Dr Thorne were no longer here. How he wished they were present: both men would have felt vindicated after what Jnr could have shown them. After all, without them, none of this would be happening.

Beevers asked the room to quieten down and listen to his announcement.

Cameras were flicking as he spoke. Jnr wasn't really listening: he was in his own little world imagining life after this event.

"Hello, ladies and gentlemen, friends and colleagues, thank you for coming to this historical event, which you are going to be amazed at. Twelve years ago on our first manned mission to Mars, you may recall an incident: we lost one of our astronauts in a freak accident upon the planet. That person was Dr David Archer. We searched for years in the hope of finding him. Unfortunately, as you may recall, it never happened. Dr Archer had disappeared into the blackness of space, forever.

"Well, that was until recently." Beevers turned to Jnr with a huge smile upon his face.

"May I present Dr David Archer?"

Jnr stood up and walked towards the podium, hand held high as he waved to the audience.

Cameras flashed like crazy, and the noise in the room picked up to deafening proportions!

Beevers waited for the commotion to settle before continuing.

"Thank you, thank you. If we could please settle down a little. Dr Archer has an incredible story to share with you."

Chapter 25 – Jnr's In Demand

Jnr was headline news all around the world: every household knew of him now. The scientific community couldn't get enough of him: he was to attend meetings with the world leaders of science across the globe.

Sure enough, the press had taken Jnr apart for months after the conference. He was getting tired of it all now: normality or something like it was Jnr's main goal at present.

Still he had not learned from Beevers anything about the message from the Vicrons.

Beevers had dodged the subject every time Jnr had called him, and because he was so far away, he could not tap into his thoughts. A meeting was in order!

"Hello, President Beevers, it's David here."

"Oh hi, Dr Archer. Nice to hear from you. How are you?"

"I'm well, thank you, and you?"

"Yes thanks, I'm good. How can I help you, David?"

"I've not heard anything at all from you regarding our meeting with the Presidents of the member states, could you tell me if any progress has been made at all?"

"I have now had the chance to speak to each president on the matter. Now we need a general meeting to discuss further the actions we will take. That's set for a month from now. It's going to be a long process, Dr Archer, I'm afraid. These things don't happen overnight," replied Beevers.

"Yes, sir, I understand that, but would you please keep me in the loop as to what developments the meeting brings? I know it's out of my hands now, but I would like to be informed as to what direction will be taken."

"Certainly, Dr Archer, you have my word on that. I have to cut your call short, I'm afraid. I'm about to leave the office, but rest assured we will speak again shortly," said Beevers.

"Ok, sir, thank you, talk soon."

Jnr hung up the call and took a second to evaluate Beevers'response.

It was then that he decided that he, too, would attend that meeting, but with a little help from his friends within.

Jnr decided to visit George once again. He trusted George: maybe, apart from his family, George was one Jnr could properly open up to.

Jnr borrowed his dad's car and drove himself down to Mansfield. He could use his ship, but he wanted to keep the power cell for as long as possible. The Vicrons said it would last about 50 years, but if he used it only in emergencies it should last a fair bit longer.

Jnr pressed the button upon the entrance to George's house.

"Hi David, come on through," Irene announced.

The huge metal gates slowly opened. There was a picture of Cyprus built into the iron gates: George's reminder of his homeland was evident everywhere you looked. Along the drive were even fig trees planted by Irene: she loved her gardening.

As Jnr jumped from the car's seat, George came over to greet him.

"Hello, David." George smiled. "Lovely to see you again."

"Hello, George, nice to see you. How are you?"

"I'm ok, David, thanks, Come, we are sitting in the garden."

It's such a lovely, quiet place here, thought Jnr. The gardens were immaculate: there were children's playhouses and swings for the grandkids, an outdoor conservatory where you could sit and read with no distractions, and an annex for visitors maybe, or extended family to stay.

Both Barry and Stavros were sitting with George watching their kids play in the garden.

"Hello again, David," said Irene from the kitchen door."Would you like a glass of fresh, cold, cloudy lemonade?"

"Oh yes, please, that sounds lovely, thank you," replied our ever-polite Jnr.

George introduced his sons to Jnr who both extended their welcomes and shook his hand.

"So, David, it's all out in the open now, how do you feel about it?" asked George.

"Well, it's like a weight has been lifted, ofcourse, but I can't help thinking that it may all be in vain," remarked Jnr.

"Why do you say that?"

"Obviously my getting home was important, but the message that I've relayed from Kandok hasn't made much of an impact up to now. Yes, I know these things are difficult, but I can't help thinking that the member states will ignore what's been foretold."

"Why do you think that, David?" asked Stavros.

"I don't know, Stavros. Maybe I think it's just our nature: greed, control, war. Will we be able to change before it's too late? I just don't know the answer."

"Dad tells us you can move things with your mind, David. Can you show us?" asked Barry rather excitedly.

Jnr smiled and raised Barry's glass of lemonade into his hand.

"Wow," said Barry with a shocked look upon his face.

"Watch this," said Jnr.

As the guys looked on, Jnr looked at their kids playing football on the grass. He shouted and asked them to stand still. Suddenly they all started to rise from the ground, nice and slow.

"Are you ok?" he asked them.

They all had the giggles, they were loving it. "Yes, yes," they answered.

Irene had joined them and the whole family watched the kids floating in the air.

"Higher, higher!" shouted Alexie.

"No, Alexie, you don't need to go higher," said Irene with a little panic in her voice.

Jnr smiled at Irene and said, "Don't worry, Irene, they're safe. Would you like to join them?"

The guys laughed. "Yes, Mum. You have a go," said Stavros.

"No, I don't think so, son. Please be careful with them, David."

"Don't worry, Irene. I could literally fall asleep and the kids would still be totally safe. I promise," replied Jnr.

Georgio, Jacob, Alexie and Xenayia were floating around in circles, giggling to each other, linking arms as they went round and round.

"That's amazing," said Barry.

Jnr gently put the kids back onto the grass, softly.

"Again, again!" shouted Georgio.

"How the hell do you do that, David?" asked Stavros.

"It's hard to explain, really, but what I'm doing is connecting with the energy of an object or mass and controlling that energy with my mind. I'm getting help from within, too."

"With the nanos," said Stavros.

"Yes, the nanos plus the Aug chip I had fitted. In years to come, humans will also be able to achieve this, but when I say years – well, I mean thousands of years into the future, provided we last that long!"

"Why do you say 'if we last that long'?" asked Irene.

"The Vicrons nearly wiped themselves out, and they say that if we don't change our ways, then we may do the same, so unless we change, war will still continue. They say that any civilisation will come to a point in time when they will either blow themselves to oblivion, or pass the danger stage and progress into a peaceful existence."

"So that's why you returned, then, David. Do you think anything will change?" asked Barry.

"I really don't know, Barry, I can only hope so."

Jnr stayed for dinner. The food was impeccable as always, and the conversation centred around Jnr, but he diverted it away from himself whenever he had the chance: for Jnr it seemed that he sounded like a broken record.

As he drove back home he decided it was time to start making some moves. He desperately wanted to know what Beevers and the rest of the members were up to. What were they planning?

Jnr told George of his plan to attend the meeting to find out more. George advised him to be careful.

The following week Jnr was invited as a guest speaker at the World Science Festival along with Prof Brian Greene, Prof Lawrence Krauss and one of his favourites, Prof Michio Kaku. He was up against the best, but for all their knowledge of the universe, our Jnr was way out in front. He decided to turn up in his ship for everyone to see: a surprise for them all.

Jnr had let the organisers know of his intentions, but it was to be kept quiet. If it was leaked, then it would not happen, so in everyone's interest it had to be treated like a top secret.

Jnr flew across the Atlantic Ocean very low so as not to be detected: his cover would be blown if not. He had the ship in invisible mode as usual as he tore across the ocean.

As he came into land he saw the crowds entering the facility to where this festival was being held; an area had been roped off for Jnr's ship. He dropped the cloak so his ship could now be seen arriving, and slowly he brought it down. All the crowd stopped to watch the event unfold, cheering and waving as he came down to Earth.

Jnr jumped from the cockpit and walked over to the ropes. There stood three officials whose job was to watch that no one jumped the ropes to get a closer look at the craft.

"Hi guys, I'm Dr Archer."

"Nice to meet you, Dr Archer. My name is Dan, I'm in charge of this watch. Rest assured your craft will be in safe hands."

"Good, please make sure no one – and I do mean no one – approaches my ship, and that includes you guys, Dan, ok?"

"Yes, sir, you have my word," replied Dan.

Jnr made his way towards the entrance but was immediately recognised by the crowd. They mobbed him for autographs. Jnr obliged, albeit reluctantly.

"Dr Archer, over here!" shouted his old friend, Dr Seabank.

Jnr waved and started to make his way over to Seabank, still signing booklets as he went.

Both men shook hands and embraced each other.

"I'm so glad to see you again, David. Come, let's get backstage and away from the crowd," said Seabank.

Jnr followed Dr Seabank through a side door which led round behind the main stage to where he saw the star professors sitting chatting.

"Wow, what a journey you've been on. I bet you have so much to teach us, David, but first let me introduce you to the gang. Both you and I can catch up later when all the circus has gone."

"Excuse me, gentlemen, may I introduce Dr David Archer?"

All three men rose to their feet and in turn shook Jnr's hand.

They all took their seats. "Would you like a drink fetching, David, before we go out onstage?" asked Seabank.

"Yes, may I have some water, please?" requested Jnr.

"Well, Dr Archer, what a roller coaster of a life you have had up to now." Greene smiled.

Jnr just simply smiled and nodded.

"If I may ask, Dr Archer, could we please have a little of your time after this event? I'm sure each and everyone of us has questions to ask that you may indeed be able to help with," asked Kaku.

"Certainly, Dr Kaku, it would be my pleasure."

The team of scientists discussed as to what format was going to be used during the presentation.

A technician came forward and announced that they would be called in around ten minutes from now: the presenter was to open with a speech and then the guys would be introduced separately onto the stage.

The discussion was very lively and informative, but Jnr took a back seat. Everyone knew his story now and he didn't want to steal the limelight; besides, he enjoyed listening to new hypotheses being cooked up after Jnr's knowledge had been spewed out in past events. The science community was having to change the way it thought and proceeded from now on.

After the presentation, Jnr joined the professors in a private room where they could talk. Dr Seabank was allowed in at Jnr's request.

He could tell this was to be a much livelier discussion than what had just passed by the thoughts in the minds of the three guys sitting around the table.

After answering, to the best of his ability, the questions posed by each professor, Jnr decided to show them what he had learned. Firstly, he manoeuvred objects around the room and explained the science behind it. Also Jnr spoke to each one through their minds which they were amazed at, especially Dr Kaku who had worked on this very subject in his books. But now was the time, thought Jnr, to step it up a little.

"Ok, guys, I'm going to answer a question that has been asked a million times over. What is dark matter? The answer, gentlemen, is gravity! You see, gravity moves freely between branes, but it moves in other dimensions, too, so therefore the gravity from a neighbouring dimension cannot be seen in our universe, by us, the observers in our dimension."

The scientists sat silently, taking in what Jnr had just said.

He got up and walked to the window: from there he could see his ship. Jnr opened the window and turned to the guys and said, "This will amaze you!"

Jnr commanded the ship to come to the window. It positioned itself so that the nose-cone was literally a foot from the glass. Out of nowhere a stream of what looked like black liquid entered through the window and onto the floor; it gathered in size until the fluid stopped running.

Jnr walked back to his chair and looked upon the object and simply said, "Watch."

The fluid started to form a shape. Slowly it started to move: it was a dog. It ran around the room jumping and playing, just as a puppy would!

"What the hell is that?" asked Kaku.

"It's a dog!" Krauss laughed.

"How, Dr Archer, and what is it?" asked Greene.

"That, gentlemen, is the future of nanotechnology. I can control them with thoughts alone: I can manifest any shape I require."

The dog suddenly changed shape into a snake and made its way up onto the table.

"Hold out your hands."

They all looked confused.

"Don't worry, it won't bite." Jnr laughed.

They held out their hands, palms up. Jnr turned the snake into three balls and placed one each into the hands of the scientists.

"Ok, think of anything that you would like to see the ball convert into."

As the guys thought of something (which is quite hard when you're put on the spot), the spheres simply changed into the shape requested.

"Are you telling me, Dr Archer, that I have just controlled this object myself, by thought alone?" asked Kaku.

"No, Dr Kaku, I read your thoughts and changed the nanos myself. It's going to be many years into the future before humans can achieve this – that's if we have years left!"

"And what makes you say that, Dr Archer?" asked Krauss.

"I have, as you know, spoken to the member states of the message from the Vicrons. The problem is: will anything be done about said message?"

"That's going to take time, I should imagine. Why do you have doubts?" asked Greene.

"I suppose I'm sceptical. There is one thing that I can help with which will help humanity now, and I would like your help, professors, with this matter: nuclear fusion. This can be a reality now for everyone to share cleaner, cheaper energy, but let's keep it quiet. Do not let the powers that be find out what we are up to, not yet!"

Chapter 26 – The Truth

Jnr spent the next week with his family: he needed some rest and to get away from the media in general. He spoke at length with his parents about his decision to sneakily attend the meeting of the presidents.

"What if you're caught out, Jnr?" asked his mother.

"I won't be, Mum. I'll be invisible to everyone, I just have to remain still and quiet. No one will ever know I was there, and besides, I can't trust Beevers to give me any information. Would it be the truth? Who knows?"

"Ok, Jnr. What if you don't like what you hear? Then what?" asked Snr.

"Well, that's a good question, Dad, that's why I need to be there. I don't trust them, Dad, and I suppose with good reason: everything in our past has been done to benefit the powerful and not the poor: the rich get richer, and the poor get shafted!"

"Yes, but that's life, Jnr."

"Yes, Dad, I know, but it needs to change."

"This is what I'm saying: it probably won't. You can lead a horse to water, Jnr, but you can't make it drink."

"Yeah, I know that, but I can try, it's for everyone's benefit in the end."

"Ok, let's say you attend this meeting and all you hear is bad news, then what?" asked Snr.

"Dad, I really don't know, I haven't got that far yet. One thing for sure: if they don't take Kandok's advice, then I think they might turn their attention to me!"

"Whatever do you mean, Jnr?" asked Anne with a worried look upon her face.

"Mum, I could teach them a lot, but for all the wrong reasons. They would love to take me apart and take the technology I have, which they could use for their own selfish needs," replied Jnr.

"Oh I see," said Anne.

"With my knowledge they would be way out in front of the rest of the world: they would be untouchable."

"I want it to be used for good, Mum, not for war and greed," said Jnr rather angrily.

"With this meeting I get to find out which way they are going to go: with me or against me."

Jnr had done some homework on the internet: he knew where the meeting was to be held, plus he had the blueprints of the building at his disposal. A locked door was to be his entry, which was located on the roof.

He felt quite nervous of the thought of getting caught, but the reward was worth it.

The time had come: the meeting was to be held an hour from now, so Jnr told his parents that he was off on his mission.

Using his ship, Jnr silently brought it to a standstill upon the roof, obviously in invisible mode. He climbed out and sent the ship up out of the way for now.

There were cameras everywhere, plus they used thermal detection, not a problem for our Jnr, but he needed to open the door! This posed a problem straight away. He would need to unlock the door without the cameras spotting it because he knew an alarm would be triggered to the control room once opened. If he got through quickly and locked the door back up without the door being seen open by the cameras, then it could be passed off as a fault within the system. Luckily for Jnr, the camera was not in a fixed position, so as soon as it faced away from the door, only then could he proceed.

Jnr stood by the door watching and calculating how long it took the camera to swing from one side to the other, away from the door. He was panting a little: nerves at last had got to him. No time for that, though. There was no turning back now.

Using his mind, he unlocked the door. The camera had moved away, and quickly he went through. While running down one flight of stairs he locked the door. There was a corridor running away from him and one to the right with a door. He opened it to find a storage room for cleaning equipment, he stepped in and stood still waiting to hear if anyone was approaching.

Suddenly he heard footsteps, then voices.

As he thought, the guards had been alerted: they checked the door.

"Control, this is Paskez. The door is locked and we are doing a sweep of the upper floor now."

Jnr heard footsteps coming his way, and the door slowly opened.

The guard looked into the small room with his gun held out in front of him. He stood still, surveying the surroundings.

Jnr dared not breathe: he could not move or he would be seen!

The guard turned and closed the door.

"Control, nothing here, must have been a false alarm," said Paskez.

The footsteps disappeared.

Jnr breathed out a sigh of relief: so far, so good.

He would now have to make his way down two floors to the main room without being spotted. Even though he was invisible, any quick movement could be a giveaway: his outline would be spotted against a still background.

After a few minutes he set off. Slowly he walked along the corridor towards the stairs: no one in sight so far.

As he came to the next level he saw a guard walking down the corridor away from him: the stairs lay just ahead, between himself and the guard. Silently he walked towards the stairs. As his hand caught a door handle, the guard spun around. Jnr watched as the guard stared in his direction: fortunately, the light wasn't fantastic, so no chance of him being seen. The guard turned and carried on down the corridor.

Jnr quickly made his way to the stairs and started to go down. He now heard voices below – quite loud actually. He knew he was getting close.

This level was much wider and there were more guards standing outside the main room, talking to people as they entered, checking credentials. Even though the presidents of the member states were very much known to everyone in the new world, they had to be careful. Infiltrators were everywhere, and they would love to get into this room: security was very tight for this reason.

Jnr made his way extremely slowly towards the door: any mistake now could be fatal. He waited until another president came so that the guards would be occupied, and then he could make a pass into the room.

His chance came as none other than President Beevers walked towards the guards. They obviously knew who he was and both guards walked forward to shake his hand – enough room for Jnr to pass unnoticed. He made it through!

Inside the room there was a huge table with seats for each president and, fortunately for Jnr, they were all busy catching up and chatting. He moved slowly and low to the corner of the room where a statue stood. He crept behind and sat upon the floor: a perfect spot.

Once the presidents had greeted each other they sat, the door was closed, and it was time for business.

Beevers opened up the talks and he didn't mess about.

"Ladies and gentlemen, presidents of the member states, I am very pleased you are all here to discuss a very serious situation regarding Dr David Archer. I have spoken to each and every one of you individually, but now it's time we discussed out loud between ourselves as to the outcome of Dr Archer's message from the Vicrons.

"There can be no reason to my knowledge to disbelieve what Dr Archer has told us, and indeed shown us, from his experience; however, what he or the Vicrons have asked seems a tall order to achieve, especially in a short time frame. I would like to hear your opinion on this matter," asked Beevers."Could I please see a show of hands for each of you who agrees that the conclusion, to be sort, should be one of peace and equality for every person upon the planet as stated by the Vicrons?"

Beevers counted the raised hands which came to twenty-eight.

"Ok, most seem to be in favour. Could I ask one of you who kept your hand down to explain why you do not agree?"

The remaining presidents looked around the table, hoping one of the others would get up to speak; reluctantly one did.

"I would like to know how we are supposed to bring about change in such a way to accommodate fairness and equality to all. It's taken many years to get to the point where we are now. Yes, there are issues but the idea, in principle, simply cannot work!" He took his seat.

Another president rose.

"I agree. For example, the nations which do not belong to our member states would have equal rights. Who would police such a project? How could these countries be trusted? Why should we extend our hand to help these countries? Obviously in an ideal world we should all coexist but it's never worked in the past. How can we possibly believe it can happen in our future?"

Beevers stood. "This is why we are here. Yes, it will take many years to accomplish, and there will be mistakes. I, for one, agree with some of your points, but I would also like to think that for our future generations, plus the most important benefactor which would be our planet, we could at least debate the pros and cons of this request."

Jnr sat trying his best not to open his mouth. Also, he needed to control his thoughts. He so wanted to plant words into the mind of Beevers, but that would give the game up.

The presidents debated and argued for what seemed like an eternity as Jnr felt anger raging throughout his body. Even now, after all they had been told, they still squabbled over petty rights. Who controls what? Why should they help the poorer countries? How can peace benefit them?

Jnr wondered if Kandok was clutching at straws with his ideas for the human race. Maybe even before Jnr set off back to Earth, Kandok knew what the outcome would be: had it all been in vain?

"President Beevers," said one of the lady presidents as she stood to address the room, "one thing that puzzles me is Dr Archer. Let me explain. Dr Archer has had an ordeal that can only be described as a miracle. He has come to us with this message of hope for our future, yet he is in control of technology which is of huge benefit to mankind, and yet no mention of sharing this technology with us. He is in control of a spacecraft which he will allow no one to approach, a craft running on nuclear fusion. Could it be used against us? Why does he not allow this to be shared information? He has no chip within his body, in fact he is the only person within our member states who is not chipped. Why? Is he hiding something from us?"

Beevers rose from his chair.

"I've met with Dr Archer on many occasions. To me he seems sincere. His credentials are impeccable, as is his character. I personally think that Dr Archer will assess the situation before committing himself in sharing these technologies," replied Beevers.

"That's not good enough, President Beevers," stated another member.

"I, for one, declare that the technology Dr Archer has in his possession should be turned over immediately, and furthermore, he has no right to keep it from us. He has to abide by our laws like everyone else within the member states, microchipped or not!"

"How do we know this is not a carefully concocted plan of the Vicrons to infiltrate our way of life, or even Earth for our resources for that matter?" asked another.

Jnr was getting quite frustrated by this point. How he wanted to show himself and join the conversation, but no, he would have to bite his tongue, at least for now.

"Ladies and gentlemen, please. Dr Archer has put his trust in me to deliver his message and to seek a resolution to our problem with constructive debate. He has also stated that at anytime we may call on him for further discussion, so he may explain his actions to the presidents of our member states directly," explained Beevers.

Jnr listened into the thoughts from the presidents. He could see that many didn't doubt his story, but also that some of the presidents felt threatened: they wanted control of what Jnr had. Furthermore, some of their thoughts were quite unsettling.

One thing for sure was that Jnr could now sense that Beevers was at least on his side, or, to put it another way, Beevers wasn't against him.

After an hour or two of serious debate it was decided that Jnr would indeed have to comply with the President's request which was to give up his ship!

Beevers asked, "What if Dr Archer doesn't comply?"

"Then, President Beevers, it will be taken out of your control. Dr Archer has no right to keep important information and technology from us. There is too much at stake. He will be made to hand over his ship and if he rejects our request, then steps will be taken against him!"

"I see," replied Beevers.

"May I ask, are the rest of the members in agreement with this request?"

They all looked at one another and then nodded in agreement.

"Alright, I will speak to Dr Archer. I conclude this meeting over!"

Beevers walked from the room. He was quite angry: Jnr could sense it.

Jnr sat and waited for everyone to leave the room; his head was spinning. Kandok had told him under no circumstances was he to relinquish any technology from Vicron. All kinds of thoughts were rushing through his mind. If he was put in a no-win situation he might have to give up his technology against Kandok's wishes: this could be bad.

Chapter 27 – Time To Take Action

Back home, Jnr told his parents of the meeting. What should he do? Confront Beevers? Wait to see if Beevers contacted him with the decision of the presidents?

"Jnr, why don't you call him?" asked his father.

"I don't know whether to wait a couple of days to see if he calls me first."

"And if he doesn't?"

"Then I will have to, Dad, but it's not really going to help, is it? I already know where this is going. I need a backup plan."

"What do you mean by that, Jnr?" asked Anne.

"Well, if they decide to turn against me, then I need to be able to have someone in high places who could help."

"Like who?" asked Snr.

"I don't know, not yet, but I need to be able to rely on someone to help if I'm taken out of the picture."

"Jnr, if President Beevers can't help, then who can?"

"I have an idea, but for now I'm going to keep it quiet. Do you fancy a ride in my ship, Dad?"

"Are you serious, Jnr?"

"Yes, I want to show you something."

"Well, I suppose so, then, yeah, why not?"

Jnr ordered the ship down and both guys jumped in: with a quick thought a new seat appeared for Snr.

"Where's the seatbelt, Jnr?"

Jnr laughed. "You don't need one, there's no traffic where we are going."

Jnr set the ship off to the upper atmosphere and cruised along, explaining to his dad what they were seeing. As the air was thinner up there you could see more clearly the blackness of space.

"Where are we going, Jnr?"

"Don't worry, Dad, I'm not taking you to Mars. You will see soon enough."

Jnr brought down his ship and landed in a clearing next to a river. Both men hopped out.

"Where are we?" asked Snr.

"Dad, we are in the wilds of Alaska. Come, I want to show you what I've been up to in my spare time."

Up in front, Snr could see a huge log cabin. More like a log house: it was huge.

"Well, Dad, what do you think?"

"Is this yours, Jnr?"

"Yes, I bought the land, obviously not in my name, plus it's untraceable back to me. I built it – well, if I'm being honest, the nanos built it," answered Jnr."Come inside, you won't believe how nice and cosy it is, Dad."

Snr couldn't believe his eyes: the place was beautiful, wooden furniture and a huge dining table, plus a kitchen looking like something out of an old western film.

"Why, Jnr? What is this place?"

"It's an escape for us, if anything goes wrong with my plan, we will need somewhere to lay low. No one knows this is here. We are miles from anyone: a perfect hideout if you like."

"How have you had the time to do this?"

"It only took a week to build, Dad, I used my telekinesis to gather the wood and the nanos completed the build for me, cool. Eh?"

"Plus, all the decor I collected from around the world in different places – easy when you have my mode of transport."

"You've kept this quiet, son."

"I had to: you are the only person who knows of its existence, and until the day comes when we need to move here, then it has to remain that way, Dad."

"Do you really think it could come to that, Jnr? I mean why would you take such drastic measures?"

"They could never hold me anywhere, Dad, but my family – well, use your imagination. I don't trust them at all.I'm not going to let you suffer for my decisions, none of you."

"Ok, I understand. I'm proud, lad, it's a good plan." His father smiled.

"I don't see any taps: are there no amenities?"

"No, there's a massive stockpile of logs at the rear, plus I've put a fireplace in every room and we will boil water from the river. It's some of the cleanest water you will ever find, Dad."

"What about TV?" Snr laughed.

"Well, we will have to read and converse, Dad, like people did years back. You will enjoy it, don't worry. Anyway, hopefully it might not come to that and besides, I could put an energy source in if it becomes too boring."

"You've been a busy lad, Jnr. Your mum would love it here."

"If everything goes ok we could use this place for breaks so it's not going to waste," exclaimed Jnr.

"Are there any fish in that river?"

"Yes there are. That's why I built it here: salmon, Dad, loads of fresh, beautiful, free salmon."

"Ah good, we will have to bring your granddad Roy's fishing tackle, then."

"Yeah, good idea, I wish he was here to see this place: he would fish on that river everyday, I imagine." Jnr smiled.

"True, son. Yes he would, bless him."

"Ok, let's drop you back off at home, Dad. I'm going to see Beevers: it's time I find out the truth."

Back at his parents, Jnr called Beevers and arranged a meeting at his office for the following day; Beevers obliged. It was four in the afternoon there, so it was quite early over in the States. Jnr decided his next move was to speak with a man who he thought could help his cause.

Dr Lawrence Krauss lectures out of Arizona State University and is the director of the Origins Project. He is also a theoretical physicist. On top of his many achievements he is also an atheist, much like our Jnr, and because they have already met and enjoyed each other's company, he knew Lawrence was his best bet. Jnr had read his thoughts and so he knew that Lawrence was looking at Jnr with a scientific mind. He had questions for Jnr.

Jnr ejected from his ship within the university grounds, unnoticed of course, and made his way to the main entrance. He found that Lawrence took his lunch break at the exact same time everyday, so he decided to wait outside the main entrance for him. While waiting for the professor to appear, Jnr called Beevers' office to confirm their appointment for later that day.

As he hung up his call, Lawrence came out withhis lunch in hand accompanied by one of his students – poor Lawrence couldn't even have his lunch without someone pestering for information.

Jnr spoke to Professor Krauss through his mind.

"Lawrence, please try not to look surprised or speak out. It's me, Dr Archer. Could you lose the student? We need to talk."

Lawrence tried his best but he did look quite blank for a second before understanding the situation. He explained to the student that he needed to make a few private calls, and so asked if he could be alone, to which the student obliged. Lawrence looked around before asking with his own thoughts, "Where are you, David?"

"Keep walking forwards and you'll see me sitting on a bench, I'm only 50 yards from you: can you see me waving?"

Lawrence spotted Jnr and waved back with a smile.

Jnr stood from the bench to face him and both guys shook hands.

"Nice to see you, David: why didn't you call my office and make an appointment? Would have been easier, you know."

"Yes true, but I'm here today for a meeting with President Beevers so I thought on the off chance I might catch you first, plus I want to keep this meeting between ourselves," replied Jnr.

"Hmm, that sounds interesting, David, how may I help?"

"Ok, why don't you eat as I speak, as I don't want to interrupt your lunch."

"That's ok, David. I like to sit on the grass to eat lunch, part of my daily routine. Come, let's find a quiet spot," said Krauss.

Both guys marched off to find a suitable spot, quiet with no one to interrupt.

"Here will do, David. Please sit, let's talk."

Both guys sat cross-legged facing one another.

"Before you tell me why you are here, I have a question for you, David, if I may?"

"Of course, Prof Krauss."

"You call me Lawrence, David, ok?"

"Yes, Lawrence, ok, I will answer your question of the lifetime of the universe."

Lawrence laughed so hard the crumbs of his sandwich shot from his mouth."Oh, I'm sorry, David, I keep forgetting that you know what I'm going to ask before I ask it, it's hard to hide anything from you."

"The universe is not infinite, as is predicted by many: we live on a membrane, as I have already stated, but what I haven't told anyone yet is that the membrane is double-sided."

Lawrence looked puzzled for a second before asking Jnr to continue.

"From the moment of the BigBang the universe expanded for what seemed to us like forever. The light from all galaxies and stars will indeed redshift until it's no longer seen by us, the observers, but that's not the end. It will expand to the point of arriving on the back side of the brane, so the side we once occupied becomes again empty!"

"So everything simply travels along from one side to another? What, forever?" asked Lawrence.

"Well, no, actually, on the empty side another BigBang will create a new universe similar to ours and time will again begin for that new creation," explained Jnr.

"So this event just keeps repeating?"

"Again no, simply because there is not enough room on a single brane for multiple universes to exist: they will eventually crash into one another and merge into one massive universe. The Vicrons believe that two big bangs per brane are the maximum any one membrane can take."

"So where does gravity fit into all this?" asked Lawrence.

"Gravity exists between branes and throughout the multiverse, and it will always weaken because of the ever-expanding multiverse."

Lawrence sat with his mouth open, not chewing, just hanging there, open.

"One more tantalising morsel for you, Lawrence, given enough time and enough energy, a wormhole may be created through the membrane, so in effect one could make contact with other beings in a different universe, which occupy the same brane, and this complies with Einstein's laws."

Lawrence looked bewildered.

"Ok, Lawrence, I can hear your mind doing overtime but I need to talk to you about a different subject. We can talk science anytime," said Jnr.

"Ok, David, how can I help you?"

"I attended a meeting of the presidents of the member states at which I found that the message from the Vicrons will most probably not be heeded. At the end of the meeting it was decided that I should give up the Vicron technology to be used for God knows what. That's not what I was sent back for. I'm giving them nothing, Lawrence."

"Good, David, I agree. Can I ask: did they say these exact words while you were in their presence?"

"Well, no, Lawrence I went incognito." Jnr smiled.

Lawrence looked puzzled.

Jnr quickly went invisible for a couple of seconds then reappeared.

Lawrence looked at Jnr with amazement. "How the hell did you do that?"

"I use the nanos, I don't have time to explain but I sneaked in on their meeting and heard every word: today I'm going to see Beevers to see if he is with me or not. I need to know because it will affect my decisions from then on.

This is the reason I wanted to talk to you, Lawrence. You seem a very trustworthy person and I see no malice in your thoughts, if I have to go into hiding, then I need someone I can trust to help bring about change scientifically into our world. I want to show you, for example, how to create nuclear fusion both safely and efficiently. This will help many people around the world, Lawrence: cheap, clean energy, and more importantly, the Earth will benefit, too."

"Oh I agree, David, but how do you think I could achieve this unnoticed?"

"That I don't have an answer to yet, Lawrence."

"You know, Lawrence, I wish I could take you to Vicron: what an amazing race of people and such a beautiful planet. No greed or wars, no poverty, no crime, no starving children, no religion which you would especially appreciate." Jnr laughed. "No sickness, no diseases of any kind. Only old age. I miss Vicron already."

"Sounds fantastic. Could you never go back, David?"

"No, I'm afraid not. That was their most important request for us earthlings, to not search them out and visit, even if we could."

"Why not?"

"The Vicrons have nothing to gain from us, Lawrence."

"Ok yes, I agree wholeheartedly, David."

"So Lawrence, will you help me if they won't?"

"It would be my pleasure, David. How I'm going to help I don't know, but yes, I'm with you."

"Thank you, this means a lot to me. Right, I'm off to see Beevers, I will contact you as soon as I know what direction I will be taking, so thank you for this chat – oh and remember, please keep this between us for now, enjoy your lunch in peace now, Lawrence." Jnr smiled.

Lawrence also smiled and both guys shook hands before Jnr set off on his mission.

Upon arriving at President Beevers' office, Jnr was offered a coffee by the secretary while he sat and waited for his meeting. Now Jnr would find out what the verdict of the member states will be. He felt apprehension, on the one hand, and hope on the other. How great life would be for all humanity, and let's not forget planet Earth, which we are mere visitors to in our short lives. The problem is that governments don't see this point of view: greed and corruption exist in all governments, the needs of now are far more important to them than the needs of the future.

"Dr Archer, President Beevers will see you now. This way please," asked the secretary.

Jnr knew exactly where to go: after all, this was not his first visit. But that's her job, he supposed.

"Ah, Dr Archer, please take a seat," said Beevers, pointing to a chair.

"Would you like a drink, David?"

"No, thanks, I'm ok for now," replied Jnr.

"Very well, let's get down to business, then, David. The members have decided that the message you bring from the Vicrons must be acted upon for the greater good: everyone is in agreement with that fact, but the members are worried about the technology you have in your possession," said Beevers.

"'Worried'? What does that mean exactly?"

"They see it as a potential future threat, David. I've said this before, until we have carried out tests to determine whether in fact the technology is a threat or not the members are reluctant to move forward."

"Oh I see. So where do we go from here? My ship will not be handed over. I don't trust them, President Beevers."

"I have an idea, David, which may suit both parties, if I may?"

"Ok, I'm listening," replied Jnr.

"Would you agree for an examination of the craft, by only a handful of scientists in the presence of just you and me?" asked Beevers.

Jnr thought for a moment before answering the question. All the while he searched through Beevers' thoughts for any kind of malice, but up to now none was evident.

"That may be a possibility, President Beevers: it will have to be on my terms, you understand."

"Yes, David, of course. I think this is the way forward. Once the possibility of a threat has been eradicated, then we may move forward onto the next step in the process."

"I will put together the team of scientists and in the meantime, maybe you could decide on where this will take place, and more importantly, when," said Beevers.

"Ok, sir, let me know when you're ready and then we can proceed," replied Jnr.

Jnr left the office feeling quite confident of the plan suggested by Beevers: it would be on Jnr's terms at a place of his choosing. Still in the back of his mind Kandok's advice kept niggling at him: was this the way forward, and what could possibly go wrong?

Chapter 28 – The Inspection

Since his meeting with Beevers, Jnr had to decide where the investigation of his ship would take place: was it to be a secluded spot or a built-up area?

He decided on speaking to both George and Lawrence for some advice.

Both agreed on a secluded position. Jnr would have the advantage of seeing anyone approaching, giving him time to make his exit, if the need arose.

Jnr hoped this would be a turning point in his plan to bring about change in the attitude of the members, to adhere to Kandok's advice.

Jnr called Beevers and gave him co-ordinates for the designated place of the meeting:

37*14'06 N 115*46'40'W

He advised Beevers as to the rules of the game: only him plus the scientists were to attend at exactly 11am, in three days' time. Beevers agreed: the meeting was set.

Over the next few days, Jnr spent quality time with his parents. He spoke in length to his father about the upcoming meeting, and also advised him that if the meeting went wrong and Jnr is not heard from, then Snr was to take the family immediately to the cabin in Alaska.

"It probably won't come to that, Jnr: after all, they are not interested in us," said Snr.

"Dad, they want what I have. They will stop at nothing to get it. I simply do not trust them."

"Can I ask you something, Jnr?"

"You don't need my permission and I cannot believe you're thinking that, Dad."

"Would you please not do that, Jnr? I sometimes feel like I can't talk to you properly anymore: stop using my thoughts and talk."

"Ok, but why would you ask me to give up the ship? Have you not understood what this is all about? Can you not see where this is going?" asked Jnr.

"Yes, Jnr, I have, but have you thought about giving them a chance? I mean, what if they actually mean well after all?"

"I sneaked into their meeting, remember: they were not interested in Kandok's advice, they are only interested in the technology. I could sense that from the very start of the meeting."

"All I'm saying is that if the meeting goes wrong, then I want my family out of reach, off the grid. I do not want them using you as a bargaining tool. Yes, it may go well and that's what I want. I'm just being cautious, Dad."

"Alright, Jnr, I get your point, I understand."

The day of the meeting came so Jnr set off early: he wanted to scout out the area and to watch Beevers approach, to make sure they were alone.

Once again he flew across the ocean to the US. It would only take an hour at the speed he could muster, unlike the eight hours' flight in a conventional plane.

Sometimes Jnr would cruise along quite slowly, looking for signs of interest. One of his favourite sights was blue whales coming to the surface to breathe, before diving once again to the depths. The whales were huge, but he also felt sadness at their sight. The largest creature ever to have graced our blue planet and they were under threat: human intervention yet again.

When you think about it, we are a plague to this planet and all life on it.

Jnr would sometimes drift away with thoughts on how Earth could one day have the same future as Vicron, if only Kandok's advice was taken on-board: no more war, no starving people, peace and prosperity for everyone, no more stone-aged religious beliefs which cause almost all the wars of today.

Jnr had arrived at the set co-ordinates early, so he decided to do a sweep over the entire area: everything was quiet, just the way he wanted.

Parking up the ship next to the road Beevers would be approaching on, Jnr decided to do a spot of sunbathing until the team arrived, killing time.

Jnr's mobile jumped into action.

"Hello, Dr Archer, we are close to the co-ordinates: can I ask why Area 51?"

"Hello, sir, it's the most secret place on the planet, so why not? I will find you and we shall conduct the meeting out in the open."

"Shall we park up and wait for you on the road, then?" asked Beevers.

"No, just pull up off the road, I'll find you."

Jnr put back on his shirt and headed out to find the team; but first another sweep, just to make sure.

Jnr easily spotted the van parked alongside the road: he swung the ship round and landed twenty yards or so away from their position. He jumped out and made his way over.

"Hi, Dr Archer, nice spot you've picked."

"Hello again, President Beevers."

"Come, Jnr, let me introduce you to our scientists."

Jnr shook the hands of the team while at the same time scanning their minds for any deviant signs: there were none, they were only there to complete their duties and they were excited to be meeting Jnr: history was being made, right there.

"Ok, here are the rules. You may touch anything in or on the ship, but you're not allowed any samples of any kind, plus you couldn't get one even if you tried. Also, once your investigation is over, I will reveal the power source of this craft for your viewing. Any questions?" asked Jnr.

"May I ask a question please?" asked one of the scientists.

"Yes, you may."

"How is it possible for you to connect with this craft from a distance?"

"Ah, good question. Think of it like entanglement: spooky action at a distance." Jnr smiled; the team smiled and understood Jnr's reply. Beevers looked baffled – never mind.

Jnr turned and faced the ship. Suddenly a door appeared.

"Dr Archer, how does the craft change shape like that?"

"Again, the nanos are linked to me and are in my control. I can manipulate them in anyway I see fit, from thought alone."

"Ok, guys, the ship's all yours."

The team went about their business taking photographs and measurements.

Both Beevers and Jnr made small talk while the team carried on with their investigation.

One of the team made his way over to Jnr.

"Dr Archer, this craft has no controls. How therefore do you fly this thing?"

"Nanomites, my friend. Without me this craft is completely useless."

It didn't take long for the team to finish as there was not much to look at, really, so Jnr asked them to follow him to the back of the craft.

"I must ask you to refrain from taking pictures of the engine of this craft for now: all will be revealed at a later stage," said Jnr.

Suddenly the craft became transparent: the power source was revealed, and the team looked upon the craft with bemusement.

"That's it," said one scientist. "That's the only power source of this craft, it's so small."

"Yes, that's right, there is a nuclear fusion-powered engine, state-of-the-art."

"How long is it likely to last, Dr Archer?"

"The Vicrons say around fifty years. I hope by then we have advanced so I may top it up. This technology is very important, President Beevers. Its applications will benefit us in so many ways."

"How long would it take to build a reactor big enough to, say, power a city?" asked Beevers.

"Around a year. It's quite possible we could have a fully operational reactor, which in turn could power a city like New York, running at a fraction of today's costs, and with no detriment to the environment."

"That's good news, Dr Archer. We must therefore get to work with this project as soon as possible," replied Beevers.

"All in good time, President Beevers, until I'm assured that the rest of the presidents are in favour of Kandok's plan, this technology remains with me."

"Well, then, Dr Archer, you will have to leave that with me. I will request a further meeting , and once the science team has presented its findings, maybe then we may proceed."

As the group were taking, Jnr noticed a faint hum: he looked in all directions but could see nothing.

The sound grew louder and now the rest noticed it, too. Jnr spun round and faced Beevers. "What is this, President Beevers?"

"Dr Archer, I assure you this has nothing to do with me or the team: read my thoughts, you will know I'm telling the truth."

He was telling the truth: Jnr found nothing.

Choppers appeared in formation, encircling the whole team.

"Please stand still. No one move or all will be shot," came the announcement.

Jnr stood and thought, *Should I make a run for it? Will the team ,including Beevers, be executed?*

The choppers came down to the ground, guns trained on the team with continued commands being thrown from the loudspeaker.

Out of one chopper came the one who appeared to be in charge.

"Hello, President Beevers, Dr Archer, my name is Sgt Mellows. I've been ordered to take you into the base."

"On whose authority, may I ask?" said Beevers with a tone of disgust in his voice.

"The presidents of the member states, sir," replied Mellows.

"Well, that's strange, as I am a member of said state. I know nothing of this."

"I'm very sorry, sir: they are my orders. The ship will remain here for now. Please, gentlemen, this way if you will," said Sgt Mellows, pointing towards the waiting choppers.

Jnr immediately sent the craft off, up and out of harm's reach.

"Dr Archer, that craft must remain grounded: have it returned now."

"No, Sgt. The ship will stay where it is for now, I'm sorry."

"Very well, have it your way, Dr Archer. This way please, gentlemen."

Both the president and Jnr took one chopper while the science team took another.

On the journey to the Area 51 base everyone kept quiet; Jnr did the same, but at the same time he searched into the minds of the two guys accompanying him on this little trip, hoping they would slip up and give him something to go on.

Neither had anything to hide, but Beevers was angry: you could tell just by looking at him. Mellows was happy that his little mission had gone according to plan.

"President Beevers, don't speak, use your thoughts," said Jnr.

President Beevers gave a little nod.

"Who did you tell about this meeting?"

"The only people who knew where the presidents, but the location was kept to myself."

"Alright, you have somehow been tracked, then. It looks like they don't trust you either, sir."

"Why wouldn't they trust me? I have always carried out my duties with the utmost precision in respect of the members. I've hidden nothing from them."

"I don't know as of yet, but I'm sure we will find out soon enough. One thing for sure is that you have been kept out of the loop. For one reason or another, they didn't want you in on this, did they?"

The helicopter came in and landed within Area 51, next to a hangar. The sergeant asked the men to follow him; the science team were taken in a different direction.

Once inside the building, the two men were taken into a room. The rest of the presidents sat awaiting their arrival.

"What is the meaning of this? Who ordered this without my knowledge?" asked Beevers.

"Please, President Beevers, take a seat, and you, too, Dr Archer," asked a lady president.

Within the agreements of the members, no president is above another: this was the reason why Beevers was so annoyed. Anytime an important decision was taken, it was taken together: this was their most valued law.

"President Beevers, we felt it was time to step in and take measures without your consent. We feel that you are too involved with Dr Archer, which may affect your decisions regarding this matter," said President DeHulme.

"I don't understand. Have I not completed this matter with honesty and integrity?" asked Beevers.

"Yes, sir, you have, but its obvious to us that Dr Archer wants full control of the situation: that we cannot allow. We need that ship, and this seemed to us the perfect situation for us to intervene."

"May I ask to how you think you may acquire the ship?" asked Jnr.

"Well, Dr Archer, let us make this clear: one way or another, we will have your ship."

Chapter 29 – Locked Up

Jnr was being held in a ten by six cell which had a bed, a table and a chair, a TV and a few books to keep him company. There was a window which looked out across the plains to the hills in the distance. It was around six inches thick, so no getting out that way without being heard.

He had been told that until he conformed to the request of the members, he would be held indefinitely.

Every day, twice a day, Sgt Mellows was to question Jnr and to somehow get Jnr to bring the ship down to Earth. It was not going to be an easy task!

"Can I ask, Dr Archer, why you feel like you have authority over the members about this matter? I mean why not just hand the ship over? What are you hiding from us?"

"Sgt Mellows, I have explained enough my reasons why. With my ship's technology the members will have a distinct advantage over any oppressors: that's not going to happen, I'm afraid," replied Jnr.

"But what does it matter to you, Dr Archer?"

"It's not about me, Sgt. The message I was given, loud and clear was that under no circumstances should the Vicron technology fall into the wrong hands."

"Ok, but we are not the wrong hands, Jnr."

"Sgt Mellows, you are following orders, which I understand. You obviously believe the members have all the right answers and are acting on humanity's behalf, but the Vicrons have a better vision for everyone, not just the selected ones."

"Dr Archer, our enemies will not listen, not now, not ever. They could never be trusted. Many times they were told to conform to the member states and in return they would have peace and prosperity, so please enlighten me: why should we help them if they are not willing to help themselves?"

"You mean they are not willing to conform. Would they be offered a fair deal? I doubt it."

"Sgt, how long am I to be kept here?"

"As long as it takes, Dr Archer!"

The Sgt walked off and left Jnr alone once again.

Our Jnr wanted to speak to his parents so badly. Of course, his father knew what to do if Jnr was not heard from.

He wondered if President Beevers could help him in anyway.

Jnr could escape this cell anytime he wanted, but for now it was a good place to be. Sooner or later he would know where he stood. The only problem was that Jnr knew that the members would be watching his family. If he did not play ball, then they may pay the price. His father had his orders from Jnr before he left for the inspection: had they left for Alaska already?

"Hello again, Sgt Mellows. Here again for more interrogation?"

"No, Dr Archer, I've brought you some food and water. I thought maybe while you eat we could have an informal chat," replied the Sgt.

Jnr knew this tactic, the softly softly approach, to befriend Jnr into spilling the beans.

"Ok, Sgt, what delightful concoction have they sent me this time?"

"Nothing but the best for you, sir: fresh red snapper with a Mediterranean salad and fresh bread: perfect for you."

"Well, thank you, Sgt, it does sound lovely."

The Sgt passed Jnr's food through the small compartment.

Taking the tray of food, he made his way over to the table and sat to eat.

"Dr Archer, I would like you to know that for me this is not personal. I believe you have had an amazing experience and you have seen things no human will probably ever see again, I imagine it was both terrifying and fantastic at the same time. I also do understand the message you or the Vicrons are passing to our world, but I cannot see how you think it can be implemented straight away. It would take years to make those changes you are suggesting."

"Yes indeed, Sgt, it would, but those changes need to take place and the sooner, the better."

"Well, yes, but I don't see how it can happen. For example, the eating of meat: cattle are bread for our consumption, they were created for food."

"True, but already the effect of methane from cattle is adding to the demise of our atmosphere. The human population is still growing too fast which, in turn, means more cattle to feed them, which again means more land required to keep the cattle. There is not enough room for more: forests are being destroyed to house more cattle, which means less oxygen and more methane. It cannot continue," replied Jnr.

"Ok, I see your point there, but what about the countries that are not members? They are always attacking us. Why should we join with them? They have nothing to offer."

"Sgt, when I left there were populations of starving people, children dying in hundreds of thousands, with no food or water, the basic requirements of human existence. I see it hasn't changed. You are right, they have nothing to offer: they are poor countries, but they are as human as you and me! Why should they suffer because they were born in a country that has civil wars raging, famine due to weather – why shouldn't they be helped?"

"Again, I suppose I agree, Dr Archer. I just don't think the members will."

"This is the problem, isn't it? This is why the technology I hold will not be passed over to be used for the wrong reasons, Sgt."

"Ok, Dr Archer, that's your choice to make but remember, you may be held here until you do," remarked Sgt Mellows.

"That's alright, Sgt, I get my food and drink for free, no bills to pay and I even have a nice view. What more can a man want?" Jnr laughed.

"I do like your sense of humour, Dr Archer, but will it be enough to see you through your stay here? I doubt it," replied Sgt Mellows as he walked away.

Jnr lay upon his bed with his hands behind his head. In his cell there were four cameras, one at each corner of the room, giving a 360-degree field of vision for the guards to keep an eye on him. He guessed that the walls were around two feet thick, which wouldn't be a problem for our Jnr with the help of his loyal nanos.

The problem now was: had his parents started their journey to Alaska? Should Jnr wait a little longer or trust that his dad had done what he'd been told?

If Jnr's dad had taken the decision to go, he hoped that he would have been thoughtful enough to cover his tracks.

Meanwhile, at the Ted Stevens Anchorage International Airport, Jnr's family were just coming in to land. David Snr had indeed taken that crucial first step, just as Jnr had instructed.

It didn't take too long for them to make it through departures, and the first job on Snr's list was to hire a car. After that, he would try Jnr again.

David Snr began to also feel paranoia set in. They would know that they had left for a two-week holiday in Canada. Could they also know their location due to the phone signal? He now had to start thinking like someone who wanted to remain anonymous.

David Snr had the coordinates written down in his wallet but how would they find it? He cannot use his phone as it could be detected. *Ok, I have to buy a GPS device,* he thought to himself.

Snr sat down with Anne and Jean and told them they had a 30-minute wait for the car to be readied.

"Anyone fancy a drink or some food?" asked Dave.

"Yes, I'll have a cup of tea and a sandwich, love. What about you, Jean?"

"I'll have the same, David," replied Jean.

Snr trotted off to the canteen area and bought everyone's food.

"Here you go. I got a pot of tea for you, but be careful, it's quite hot."

As he sat eating his own food, he had a realisation: he had just used his card to purchase the food. That he could not do from now on, as it could be tracked!

The problem now was that they needed cash and of course there was a daily limit on his card. For now he would have to use his limit and get both Anne and Jean to do the same, but he needed more: he could not keep using his card daily.

Now Dave's mind was working overtime. He realised that he could not keep the hire car as it would have a tracker, so the first job was to book into a hotel for the night and, while there, he needed to buy a car. It should be ready the same day.

"I'm going to try to get hold of Jnr again. I wish he would answer," said Anne.

Back at the cell Jnr decided it was time he left: he was not getting any information, so it was not worth staying. He would wait until late so that the guards watching the monitors would probably be watching something on TV: they could not surely sit and watch every move Jnr made for an eight-hour shift.

Jnr had it planned: easy really. The time had come. There was no noise coming from the corridors: all was quiet. Jnr sat down on the floor with his back to the wall, reading a book. He instructed the nanomites to exit from his body and onto the wall. There they were to cut through the brickwork: they did as they were told.

The nanos cut a perfect silhouette of Jnr's shape. He ordered the ship to land just outside in invisible mode. As the nanos made their way through, they hit a metal sheet within the wall: the alarm started to ring out!

Jnr pushed hard with his back onto the wall: it fell through. Quickly he gathered up the nanos and jumped into the ship. Already two guards were almost upon him, and they opened fire. Bullets bounced off the craft: one caught his shoulder but it ricocheted off him. Once inside, he shot off upwards into the night sky.

"Wow," said Jnr, "that was crazy." He giggled excitedly with nervousness. The adrenaline had kicked in, and his legs were shaking.

Jnr was now free. He had to call his dad: he needed to know what they were up to, so the nearest town would have to do.

It wasn't long before he'd found a small town. He landed the ship in disguise mode as usual, and set off to look for a phone box.

He found one but he had a problem: no money! It looked like the nanos would have to earn their keep yet again.

Once the nanos had unlocked the cash box, Jnr borrowed a few dollars and dialled his dad's number.

Dave's phone started to ring."I don't recognise the number," said Dave.

He rejected the call; Jnr tried again.

"Answer it, Dave, it could be Jnr," said Anne.

"What if it's not?"

"What if it is?" said Anne, this time rather angrily.

"Hello."

"Hello, Dad, it's Jnr."

"Jnr, thank God for that, where are you?"

Both Anne and Jean held hands, looking very relieved.

"Never mind, Dad. More importantly, where are you?"

"We are in Canada, at the airport: we landed only a short while ago."

"Ok good, Dad. I'm so glad you have. I told you this would go wrong, didn't I?"

"Why? What do you mean? Where are you?" asked Snr.

"They arrested me, Dad: now they will stop at nothing. After this call, Dad, you must snap your sim card and throw your phone away."

"Ok, Jnr."

"Make sure no one else has a phone, too. Write down the numbers you need and throw the mobiles in a bin, and Dad, do not under any circumstances use any cards," stated Jnr.

"I need to buy a few bits and get some cash, Jnr, so I will have to use it today but then I will bin them, too."

"Ok, but make sure you do. I will meet you at the cabin. I'll be there when you get there. Oh, and get some food and water on your way."

"Ok, son, see you there."

Snr explained to Anne and Jean what Jnr had told them, and that they had to make their way over to the cabin.

He had a plan of how to get some serious cash.

They set off in the rental car and the first stop was a car sales showroom. Snr was now in full secret agent mode: he figured the rental car would have a tracker fitted!

"Ok, you two wait here: sit in the sun for awhile. I need to sort another car out."

"Why, David? We have a car," asked Anne.

"I'll explain later, love. I won't be too long."

Snr made his way into the showroom. Being a mechanic all his life he knew exactly what he wanted.

"Goodday, sir, how may I help you?" asked the salesman.

"Hi, you have a Ford Cab outside in black for $33,500, I would like that please," he confidently replied.

"Ah yes, sir, I know the one, two years old and only covered 30,000 kilometres. One owner from new."

"Ok, sounds good. That will do, then."

"Would you like to take it out, sir?"

"No thanks. I've been a mechanic for the majority of my life. I know that vehicle probably better than you. When can you have the vehicle ready?"

"I can have it ready for collection by the morning, sir."

"Fantastic. Let's do this, then," said Snr.

"It doesn't have one of those black boxes fitted, does it? I don't want fines for speeding."

"No, sir. Only new vehicles get them as standard now."

"So, no trackers, then?"

"No, nothing at all, sir."

Both men walked into the office.

"How are you wanting to pay for this vehicle, sir?"

"Bank transfer. Could you allow me to call my business manager to arrange the payment?" asked Snr.

"Yes, sir, of course."

"Before we go any further, do you carry cash here?"

"I'm sorry, sir, I don't understand."

"I would like you to put the price of the cab at $50,000. I need the rest for the casino and I'd rather pay cash. I don't want my wife knowing."

"Oh right, sir, I understand, but that's not something we could normally do," said the salesman, looking at Snr rather suspiciously.

"Look, do this for me and I'll give you a couple of grand as a thank-you, ok?"

"Ok, sir, I'll see what I can do."

Dave smiled to himself. *Funny how he can do it now,* he thought.

With the bank transfer in place, Snr and his family set off to a local hotel for the night.

On the way Snr stopped off at a hunting store: there he picked up a GPS, a satellite phone and a gun! Of course, he wasn't about to tell his family about it – but you never know, it might come in handy!

Chapter 30 – On The Run

Back at the log cabin, Jnr was getting to grips with the current situation. It had indeed gone pear-shaped, his whole plot.

The fact that he had got his family safe gave him hope, but what was he to do now?

Jnr was now classed as 'on the run'. His face would be posted everywhere. The presidents of the member states are not going to simply sit back and let Jnr slip into the night. No, they would stop at nothing now to have him arrested.

One thing for sure was that Jnr and his family could not live out the rest of their lives in the cabin - even though it sounded like heaven. Sooner or later they would be found!

Just then he heard the low rumble of an engine approaching: quickly he dashed to a window, his heart pounding to the point of leaping from his chest. As he watched the 4x4 heading his way, he realised that his palms were sweating. This was a new sensation for Jnr, one he didn't relish.

As it came to a stop he realised that it was his dad driving: relief came instantaneously. He stood back and watched as his family climbed from the vehicle. Once he was sure they were alone, he sped from the cabin with excitement, happy to see his family safe.

After the hugs and kisses, Jnr asked the ladies to go into the cabin while the guys brought in the luggage.

"Why are Charles and Sophia not here? That was the plan, Dad."

"You know what he's like, Jnr. No way I could convince him to come: his precious university would not have approved."

"That's just great. Now I'm going to have to fetch them myself, which is risky," moaned Jnr." Dad, we have to change the colour and the reg plate of this car as soon as possible."

"And how are we supposed to do that out here in the middle of nowhere, Jnr?"

"Don't worry, I'll sort it."

"That was one of the most awful drives I've ever done: do you know how long it's taken to get here?"

"I can imagine, but it is out in the sticks, Dad, which is what we need right now."

"Come on, let's take these in. I'm starving."

Inside the cabin his mother and grandmother had already done a full sweep and they were impressed.

"Its lovely, Jnr. Did you do all this yourself?" asked Jean.

"Yes, Grandma, I had a good teacher." Jnr smiled at his mum.

"I better cook us some dinner, then, I suppose. Will you get the fire started, please, Dave?" asked Anne, "It's quite cold at the moment."

With the fire sorted, Jnr sat chatting to his dad about what to do next. His grandparents would have to join them whether they liked it or not. Convincing them would not be an easy task.

As they sat to eat, Jnr realised that this was the closest the family had been in a long time. No Granddad Roy, though. He missed him, even though he was a stubborn so-and-so.

After dinner, the family sat and talked together mostly about the future: what did it hold? They all agreed with the Vicrons' way of life and what a difference it would make to our world, but they, too, could not see a way forward, especially with the tight grip the presidents had at the moment.

Jnr decided he would go early in the morning for his grandparents: around 3 he would set off for the UK.

So it was time for bed for everyone. Jnr kept his plan to himself for now.

3 o'clock came and Jnr was awake already: infact, he hadn't slept well at all.

Ok, first job, sort out a new number plate, then kidnap my grandparents against their will, and all this while trying not to be recognised, pondered Jnr. *This should be fun!*

Sneaking past the bedrooms as quietly as possible, Jnr made his way outside. No need to lock the door: no one will be visiting out here.

He called the ship down and jumped in: yet another trip across the pond.

Walking into Halfords with sunglasses and a cap on at ten past six must have looked odd, but fortunately the staff didn't look interested enough to take much notice. He asked the young lad behind the counter for a new number plate: he was told it would take around ten minutes.

With that out the way he headed out for phase two of his plan: this was not going to be as easy.

Behind his grandparents' home were fields, lots of quiet open space. Jnr decided that this was the best way into their home without being noticed: after all, he suspected they would be watching.

He kept the craft high and proceeded quite slowly, eying up the situation before landing. Jnr knew this estate well and if there was anything out of the norm, then he should spot it.

And spot it he did!

A white van with some writing on the side sat on the courseway two doors down: it could be a plumber or painter just going about his business, but Jnr had his doubts.

On the driveway of a couple of the properties were parked cars that Jnr had never noticed before: they were plain in colour, mostly black, boring-looking even. Usually only high-end vehicles adorned these driveways, so to Jnr these could be surveillance.

He decided to float in position around 200 feet for a while so as to spot any unusual movement below. Agents get bored sitting for so long: sooner or later they might slip up and give themselves away, he hoped.

Below in the fields he noticed that two couples walking dogs had completed the same loop around the field maybe a dozen times. *That's a dead giveaway,* thought Jnr.

Further across there was another field that looked empty: that's where he will land.

Stealth mode once again for both Jnr and his ship: it shouldn't be a problem getting to the house, but after that he would have to make it up as he went.

He waited until the agents walking the dogs crossed paths at the bottom end of the field before he made his way slowly towards the back of the house: so far, so good.

As he made his way down his granddad's long garden, he could see that Charles was sitting in the conservatory, on his laptop as usual. His grandmother was probably in one of two locations, either cooking or sitting in the lounge watching *Coronation Street*.

Still no sign of anyone, so Jnr crept to the side of the conservatory and used his thoughts to listen in on activity from inside the home.

He was right, his grandma was making some food, but she wasn't alone: an agent was sitting in the kitchen with her, making small talk. Jnr dare not communicate with her right now: she would probably give the game away.

Concentrating, he used his mind to speak with Charles.

"Granddad, it's me, Jnr. Please don't speak or look around, just keep staring at your laptop. Use your thoughts to speak to me."

"Ok, David, what are you doing here? They are in the next room and all around the house. You are wanted: they will catch you, David."

"They cannot see or hear me, Granddad, so we need to not make any silly moves, or yes, I will get caught. Why didn't you come with my parents?"

"Why would I, David? I'm needed at work and so is your grandmother. We have nothing to fear."

"Is that right, Granddad? What is he doing in the kitchen, then? Are you even allowed to go out alone?"

"They only leave one in the house, and be careful, David, because there are more of them watching the house. I suppose they are waiting to see if you show up. Yes, we both go to work by ourselves but they always keep one inside, all night."

"I need to figure out a way to get you both out without raising the alarm, Granddad."

"What if we don't want to go, David. We're not in any danger."

"Maybe not at the moment, but what if they become desperate? They could turn nasty, Granddad, and that I couldn't live with. It's me they want: this has nothing to do with you."

"I understand but I don't want to up and go, I have too much to do at university and besides, I'm sure we can put up with them for a while longer."

Jnr heard a noise coming from the side of the house.

He moved slowly to the edge of the building and looked down the side of the house towards the driveway. He can see four guys advancing his way with what looked like SWAT uniforms on, completely dark in colour with night vision scopes on.

He stood still, shallow breathing and heart racing, but he knew he couldn't be seen, so no need to panic just yet. Somehow he needed to get up high, out of the way.

Suddenly out of nowhere a net was fired from one of the SWAT team's guns. Jnr simply stopped it: the net lingered in thin air to the bemusement of the squad, which gave Jnr a split second to think, but now he started to panic!

"He's here!" shouted one of the SWAT team.

223

Jnr turned and ran as fast as he could up the garden. He called the ship over from the adjacent field to meet him at the end of his granddad's garden.

Shots started flying past as he raced along.

How can they see me? wondered Jnr as panic really started to take effect.

As he jumped into the ship, the dog walkers appeared out of nowhere, shouting, "Stop, Dr Archer, do not run!"

Jnr didn't stop, so they opened fire. A couple of bullets hit him but to no avail, they deflected away with the help of his nanos, but still hurt for a second, though.

The four-man team were closing in behind, shooting as they went.

Jumping into the ship he made a quick exit and headed away from the commotion. His heart was pacing: using shallow breaths, he steadied it.

That's blown it. Now they know I will be back. How on Earth am I going to rescue my grandparents now? Security will be tightened after this failed attempt.

After flying in no particular direction for awhile, Jnr decided that he needed to speak to Beevers, which meant he needed the satellite phone, which was in Alaska.

Heading back to the cabin, Jnr had a quiet time to think: what was he to do now? Who could help his situation? Everyone thought he was the bad guy, according to the news.

Jnr was now a fugitive. He came back home with a clear simple message, a message from people who have already been through the same history as our own, people who have learned from past mistakes, people willing to help.

Jnr didn't have to come back to this crazy, mixed-up world, but he did: was it a mistake? Can humanity be saved from themselves? All Jnr wanted to do was help, but it seemed it might be to no avail.

Entering the cabin, Jnr looked exhausted.

"Where have you been, David?" asked Anne.

"I tried to get Grandma and Grandpa to come here with us, Mum."

"Why, Jnr? They didn't want to come: your father begged them to, but still no."

"I know, Mum, but I'm worried about them. They may use them against me, as a bargaining tool. I don't want that on my conscience. Granddad thinks he has nothing to fear, but I don't trust them at all."

"What do you mean, use them?" asked Jean.

"Nothing bad, Grandma, but what if they hold them against their will, hoping to get to me, having people around them all the time like they have now?"

"Like how, Jnr?"said Anne, looking rather concerned.

"At the house they were being watched: one guy in the house and a few in the grounds around the back and front, waiting for me to turn up. They know I won't leave them, Mum."

"You might have to for now, Jnr,"said Dave.

"I'm going to call President Beevers, I'll take the satellite phone and call from a distance: they might find the source of the signal. I need to know what they want of me, Dad."

"If you say so, Jnr, but I don't know what you expect to hear. They are not likely to help now, are they?"

"I guess not, but I think it's worth a call."

Jnr decided to change the number plate on the new car first to give him chance to think. He also sent his trusty nanos to work on the paint job: they chewed the colour right out of the vehicle, and it was now silver.

Jnr dropped in just over the border to make the call to Beevers.

"Hello, President Beevers, this is Dr Archer."

"Hello, David, this is out of the blue. Where are you?"

"I'm in the States at the moment: we need to talk."

"Certainly, David, but I'm afraid I've been taken out of the equation for now: it seems I'm not trusted either."

"I'm sorry about that, sir, but I told you from the start my position on this matter. I will not be held and I will not let the Vicron technology be taken, ever," replied Jnr.

"I see, David. Well, let me tell you that every step possible is being taken for your capture, no matter what that implies. From now on you are to speak with DeHulme: he is in control now. I can give you his direct number if you wish."

"Does that include shoot to kill, which is what happened at my grandparents' home?"

"It seems so, David. Like I said, I have no say in the matter now. The best advice I can offer you is to give yourself up before someone does get hurt."

"That's not about to happen, President Beevers, not now, not ever."

"Ok, David, that's your choice, I am sorry, Dr Archer, and believe me when I say I wish you the best of luck in whatever you decide."

Jnr decided that a long, steady flight was in order. He needed time alone to think, so he took his craft up to the roof of the stratosphere: it was all quiet and calm up there. As he glided along he looked down upon the Earth. What a beautiful sight: a big, blue, beautiful planet from which he now felt detached. Could he ever live out his life in peace? He had a plan up his sleeve, but it was a last resort. For now his main priority was getting his grandparents to join the rest of the family back at the cabin.

Charles and Sophia travelled to work by themselves; they are not accompanied by an agent. Yes, sure they will be watched, but Jnr thought this would be the way he could complete his kidnapping attempt – not yet, though, he would be expected.

Jnr spent a whole week back at the cabin, relaxing: both he and his father fished for salmon everyday, while the salmon are active, migrating upstream to their final destination to spawn. Jean and Anne spent their time reading mostly. If not reading, they liked to walk along the river's edge: it's so peaceful here, with clean air to breathe.

Meanwhile, back in the States, the presidents had gathered for an emergency meeting: the agenda of the meeting was Jnr and, more importantly, how to capture Jnr.

The decision was made and agreed upon by all the presidents: Jnr had to be captured, dead or alive!

Chapter 31 – The Rescue

Jnr decided to watch his grandparents over a span of a few weeks. They travelled to work separately which didn't help the situation, but Jnr was determined to make his family safe. Sophia had a space in an underground car park which could help, but Charles parked out in the open.

Doubts were creeping into Jnr's mind: he knew that they did not want to come with him. Were they really in danger or was it Jnr's selfish needs that were driving him right now?

Were they actually safer living their lives the way they wanted? Would the presidents stoop as low as to use them as a bargaining tool? Would they be any safer back at the cabin? All these questions floated around Jnr's mind and he started to wonder if he was doing the right thing. Should he leave his grandparents be and give himself up, too, so he may share his knowledge? What's the worst that could happen if the member states acquired the Vicron technology?

Kandok's words were ever-present in his mind: 'do not let the humans get hold of our technology, no matter what', were his words. Even though he knew that humans cannot be trusted with power, he often imagined if the advancements that this technology could bring were worth sharing, after all, would Kandok intervene? But deep down he knew that Kandok was right and besides, with the current situation with the world against him, why would he take the risk?

Sophia pulled into the car park and proceeded to her spot: Jnr was waiting. There were cameras operating, but no agents to be seen. He knew they would have followed her there, and one agent awaited her in the building, so this was his only chance. He sneaked in close in stealth mode as Sophia climbed from her car, hoping she did not jump with surprise.

"Grandma, it's Jnr. Please don't make any sudden movements and do not speak: use your mind to speak with me. Go into your boot and look like you're looking for something."

"Oh Jnr, why are you here? Charles has asked you not to come, it's too dangerous for you," said Sophia as she opened her boot and rummaged through the contents.

"I'm going to ask one question, Grandma: did you want to stay, or was it Granddad who made you?"

"Charles said there was no need for us to come with you, but yes, Jnr, I wanted to go. I don't like it at all now: we are being watched night and day."

"Then there's not much time: walk out of the car park, Grandma, and I'll be there at the exit with the ship, waiting for you."

"What about your granddad? Are we going to fetch him, too?"

"Yes we will, I promise. Now please walk out slowly. Do not draw any attention to yourself, just act normal. Now go," said Jnr.

Jnr made his way along the wall at speed. He ordered the ship to the car park entrance. So far, so good: no one in sight but they could not hang around. The agent in the school would have noticed that Sophia was not on time.

He waited until Sophia was close, then jumped on the ship. He uncloaked the door's entrance so his grandma could see where she was to go. As she climbed in, the agent from inside the school came running towards the ship through the car park.

"Stop, do not leave, you will be shot down!" he screamed while running.

Jnr pulled Sophia in and shot off into the sky.

"Are you ok, Grandma?"

"Yes, Jnr, I'm fine. Are we going to get Charles now?"

"Yes, take a seat, Grandma, and strap yourself in: we need to hurry."

It only took a few minutes to arrive at the university but still it was too late. Charles was standing beside his car, but was totally surrounded by armed personnel, guns pointing at him as Jnr pulled the ship down to around twenty feet from his position.

"Granddad, I'm sorry, I got here as quick as I could."

"But why, Jnr? I asked you time and time again not to. Where is Sophia?"

"She is here with me: she wanted to come, Granddad."

"No, Jnr, she didn't. We decided together to stay: that was not your decision to make."

"Don't worry. I will find a way to sort this, Granddad, I promise."

"How, Jnr? Look around: you will be shot if you leave that ship, and now I will be taken in. You have just made things far more dangerous than they needed to be."

"Who is in charge here?" asked Jnr.

All the armed guards looked at one another, puzzled. They knew of Jnr's abilities, but still it was very different to actually experiencing it first-hand.

"I'm in command, Dr Archer. My name is Sgt Harris. Please come out and speak with me face to face."

"No, Sgt Harris, I will not leave this ship. I'm here for my grandfather. I do not want any trouble with you, I only want for his safety."

"There doesn't need to be any trouble: I simply want to talk. I cannot allow you to take him and besides, he has already stated that he doesn't want to leave."

"I have his wife here with me. They don't need to be involved in this. Please let me take him, I will come back and speak to President DeHulme, I promise."

Jnr read the thoughts of the sergeant and he didn't like what he saw. He was thinking of shooting Charles the minute Jnr made a move. At that very moment Jnr realised just how serious it was, and he had put his granddad right in the firing line.

"Granddad, I'm going to make a move, the soldiers won't be able to fire. You will float up to the ship. Please don't worry: this will turn out fine."

"Alright, Jnr. Only because you have Sophia with you I'm allowing this: do it now."

Jnr used his telekinesis. First he took the guns from the soldiers. They came away from their hands and crashed down to the ground. Then Jnr froze them stiff, and they could not move.

He raised his granddad up towards the ship. Sophia was looking on, panicking for her husband. "Please be careful, Jnr!" she cried.

Charles came up alongside the ship. Jnr got up from his seat and made his way over to the door to help his granddad in. Sophia stood facing her husband, nervous with excitement as he neared the door.

Charles reached out to grab Jnr's hand. A shot rang out, Charles opened his eyes wide with shock. He gasped loudly. Everything suddenly became slow motion. The shot had hit him in the back: it was fired from a sniper. Both Jnr and Sophia reached out and pulled him in. Jnr didn't waste time, he sped away from the area.

Charles lay writhing in pain upon the floor. Sophia held his hand crying hysterically: he was struggling for breath. He looked up at Jnr and spoke with his mind. "Take your grandma back with you and please promise me, Jnr, keep her safe."

"I will, Granddad. I promise, but first I'm taking you to the hospital."

"Its too late, Jnr. I love you and don't blame yourself: you did the right thing."

Charles looked upon his wife with tears running down his face. He then closed his eyes for the last time.

Chapter 32 – A Step Too Far

Landing the ship next to the cabin, Jnr helped his grandmother as she was too distraught to walk without him. Anne stood in the doorway: she could tell there was something wrong. She had only seen her mother in this kind of state twice in her life. Her father was not there. Anne felt suddenly dizzy: she fainted. Dave was standing beside her, so he caught her from her fall and gently carried her to the sofa.

Jean held out her arms to comfort Sophia, all the while asking what had happened: where was Charles?

Jnr looked through teary eyes at everyone. "He's dead. They shot him."

Dave looked at his own son with a look of disbelief. Jnr knew that look: he was at fault as far as his father was concerned.

Both Jean and Jnr helped Sophia into the cabin. They sat her upon the sofa.

"Jnr, I cannot believe this. Charles did not want a part in this and now look: you are going to have to give yourself up. I'm afraid this has to stop before anyone else is hurt," said Dave.

"Dad, are you crazy? What has this all been about? Greed, Dad. They want what I have, no matter what. Why should I give it up?"

"Why not, Jnr? You don't owe this Kandok anything and how the hell would he know anyway? What does it matter?"

"What does it matter? How about Earth's future, Dad? With this technology the whole world could be at stake. If they would only follow the advice from Vicron, everyone could live in peace. The way it's going now, it's not got any future. That's why, Dad."

"Of course, Jnr, I'm with you but when it comes to my family, which includes you, I will not let any more harm come to any of us. I will not let that happen."

"What does that mean exactly?" asked Jnr.

"It means, Jnr, that if push comes to shove, I will let the members know of our location. That way, no one else will be harmed."

"You do realise, Dad, that I cannot and will not be captured, don't you?"

"Yes, son, I do, that's your choice to make. But what are you to do, run forever?"

"I'm going to speak to DeHulme. If I get no joy and you don't hear from me for a week or so, you will know I have gone my own way: that way, you all can return to your normal lives. I can look after myself and I will contact you when I think the time is right. Hopefully I can work something out with the presidents so it may not come to that."

"Ok, Jnr, that makes good sense to me. It's time to end this."

Jnr and Dave buried Charles close to the river. Kind words were said by all, and it was an immensely sad moment for all the family. Jnr felt guilty ofcourse: he had only wanted to protect his family, but it had now gone too far. A life had been taken as a direct result of Jnr's actions. They all looked at him with anger now. Snr was right: something needed to be done.

Taking to the sky once again, Jnr took the satellite phone and headed over the border to the US.

He dialled in the direct number to DeHulme.

"Hello, President, DeHulme. This is Dr Archer."

"Hello, Dr Archer. I wondered how long it would take for this call. You want to hand yourself over, I take it, now you have witnessed just how serious this situation has become?"

"I was actually hoping you and I could talk privately. There must be a way to move forward without any more bloodshed."

"There is a way, David: hand yourself in and that's it, problem solved, no one else needs be involved."

"Can we meet, somewhere quiet, just yourself and I?"

"For what reason, David? Just come in and we may talk then."

"I want to speak to you alone first.. If I'm happy with the outcome, then yes, I will come in peacefully."

"Ok, if you wish: where would you like this meeting?" asked DeHulme.

"Central Park, on the bridge at exactly 4pm."

"Alright, Dr Archer. You have your wish: 4 o'clock then. Bye for now."

"Before you go, President DeHulme, do I have your word that you will be alone?"

"Yes, Dr Archer, you have my word."

Jnr turned up early: it was a perfect afternoon for a walk around the park, plus he brought a little snack with him which he sat on the grass to eat. He pondered the outcome of this meeting. After all, he already knew the answer: DeHulme wouldn't listen. He didn't before, so why would he now?

Since returning to Earth nothing had really changed: he had the power in his hands to help the whole planet with its future energy supply, a cleaner, cheaper source which would also help with the planet's atmospheric regeneration. He knew it would be an enormous task to ask the world's leaders to change on his and Kandok's say-so. Nevertheless, he had to try.

4 o'clock approached and so he made his way over to the bridge. DeHulme was not there yet, but there were ten minutes to go. While approaching he checked everywhere for signs of agents, but he could see none: they were either very good at concealment or he had stuck to his word and had, indeed, come alone.

Jnr stood with hands outstretched, leaning over the bridge while looking down at the water. Fish were slowly making their way along whilst little creatures sped across the surface upon the lily pads. *If Jib was here he could tell me what those creatures were, even their Latin names,* thought Jnr. He missed his friends.

Jnr was that deeply engaged in thought that he hadn't noticed that soldiers had crept up on his position from either side; also a helicopter was fast approaching. Suddenly Jnr stood bolt upright: no, he hadn't seen them but he did pick up on their thoughts as they closed in.

"Dr Archer, please raise your hands above your head and stay where you are. If you do not comply we have full authority to fire our weapons," said one of the very nervous soldiers.

Jnr was fuming. DeHulme had double-crossed him, even after giving his word.

"Firstly, you do not need to fire upon me as I am unharmed. Also I will not use any force towards you unless I'm provoked. I will not be taken in, so please be aware that I will protect myself against any attack," replied Jnr.

"Please give yourself up, Dr Archer. That way, no one will be harmed. As you can see, you are totally surrounded both on the ground and from the air. It would be unwise to try to run."

From the helicopter, DeHulme looked down at the scene below: there must have been in total around 100 soldiers, all guns trained on Jnr. Three more choppers were closing in, and at least ten armoured vehicles sat behind the soldiers on either side of the bridge. It looked like a hopeless possibility for Jnr to make his getaway. Our Jnr was protected, of course, but not against this type of attack.

With a lightning-fast burst he ran towards the wall and dived over, into the river below. Shots were fired from every direction as he descended: a lot of bullets miss but a lot had found their target. He reeled in agony as he hit the water, but the pain he had to ignore. He swam towards the bottom to try and get away from the deluge of bullets entering the water all around him. It was very murky: he could only see a few feet in front of him.

Jnr made his way along the river bed. He had switched to stealth mode as he needed to come up for air. As he ascended, an explosion occurred only ten feet from him. Jnr was slammed into the bank: it knocked the wind out of him, and now he was desperate to get to the surface. The nanos could help with just about anything, but they could not supply him with air.

Breaking the surface, Jnr took a huge gulp of air but the soldiers were on him instantly. He dived down again. Somehow the soldiers could see him, but how? He called the ship over the river's edge, but as he neared the surface he could see that the choppers were attacking his ship with missiles. It was not destroyed yet, but surely it would not be able to survive a relentless barrage of missiles from all four choppers.

How the hell can they see my ship? wondered Jnr.

For now that would have to wait. He sent the ship up and out of the way of the choppers. He had more important issues at hand: his escape. Diving down deep again to the bottom, he decided to use his telekinesis upon the water: it was not as easy as a stationary object, but he had to try. Concentrating his mind on every single atom surrounding him, he forced the water into a fast flow which propelled him along quicker than the soldiers could run: this would buy him some time.

With the soldiers now behind him, Jnr started to rise to the surface for some much-needed air, and to see where he was headed. At the same time, the choppers flew up and down the river, waiting for him to show. Up ahead was a wooded area: Jnr sank beneath the surface and kept out of sight until he reached that point.

He had made it. Quickly he climbed the bank and ran as fast as he could through the trees. He could see the boundary fence. So far, so good: he hadn't been spotted. Up and over the fence he went, then he crossed the road and headed for an alley way. He could see soldiers making their way along the pavement, checking every nook and cranny as they went.

Jnr made his way through the alley and across another road towards the next alley. While running along he saw a fire escape ladder hanging down from the stairs. He started to climb: at the same time he called the ship down to the rooftop. As he climbed he heard the choppers approaching. Again they attacked his ship: he was now three-quarters of the way up, and he had to retreat as he could see the soldiers were already heading his way, but how?

He called the ship down and away from the choppers to pass underneath him. He jumped, and clumsily landed on its back. He commanded the ship to go low, away from the choppers above, but no sooner was he about to enter the ship than a soldier fired a missile launcher which collided with the underneath of the craft. It threw Jnr off into a pile of rubbish, luckily for Jnr. He quickly ran through a door which led into the kitchen of a restaurant. He didn't stop as he ran through: chefs and waiters stopped what they were doing, looking surprised as Jnr ran past.

Exiting from the main entrance, Jnr could see no soldiers yet, and across the street was a shopping mall: he made his way over, he could mix into the crowd there, it would buy him some time to think. Somehow he had to get back to the ship: there was no way of escaping without it. They knew that if they took control of Jnr's ship, the game would be over for him.

Making his way through the crowd he tried to blend in, casually looking in store windows as he passed. He knew that security would have been alerted to keep an eye out for him. He was famous, after all: most people knew of him now. One mistake he had made was that there were cameras everywhere; they had spotted him using face recognition software. Jnr made his way out to the car park. It was an outdoor, two-floor car park. Here he could bring down his ship: he called it to land on the top floor.

As he climbed the stairs he saw soldiers converging from all angles below: did he have time to jump in? As soon as he got to the top he could see the ship, but he could also see the choppers closing in. Should he make a run for it? With a quick decision he started to run but, as the choppers closed in, they opened fire. All hell broke loose: there were more choppers joining the fray, all firing missiles at his ship, and at the same time blowing everything up around it. Cars and even people were caught in the commotion. It was clear that the members were not letting anything get in the way of their goal. People's lives did not matter: they were that desperate to get control of the Vicrons' technology.

Jnr sent the ship away yet again: there was no way he was getting near it at the moment. Behind him the soldiers began closing in. They opened fire at first sight of him. He set off towards the end of the car park, bullets hitting him as he ran. He was in such pain but he couldn't stop, not now. Even though the nanos were protecting him from the outside, he felt the pain on the inside, only for a little while, but with the onslaught he was receiving there was no let-up. It was taking its toll upon his body.

Jnr cowered behind a car in the corner of the car park while bullets collided all around him. He was now panicking, out of breath and in terrible pain. The soldiers were closing in fast: he felt at such a loss, and he now feared the worse. Was he to give up before they actually killed him?

Before he could make that decision, a missile hit the car he was behind: it exploded, smashing Jnr into the barrier at the edge of the car park. Slowly he rose to his feet and managed to pull himself up and over the barrier. He fell about twenty feet to the concrete below, knocking all the air from his lungs. Jnr was exhausted: he lay still for what seemed like an eternity, though it was actually only a second or two.

Soldiers lined up along the barrier, shooting at him as he lay upon the ground. Jnr was crying. He had nothing left, and there was nothing left in the bank. His only option was to keep still and wait for the nightmare to end. Six choppers hovered, hordes of soldiers had their guns trained on Jnr. Still they kept firing: they wanted to make sure he was finished, to eliminate the threat.

Suddenly, from out of nowhere, the choppers were fired upon, and all six quickly exploded in mid-air. The soldiers started firing into the sky, but at what? There was nothing to be seen. One by one they were being eliminated. Jnr looked up but saw nothing: at the same time he felt a presence: hope appeared, which could be seen in his eyes. Most of the soldiers had been killed, and those who were left alive had backed off. They didn't have a clue as to what had just occurred, and neither did Jnr.

It was then that he realised he heard a familiar voice: it was the commander who first brought Jnr about his ship. "Dr Archer, it is I, Commander Kep. You are to come with us, back to Vicron." Jnr was lifted up into an awaiting craft which had now revealed itself: there were two of them sitting rather menacingly in the sky. Jnr was safe: he felt relief wash over him. Gently he was carried up into the interior and then laid upon a bed.

The craft shot up through the clouds and onwards out into space once again. Jnr lay upon the bed crying with both joy and sadness: he was leaving Earth behind yet again. Kandok hadn't trusted the human race: maybe we cannot be saved, maybe this is our destiny.

Jnr didn't care, he was leaving this planet and hopefully never coming back.

Thank you for your purchase of my debut novel; Path To Life

Please may I ask if you enjoyed my story, would you be so kind as to leave a review on Amazon books.

Also keep an eye out for my upcoming stories:

It Came From The Sky
We have sent many rovers around the planets for the purpose of exploration. What would happen if another race of beings sent one to Earth? Would we panic? It would answer the question: Are we alone in the universe.

A Fight For Mars
In the not too distant future, our scientists are planning to terraform Mars. What if another race of beings beat us to it? Could this spell disaster for the human species?

Subscribe at www.markchilderley.com and get informed of new releases of my future works.

Many thanks
Mark.

Printed in Great Britain
by Amazon